DARK SI[...]
"Kenyon's writing is [...]
imaginative. These are [...]

"A delicious balance of suspense and sensuality."
—*Publishers Weekly*

SEIZE THE NIGHT
"Kenyon succeeds in offering a lively read containing her signature blend of brisk action, sensual thrills, and light humor." —*Publishers Weekly*

KISS OF THE NIGHT
"With its frenetic, *Matrix*-style fight scenes and feral, leather-clad heroes, this book makes it easy to see why Kenyon's fantasy world has caught on so quickly and even inspired some readers to role-play on her Web site . . . an entertaining thrill ride." —*Publishers Weekly*

DANCE WITH THE DEVIL
"Move over, Anne Rice. Kenyon's Dark-Hunter books are changing the face of the vampire novel, making it hip, darker, and all the more appealing." —*Publishers Weekly*

"Using figures from mythology, Sherrilyn Kenyon provides a deep novel that a romantic fantasy lover will cherish. A powerful story that makes believers of skeptics that Ancient Gods and Goddesses, Dark-Hunters, Dayslayers, and other mythological characters walk among us . . . another fine myth from a superb storyteller climbing to the top." —*Baryon Magazine*

NIGHT EMBRACE
"With her steamy, action-packed Dark-Hunter novels, Kenyon is ushering in a whole new class of night dwellers . . . an abundance of hot sex and snappy dialogue keep the plot both accessible and appealing. With its courageous, unconventional characters and wry humor, this fast-moving fantasy will fill the void left by the end of the *Buffy the Vampire Slayer* series." —*Publishers Weekly*

DREAM CHASER

Sherrilyn Kenyon

St. Martin's Paperbacks

DREAM CHASER

Copyright © 2008 by Sherrilyn Kenyon.
Excerpt from *Acheron* copyright © 2008 by Sherrilyn Kenyon.

All rights reserved.

For information address St. Martin's Press, 175 Fifth Avenue, New York, NY 10010.

ISBN: 0-312-93882-9
EAN: 978-0-312-93882-6

Printed in the United States of America

St. Martin's Paperbacks edition / February 2008

St. Martin's Paperbacks are published by St. Martin's Press, 175 Fifth Avenue, New York, NY 10010.

10 9 8 7 6 5 4

PROLOGUE

Hatred is a bitter, damaging emotion. It winds itself through the blood, infecting its host and driving it forward without any reason. Its view is jaundiced and it skews even the clearest of eyesights.

Sacrifice is noble and tender. It's the action of a host who values others above himself. Sacrifice is bought through love and decency. It is truly heroic.

Vengeance is an act of violence. It allows those who have been wronged to take back some of what was lost to them. Unlike sacrifice, it gives back to the one who practices it.

Love is deceitful and sublime. In its truest form, it brings out the best in all beings. At its worst, it's a tool used to manipulate and ruin anyone who is stupid enough to hold it.

Don't be stupid.

Sacrifice is for the weak. Hatred corrupts. Love destroys. Vengeance is the gift of the strong.

Move forward, not with hatred, not with love. Move forward with purpose.

Take back what was stolen. Make those who laughed at your pain pay. Not with hatred, but with calm, cold rationale.

Hatred is your enemy. Vengeance is your friend. Hold it close and let it loose.

May the gods have mercy on those who have wronged me because I will have no mercy for them.

Xypher paused as he read the words he'd written on the floor of his cell in his own blood centuries ago. Dull and faded, they were a reminder to him of what had brought him to this time and place.

They were a sacred vow to himself.

Closing his eyes, he spread his hand out and the words dissolved into a mist that lifted from the floor only to reassemble down his left arm. Symbol by symbol, word by word, the characters, still bloodred, cut themselves into his skin. He hissed at the burn of them engraving themselves into his flesh. That pain succored him. It strengthened him.

Soon he would be free for one month. One month to track and to kill. The one he'd sacrificed himself for would pay and if he earned his reprieve in the process . . . Good.

If he didn't . . .

Well, vengeance sometimes deserved a good sacrifice. At least this time, he'd die knowing no one was laughing at him anymore.

ONE

"Have you ever wanted to put your head in a blender and turn on the liquefy switch?"

Simone Dubois frowned then laughed at Tate Bennett, the parish coroner for New Orleans, as he took a seat at the dark wood table, across from her. As always, Tate was impeccably dressed in a white button-down shirt and black slacks. His skin was dark and flawless, a gift from his Creole and Haitian heritage. With sharp, sculpted features, he was extremely good-looking and those dark eyes of his never missed a detail.

His impeccable attire was a sharp contrast to her faded jeans, navy sweater and riotous mop of dark brown curls that would never obey any style Simone attempted to beat them into. The only feature she had that she considered even remotely interesting were her hazel brown eyes that turned gold whenever the sun hit them.

She wiped her mouth on her napkin. "Honestly . . . I can't say that I have. *But* there have been a few other heads I'd like to do that to. Why?"

He dropped a folder in front of her. "How many serial killers can one city have?"

"I'm not up on those stats. Depends on the city I suppose. Are you telling me we have another one here?"

He unwrapped his silverware and placed his napkin on his lap. "I don't know. Couple of weird murders have come through my office over the last two weeks. Seemingly unrelated."

Those two words were loaded with meaning. "But . . ."

"But I have a gut feeling on this and it's not the oh-look-it's-a-bright-shiny-world kind."

Simone took a sip of her soda before she opened the file and grimaced at the grisly crime scene photos. As always, they were gory and detailed. "I just love the gifts you bring me for lunch. Other girls get diamonds. Me? I get mayhem and blood—and all before noon. Thanks, Tate."

He leaned over and stole a French fry from her plate. "Don't worry, boo, I'm buying. Besides, you're the only woman I know I can meet for lunch and talk business with. Everyone else gets squeamish."

She looked up. "You know, I'm not sure that's much of a compliment."

"Trust me, it is. If LaShonda ever comes to her senses and leaves me, you're the next Mrs. Tate."

"Again, not flattering to either of us. Should I tell LaShonda what her hubby thinks of her?" she teased.

"Please don't. She might poison my cush-cush . . . or worse, beat my tush-tush."

Simone laughed again. "Don't worry, I'd make sure and bring her to justice for it."

"I'm sure you would." He paused to order a shrimp po'boy and fries from the waitress.

Simone continued to look at the photos while he spoke to the young Goth woman who was taking his order.

Yeah, these pictures were pretty gruesome. But then these types of photos usually were. How she hated that the world was filled with people capable of doing such horrific things to others. What people could do to each other was bad enough. What the other, nonhuman inhabitants could do was a whole other nightmare. Literally.

And she was more than just a little acquainted with both kinds of monsters.

The waitress headed back toward the kitchen.

Tate leaned closer. "You getting any vibes from the other side?"

She shook her head. "You know it doesn't work that way, T. I have to be touching the body or something that belonged to the victim. Photos only give me a paper cut . . . and the willies." Shivering in sympathy for the way the poor woman had died, she closed the file and slid it back toward him.

"Want to come to the morgue with me after lunch?"

She arched one brow at his offer. "I shudder at the thought of the pickup line you must have used the night you met LaShonda. Come with me, baby, and see my collection of stiffs."

He laughed. "God, I love your sense of humor."

Too bad a married man was one of the very few people who actually got her offbeat humor. The only other person to really appreciate it was a teenaged ghost who'd been haunting her since she was ten years old.

Jesse was seated to her right, but only Simone knew that. No one else could see or hear him—oh, lucky her. Especially since Jesse was locked in a late 1980s time warp. Case in point, he was wearing a light blue blazer reminiscent of Don Johnson from *Miami Vice* with a curly black pompadour courtesy of Jon Cryer from the movie *Pretty in Pink*. Jesse was a huge John Hughes fan who made her watch way too many reruns. He completed his offbeat outfit with a skinny white keyboard satin tie and matching white checkerboard Vans.

"I don't want to go to the morgue, Simone," Jesse said from between clenched teeth. "I don't like it there."

She could certainly understand that sentiment. It was her favorite spot to visit right after the proctologist's office.

She gave Jesse a pitying look, but they both knew that she'd have no choice except to go. There was nothing she wouldn't do to bring a killer to justice and that included hanging out in the creepy city morgue instead of her lab at Tulane.

"So what's the strangest part about these murders?" she asked, trying to distract Jesse from repeating a tirade she was more than familiar with. Besides, he could go home without her—he just didn't like being in the house when she wasn't there.

Jesse could be a very needy ghost sometimes.

Tate stole another fry before he answered. "The fact that Ms. Gloria here got up and walked off her examining table."

Simone choked on the Coke she was drinking. "Excuse me?"

"You heard right. Nialls is now in a straitjacket because of it. He freaked out so badly we had to call the psych ward for him."

She coughed twice to clear her throat before she spoke again. "The victim was in a coma?"

"The victim was dead as a doornail. As you saw from the photos, her throat had been ripped out and Nialls had just opened up her chest for the autopsy. Her heart was in his hands when she started breathing."

"Uh-huh . . ." It was the only response she could manage for a moment. "And she got up and walked off . . ."

He nodded glumly. "Welcome to my world. Oh, wait, welcome to *your* world. Yours is even more bizarre than mine. At least I don't live with a ghost who has his own bedroom in my house." He glanced around the table, then lowered his voice. "Is Jesse here?"

Simone inclined her head in the direction of where her friend was seated and staring at them with a stern frown.

"Please explain to me how she got up while he was holding her heart," she said slowly.

"That's what I want *you* to tell me. See, I deal with . . . well, most days, bizarre paranormal crap. You are Queen Weird. I need the queen on this before I have to start hiring a new staff of medical examiners who don't freak out when the dead move off their tables. You know where I can find some of these unusual people? I know you hang out with them."

"Thanks, Tate. I always look forward to these ego-bolstering pep talks of ours."

"Yes, but at least you know I love you."

"Like a hole in your shoe."

He laughed. "Not true. You are the best damned medical examiner I've ever seen and you know that. If I could get you away from Tulane and hire your butt for the city, I'd do it in a heartbeat. The fact that you're the only one I can talk to about paranormal deaths is a major bonus to me. Anyone else would have me in a room next to Nialls."

Simone reached for her pickle. "True. I'm also told they have incredible drugs to help curb those hallucinations."

"Then sign me up. I could definitely use them."

So could she, but that was another story. Then again, her entire life was bizarre enough to be considered one massive hallucination.

If only it were.

Simone paused as she got that weird feeling in her gut again. She glanced about the dark restaurant, then out the window to the left of her that showed the traffic on Decatur Street. Nothing appeared out of the ordinary, but still the sensation persisted.

"Is something wrong?" Jesse asked.

"I've got that feeling again."

Tate scowled. "What feeling?"

Her face heated at his question. "I was actually talking to Jesse. But for the last couple of weeks I've had this bizarre sensation that something is watching me."

"You mean some*one*, right?"

She shook her head. "I know it sounds crazy—"

"I just had a body walk off the table mid-autopsy and you think *your* story is nuts? Yeah, boo . . ."

That was what she liked most about Tate. He made her feel almost normal. Not to mention he was the only person besides her who knew about Jesse. Of course she was also the only person outside of a small handful who knew Tate was a Squire for the Dark-Hunters—a group of immortal warriors who hunted down and executed the vampiric Daimons who preyed on human souls.

Yeah, her life was anything but normal.

So why should she even be concerned about the fact that she felt as if something evil were watching her? It probably was. And unfortunately, it wouldn't be the first time. She only wanted to make sure it wasn't the last one.

"Do you know where it's coming from?" Jesse asked.

"No. I can't pinpoint it. All I know is that it's making my skin crawl."

Tate leaned back in his chair to stare at her. "I really wish I could hear Jesse. It's so disconcerting when you two talk. Makes me wonder if he's not sitting there, mocking me."

She smiled. "Jesse only makes fun of me."

"That's not true."

She looked at Jesse. "Yes it is."

"No it's not," Tate inserted.

Simone frowned at him. "Do you even know what you're arguing?"

"Not really. It just seemed natural to add that."

She laughed. "How I *ever* got mixed up with the two of you, I'll never know." But that wasn't true. Jesse had come to her during the darkest hour of her life and he'd been with her ever since.

Tate . . . he'd been there when she'd come the closest she'd ever been to catching her mother's and brother's killer. Unfortunately, her hunch hadn't panned out and the evidence she thought would give them a clue to her mother's murderer had been too tainted to use. Even so, Tate had fought for her tooth and nail even though he hadn't known her at the time. That meant more to her than anything and they'd been friends ever since.

There was nothing she wouldn't do for him and he knew it.

Tate, LaShonda, and Jesse were the only family she had.

He leaned back and waited for the waitress to put his plate on the table and leave before he spoke again. "Are you sure it's not one of the ghosts you see eyeballing you?"

She shook her head. "No. They're never this subtle. They usually pop in, like 'yo, she-bitch, do my bidding.' This . . . this is something else."

"Evil is coming for you," Jesse said in a grim, echoing voice.

Simone narrowed her eyes on him. "I hate it when you do that."

Tate pulled back as if he were offended. "What'd I do?"

She smiled at him. "Not you. Jesse. He's using his ghost voice on me. It's extremely unnerving."

"Yes, but you still love me." Jesse winked at her.

"Of course I do. But save the voice for a haunting."

"I would if anyone else could hear me. Have you any idea how annoying that is? No, 'cause everyone hears you when you talk." He stood up and danced in the corner. "Hey, people!" he shouted. "See the freaky ghost dance." He flapped his arms around and shook his booty. "I'm bad, I'm bad, I'm bad." He stopped and looked around at the people who went on about their business, oblivious to his offbeat antics. "See. Sucks."

She passed a dry look to Jesse, who held his hands up in surrender. There were times when he was a strange cross between a nagging mother and a wife combined with a lunatic brother.

She focused her attention on Tate. "Anyway, back to the decedent . . . do the police have any leads?"

Tate shook his head. "She was found in an alley down in the Warehouse District. Her throat was lacerated with something clawlike. Too large to be animal and too jagged to be individual knife marks."

"Definitely not a Daimon attack then." Daimons were a particular breed of vampire who called New Orleans home . . . and unlike many of the others who made ambitious blood-sucking claims, these guys were real and they were deadly predators with highly developed supernatural powers. As medical examiners, she and Tate were used to seeing their handiwork come through their offices.

Her acceptance and willingness to help cover the Daimons' tracks was what kept her close to Tate. They weren't protecting the Daimons, they were keeping the rest of humanity safe by not informing them of what was really out there ready to take them down. If mankind were ever to know, they would freak out and kill innocent people, too.

The bad thing was that even though the Daimons drank blood, they didn't feed on it. They fed on actual human souls. Luckily a single human soul could keep them fed for a long time, so as a rule, they weren't out hunting victims every night.

If you could call that lucky. Which Simone did, and that more than anything said just how weird her life was.

Anytime the Daimons left their holes, the Dark-Hunters Tate worked for would seek them out, hoping to stop them from killing more people. A bonus to the Daimons' deaths was that it also freed the human souls they'd eaten so that their victims could go on to the afterlife.

Tate swabbed his fry in ketchup. "Definitely not

Daimon," he repeated. "She was drained of all her blood, and since none was found at the crime scene, we assume she died somewhere else and was dumped in the alley. You sure you can't summon her from the grave and ask her what happened?"

"That would be a voodoo priestess, Tate. The decedents come to me, not the other way around."

He stifled a look of disappointment. "We need to find the body ASAP. Her parents are on their way down from Wichita and I don't want to tell them that their little girl went AWOL from the examining table."

"Did you get anything from Nialls?"

Tate scoffed. "Nothing coherent. As you can imagine, he was a bit hysterical. All he'd say was that she smiled at him on her way out the door."

"So you don't know if she was a zombie then?"

"Thankfully, I've never seen a zombie. Much other weird shit on the job, but not that. Have you?"

"No. However, I've learned to not question things like that. If there's a legend, then there's something real behind it."

He saluted her with his drink.

"What about your Squire contacts? Have they anything to offer on this?"

Tate shook his head. "None of them know anything more about the dead walking around than you or I. Daimons don't make the dead rise. They make the living fall."

Simone looked at Jesse. "You have any suggestions?"

"Only that I wish my body were still walking around. It would make my undeath easier to bear."

"Thanks for the nonhelp, Jess. You're such a doll."

Simone didn't speak much more as they finished lunch, then headed to the morgue. Jesse opted to stay outside while she followed Tate into the crypt. Honestly, she couldn't blame Jesse for his feelings. She didn't like hanging out with the dead, either, Jesse notwithstanding. The only reason she did what she did was to help the victims and their families. Having seen her own mother and brother gunned down before her, the last thing she wanted was to stand by and let someone else's killer go free.

It was why she worked cases for the city pro bono and why she spent her life training the next generation of medical examiners at Tulane. She figured she could do more good by training other MEs to be conscientious than she could working on mundane cases. The more people who did their jobs right, the fewer criminals who would go free to slaughter again.

That philosophy was also what kept her single. Most men didn't appreciate dating a woman who was handy with both a scalpel and a shovel.

Tate opened a door in the middle of the crypt vault and pulled out an empty drawer. "She was stored in here."

"Do you have any of her personal items?"

"Let me get them."

Simone closed the drawer and turned slightly as she felt a presence behind her. It was a young woman around the age of twenty-four. Her brown hair was mussed and she looked a bit confused. It was a natural state for many of the newly deceased.

"Can I help you?" Simone asked the girl.

"Where am I?"

Simone hesitated. She never liked being the one to tell another that they were no longer alive. "What's the last thing you remember?"

"I was walking home from work."

That was a good start. If Simone could help the woman remember more details of her life right before it ended, then she might remember her death, too. "What's your name, sweetie?"

"Gloria Thieradeaux."

A chill went down her spine as Simone recognized her from the photos. This was the woman whose body had risen up and walked out of the morgue.

Merde.

The ghost looked about the room. "Why am I here?"

"I'm not sure." Any more than she was sure how her body had reanimated itself.

"Why can't I touch anything?" The agony in her voice made tears of sympathy well in Simone's eyes.

There was no avoiding the answer and no way to make it kind or gentle on the poor thing. "I'm afraid you're dead."

Gloria shook her head. "No. I just need to get home." She frowned as she looked around the room as if trying to identify something. "But I can't remember where I live. Do I know you?"

Simone paused. Something wasn't right. It was normal for a new ghost to be slightly disoriented, but Gloria was more than that. It was like a part of her was missing . . .

"Jesse!" Simone called. "I know you hate it in here, but I really, really need you."

He manifested right beside her. "Yeah, boss?"

She indicated Gloria with a tilt of her chin. "She doesn't know where she lives."

His scowl was fierce. "Do you remember when they killed you?"

"Jesse," she said under her breath, "a little tact, please."

Ignoring her, Gloria shook her head. "I don't feel dead. Are you sure I died?"

Simone passed her hand through the woman's abdomen. "Either that, Princess Leia, or you're a hologram."

Gloria stared at her in a cross between horror and disbelief. "How did you do that?"

Jesse answered for her. "We have no body. All we have is our essence and consciousness."

Gloria staggered back as if overwhelmed. "I

don't understand. How can you die and not know it?"

Jesse shrugged. "It happens. Not common, mind you. Most people know when they die, but every now and again, someone gets trapped on this plane without realizing they're dead."

Gloria shook her head in denial. "I can't be dead. I have finals."

"The Reaper waits for no one, babe," Jesse said glibly. "Believe me, I have firsthand experience there. It's a pisser, but reality for us nonetheless."

"What's going on?"

Simone turned at Tate's worried voice. He was standing behind her with a manila envelope in his hand.

"I found Gloria."

"Good, where is she?"

Simone glanced to where Jesse and Gloria stood side by side. "Well, her ghost is right in front of me. Unfortunately, she has no more clue about her body's whereabouts than we do."

Tate let out a frustrated breath. "How can that be? I mean, really, shouldn't the ghost have like a homing beacon on its body or something?"

"It would make sense. But unfortunately, the two parts separate and the spirit never wanders back to the body . . . at least not to my knowledge." Simone looked at Jesse, who nodded his head in agreement.

Tate held the envelope out to her. "So where does that leave us?"

"With one hell of a mystery." Simone took the envelope from his hands and reached inside to touch a necklace that must have belonged to Gloria. Closing her eyes, she tried to get some sense of the time and place where Gloria had passed.

Nothing happened.

She couldn't even get an emotion from it, which was highly unusual for her. Since she'd been five years old, Simone had been able to glean emotions that were attached to objects as soon as she touched them.

She dropped it back into the envelope. "I suggest you call your Squire buddies and get them started on a hunt for her body while Jesse and I try to help her remember something that might lead us to its whereabouts."

"I'll see what I can do."

Simone turned to Jesse.

"I hear you," he said before she could speak. "We're going to scout the alley where she was found for a clue."

"Exactly."

Tate paused in front of the door with a frown. "Exactly what?"

"Jesse and I are going to the Warehouse District. I'll let you know if we find anything."

"Please do." Tate held the door open so that she and her "companions" could leave.

She started down the white, Spartan hallway.

"Hey, Simone?"

She looked back at Tate who was about to head in the opposite direction. "Yes?"

"Be careful."

Those words warmed her. Tate and LaShonda were the only people in the world who would miss her if anything were to happen to her. "I'm always careful, boo. You know that."

He inclined his head to her. "Just the same, keep your stun gun loaded and call me as soon as you're done. I don't want to get another call to that alley. I've buried enough people I love. I don't want to do it again."

She smiled at his concern. "It's an alley, Tate. There are a million of them in this city. I'll be fine."

He nodded at her before he headed toward his office.

Simone took a second as that weird feeling came over her again. She'd never understood those odd sensations. But one thing she remembered clearly . . . the first time she'd had it.

"I'll be right back, baby. You wait in the car and don't move." Those were the last words her mother had said to her before she took her brother into the store.

And died.

Simone flinched as unbridled grief tore through her. *In one instant, everything can change.* It was the mantra she lived her life by and a lesson she'd learned all too well when she was only ten years old.

Never take anyone or anything for granted.

In one blink, life altered and sometimes all you could do was hang on as tightly as possible while it did its best to sling you off.

Trying not to think about that, she headed down the hall, toward the door that led to the parking lot.

Kalosis (the Atlantean Hell Realm)

Stryker walked down the dark hallway that led from his bedroom to the throne room where he held court over his Daimon army. There shouldn't be anyone in it this time of day . . .

Or night. Whichever it was. Let's face it, here in hell it didn't really matter.

In Kalosis, it was always dark since any amount of daylight was fatal to his people. That had been a curse from his father, Apollo, who in the midst of a hissy fit had condemned everyone of the Apollite race that Apollo had created to be banished from the sun.

And to die painfully at age twenty-seven. The only way an Apollite could survive past his or her twenty-seventh birthday was to take a human soul into their body. From that moment on, the Apollite mutated into a Daimon—a demonlike creature who had to continue to swallow human souls in order to stay alive.

Sure it was a crappy, cold existence, but it was so much better than the alternative.

Besides, Stryker had survived eleven thousand years as a Daimon—their existence was definitely not without its benefits. And its rewards.

Highly entertained by the thought, he paused in the entrance of his throne room as he caught sight of his sister, Satara, surrounded by a reddish haze while she sat perched on his throne. Her hair was black—something she seldom chose as a color. She mumbled words in ancient Greek as she swayed to a silent song.

Yeah . . .

He cleared his throat, but she ignored him. Unamused by her actions, he crossed his arms over his chest and closed the distance between them.

What she was chanting amused him even less than her ignoring him. "Why are you summoning a demon?"

One eye, bloodred, opened to pin him with a feral stare. "I'm not summoning. I'm controlling."

He cocked a single brow. "Really? And who has you so angry that you're sending a demon for them?"

"What do you care?" She closed her eye and continued her chant.

If they'd had a loving relationship, Stryker

might have left her to it. But he was far from a loving brother and she was ever his bane. Snapping his fingers, he made the light in the hall blinding. "If you want to kill someone, I know a few gallu demons who are dying to eat."

She let out a shrill scream before she opened her eyes and stood up from his throne. "Like they'd do anything I ask. You're an idiot for allowing the gallu to stay here. It's the same as sleeping with a pack of feral wolves at your feet. Sooner or later, they will attack and you'll be dead."

As if he were afraid of some Sumerian castoffs. "Kessar and crew don't frighten me." His sister's insatiable ambition did. There was nothing she wouldn't do to get what she wanted and he knew it. "Who are you after?"

"Hades let that bastard Xypher out of his hole."

The name was vaguely familiar, but for his life, he couldn't remember who it was. "Xypher?"

Satara rolled her eyes. "Oh, how could you forget him? He was the first Dream-Hunter I coaxed away from his duties and turned."

Stryker shook his head as he remembered the god who'd been a handful the instant he started sniffing around Satara's heels. It'd taken a number of gods to run the bastard down and kill him. "Speaking of wolves at your throat. Did I not warn you about him?"

"Oh, shut up."

Stryker rudely moved her aside so that he could take his seat on the throne. "You know, little sister, I'd be playing nice right now if I were you. After all, you're the one in hiding . . . in my house."

"I'm not in hiding."

"No? Then why are you here? Shouldn't you be on Olympus at the beck and call of Auntie Artemis?"

The fury in her eyes told him he'd struck a chord. Good. He lived to piss off people.

"Xypher has to be stopped. He will kill me if he has a chance."

"You think? You coaxed the man from his cushy god-life, caused him to be hunted and then killed and tortured for eternity. I can't imagine why he's not bringing you roses and kisses."

She curled her lip at him. "Well, at least I didn't slit open the throat of my own son."

Stryker thrust his hand out and brought her into his grasp with his demigod powers. He tightened his hold on her throat until her eyes bulged and he felt her larynx start to crush. "Xypher isn't the only man you should be afraid of." He shoved her away from him.

Satara caught herself and choked while she glared furiously. "I've given everything to you, Strykerius. I've spied for you and told you things no one else would. Now I ask for a modicum of protection and what do you do? Threaten me. Fine. I'll leave, and when Xypher kills me, I hope you'll think back on this and remember that you're the only reason you're alone in this world."

Stryker rubbed his brow, grateful he couldn't get a headache from her whiny tirade. "Oh, stop the dramatics. I've never been one for the theater. You're welcome to hide out here and release as many demons into the human world as you like. But before you completely annihilate my food source, might I offer a suggestion to you?"

"What?"

Stryker manifested a set of golden bracelets in his hand—one of three pairs that had been uncovered just two years ago. One of his generals had found them and brought them to him, not knowing what they were.

But Stryker knew, and he was reserving one pair for a very special "friend."

He held the bracelets out to her.

Taking them, she grimaced as if they were made of coal and not Atlantean gold. "What do I do with these?"

He sighed in weariness. There were times when she was brilliant and other times when he had to lead her about as if she had the intellect of a five-year-old goat. "How do you kill a god?"

"You strip his powers."

He nodded approvingly. "If you can't do that?"

"You seduce a Chthonian and tell them that the god attacked you, then laugh while the Chthonian sucks the life out of him. But I don't have time for that. Xypher is one step away from storming his way down here and killing me."

Stryker growled at her in irritation. "Stop thinking like a whore for a minute. The best way to take out an enemy is to attack his weakest point."

She put her hands on her hips. The bracelets dangled precariously from her right hand as if they were cheap knockoffs and not worth more than a human kingdom ... or her life. "He doesn't have one."

Stryker narrowed his eyes on the bracelets. "You put one of those on him and he will."

Finally interested in what he'd put in her hands, she inspected them. "What are you saying?"

"What I'm saying, Themis, is those little gold bracelets in your hands are his Achilles' heel. Pass those along to one of my Spathi Daimons and have him secure one to Xypher and the other to a mortal and all your troubles are over."

She smiled as she finally understood the significance of the bracelets. "They bind them . . . Kill the mortal and Xypher dies."

He inclined his head to her. "Even better than that, if the mortal gets more than twenty feet from him, the human dies . . . and so does he."

She laughed evilly before she approached his throne and kissed him on his cheek. "I knew I loved you for a reason."

Stryker wasn't stupid enough to believe that for even a moment. His sister was incapable of loving anyone except herself. But he'd won her over as an ally for a few days more.

Satara tossed one bracelet up and caught it in her hands. "I can't wait to see his face when he learns what these are." Then she vanished before Stryker could give her one more piece of advice.

"Choose your human wisely." The last thing she needed was to find one who actually knew how to fight them.

By the time Simone finished teaching her afternoon class and reached the alley, it was nearing dusk. There was an unseasonable biting chill to the breeze as she got out of her white Honda and stepped up on the curb. She pulled the collar of her wool coat up higher on her neck and shivered. She never liked approaching crime scenes, especially after they'd been cleared. Right now, there was nothing to mark this as a place of violence. It looked like all the other alleys in town.

That was what disturbed her most.

Gloria's life had ended abruptly right here and only Gloria and her family would ever know it. Hundreds of people would walk right past this spot without being aware of the fact that one young woman had been dumped here like so much rubbish. The thought of it made her livid and it reminded her of her own mother.

Simone flinched.

"You okay?" Jesse asked.

"Yeah. Bad chicken at lunch."

"You ate a ham and cheese sandwich."

"Oh, shush, smarty-pants. Stop being so attentive." She reached into her purse and pulled out a pair of latex gloves just in case she might find something. It would also protect her from any stray germs that might be lingering. That was one thing she continually harped on with her students. Any clothes worn to a crime scene should be treated as biohazard. In the last few years she'd brought home more contagion than she even wanted to think about and that alone made her glad she lived alone. The last thing she wanted was to make a significant other ill.

She opened her trunk and tossed her purse inside before she pulled out her ME toolbox that contained everything she'd need to preserve any evidence that might have been overlooked by the police.

Gloria cocked her head as she stared into the alley.

Simone's stomach tightened in sympathy. "You remember something?"

"There was a weird growling . . ." Her voice was quiet. Distant.

"Growling?"

Gloria nodded. "It was deep and feral, but not really like an animal."

"Was it like this?" Jesse made an inhuman ghost noise.

Gloria scowled at him. "That sounds like Darth Vader choking on a chicken bone. No."

He passed an indignant glare to Simone as she burst out laughing. "Well, it did."

"Fine, see if I help anymore."

Simone shook her head at him before she pulled out her flashlight and headed to the area where she'd seen the body photographed. There were buildings on three sides and a gutter in the center. The walkway all around was broken up. Typical alley with a lot of street traffic around it. Not to mention, anyone in the buildings could easily look out the window and see right where they were standing.

It made her wonder if there'd been a witness who'd seen the killer . . .

She glanced over to where Jesse was doing the Michael Jackson Moonwalk while he surveyed the alley and street. All the boy needed was a red leather jacket with gold studs and a sequined glove.

"Excuse me, Mr. Thriller or Beat It or whatever video you're sadly reliving . . . Is it just me or is this area way too exposed for this to be a Daimon attack?"

After giving her a hateful glare, Jesse agreed. "There's too much movement around here and they wouldn't have minded a little blood on the ground. Them bastards are sloppy eaters."

"Yeah, that's what I'm thinking, too. I believe Tate had it right when he said she died somewhere else. But the claw marks on her neck . . . that's not human. If not a Daimon, what killed her?"

"Excuse me, people," Gloria snapped. "I happen to be standing right here. Do you mind?"

Simone cringed at her insensitivity. Normally she was much more careful around her spirits. "Sorry."

Jesse approached Gloria. "But you remember being here, right?"

Gloria nodded. "I heard the noise and then tried to cross the street to get away from it."

"Good," Simone prompted. "You remember anything else?"

Gloria shook her head. "I really don't think I'm dead. I mean, I know you went through me with your hand earlier, but I remember this movie I saw with Reese Witherspoon—"

"*Just like Heaven,*" Simone supplied.

"Yeah, that was it. Everyone thought Reese was a ghost, but she was just in a coma. Maybe that's me."

Simone really wished that were the case. She looked at Jesse, hoping he could help her make Gloria comprehend that this was final and there wasn't any coming back from it no matter how much they all wished otherwise.

He gave Gloria an understanding smile. "I know how you feel. That disbelief that keeps telling you it's a dream, but you have to face the fact that you're not in a coma."

Simone sighed as she skimmed the empty alley. There was only a piece of paper and a crushed Starbucks cup. Nothing else.

"I really don't see anything helpful," she said to the ghosts. "The police must have gotten everything. Let's head back to Tate and see what his people have unearthed."

As she took a step toward her car, she heard a tsking sound behind them that sent chills over her. No one had been there before . . .

"Surely you don't want to be leaving us so soon. After all, we just got here . . . and we're looking for a good bite to eat."

Simone turned her flashlight on the man speaking.

Correction, it wasn't a man. It was a Daimon.

And he wasn't alone.

TWO

Jesse's cheeks paled. Not that, as a ghost, he had much color to begin with, so whenever he lost what little he had, it scared her.

He gave her a cheesy grin. "Looks like I was wrong about the Daimons choosing this spot, huh?"

Simone stepped back. "Yeah, Jess, bad call."

The Daimon turned toward Jesse and smiled. "How thoughtful. We have three for the price of one, guys. Guess Apollo is in a good mood tonight."

As the Daimons made a move for Gloria, Simone

pulled her stun gun from her pocket and rushed them. There was no way she was going to let them hurt the poor ghost. "Stay away from her!"

The first Daimon dodged the electric prongs that flew from the stun gun toward him, and knocked her back. Before she could counter-attack, he had the stun gun out of her hand. "Don't be jealous, baby. We'll get to you in a jiffy."

"Jiffy?" The malevolent, mocking tone sent a shiver down her spine. "What kind of pathetic wuss uses the word 'jiffy'?"

Simone froze at the voice that was so deep she felt it resonate inside her bones.

Out of the darkness moved a shadow so large, it dwarfed her. An instant later, the Daimon went flying over her head to slam into the wall next to Jesse. The Daimon hit it so hard, she was amazed he didn't splatter like a bug. And he was quickly joined by another Daimon who landed on top of him.

"Open the portal," the stranger growled at the third Daimon he now held in his fist.

"I ain't opening shit."

"Wrong answer."

The Daimon joined the other two.

The shadow bore down on her like a mountain. Sinister. Angry. Cold. Determined.

She shone the light on him and felt her breath leave her in one sudden gasp. Easily over six feet tall, he had long, black hair that was tousled around features as perfect as any actor she'd ever seen and eyes so blue they all but glowed in the darkness. He had his jaw set as if he were attempting to keep his fury leashed, and failing miserably. Every sinew of his body rippled like a feral beast on the prowl. He was seduction and he was death.

Wearing only a pair of jeans and a black T-shirt, he appeared immune to the cold. His shoulders were wide, his waist narrow, and there was an aura around him that said absolute killer. No fear.

No mercy.

Those icy blue eyes penetrated with hatred and warning. And they sent shivers over her. "This is the part where you need to run, little human. Don't look back."

Those words angered her to the same level he appeared to operate at. She wasn't incompetent or weak. "I'm not little." She elbowed the Daimon who was running at her in the throat before she flipped him onto the ground and kicked him.

The newcomer scoffed at her show of power. "Then let death become you." He turned and pulled the Daimon she'd attacked off the ground. He plowed him into the wall so hard, it left a dent in the brick. The Daimon grunted and cursed.

"Open the portal," he demanded of the Daimon, whose nose and mouth were bleeding profusely.

As if in response to his words, a bright light flashed at the rear of the alley, right in a corner.

The man dropped the Daimon in his hands and

headed for the light, but before he could enter, a giant, blond Daimon came out of it.

This wasn't one of the normal Daimons she'd seen before.

Dressed in black leather, he had the aura of a trained fighter. Of someone who was used to killing and making the death as painful as possible.

Simone couldn't move at the frightening sight. At least seven feet tall, the Daimon actually laughed and exposed his long sharp fangs at the dark-haired man an instant before he attacked him.

Fists and kicks were flying faster than she could follow. Apparently no braver than schoolgirls, the other three Daimons ran toward the street to get away from the combatants.

Simone stumbled away as the Daimon knocked the man against the wall. The man let out a huff as he collided with the stone. The Daimon landed a punch against his jaw so solid that she could feel it herself.

The man took it with a grimace before he head-butted the Daimon, who staggered back. But the Daimon didn't go far before he reached into his coat and pulled out a large gold bracelet. He snapped it around the man's wrist.

The man hissed as if the bracelet burned his skin. The Daimon kicked him back, then turned to her.

This would be a good time to take the man's advice and run like hell.

Simone didn't know what the Daimon intended, but whatever it was, it boded rotten for her. She ran for the street. The Daimon caught her and slung her to the ground. She scrambled to get away, but he was inhumanly strong and much faster than she was.

He grabbed her arm and shoved her over onto her back. She tried to kick him. It didn't work. He pushed her sleeve back to expose her forearm.

Rather than bite her, he snapped another bracelet onto her wrist. Pain tore through her arm with such ferocity that she wouldn't have been surprised to see her arm shredded.

She struggled to breathe for the pain of it.

Meanwhile the Daimon laughed at the tears that gathered in her eyes. He smiled evilly. "Time for you to die, human."

Before he could carry out his promise, Jesse picked up her toolbox and hit him across the back. The Daimon turned on him with a hiss made rabid by his razor–sharp fangs and lunged.

One heartbeat later, the stranger was there, pulling her off the ground and shoving her toward the street. "Move your ass."

"What do you think I was doing?"

"Picking your nose." He paused to sling his hand out at the Daimon after them. The leather-clad Daimon recoiled as if something invisible had blasted him.

An instant later, that same invisible force

slammed into her and sent her flying. She landed on the ground with a thud so hard, it knocked the wind from her lungs.

"Breathe, Sim, breathe," Jesse said as he appeared beside her. He grabbed the keys from her pocket and put them in her hand. "Now get your butt up!" He ran to her car and opened the door for her.

Simone followed him as fast as she could. As she got in, someone shoved her from behind. She looked back to see the dark-haired stranger. He pushed her into the passenger seat and climbed into the car after her.

Even more surprising than that, he glared at Jesse, who was still outside. "Get in, ghost-boy, or get eaten. I don't care which and I'm not waiting."

Something struck the car.

Turning to look out, Simone gasped at the sight of the leather-clad Daimon perched like a giant ornament on her white hood. He moved to punch the windshield. The man beside her gunned the engine and knocked the Daimon face first into the glass before he slammed on the brakes and sent him flying from the hood.

The man jerked the wheel and sent the car careening into traffic, over the median. Tires squealed. Cars crashed around them as horns began blaring.

Simone crossed herself and prayed as she watched headlights coming at them, fast and furious. Her hands shaking from fright, she buckled herself in while Jesse screamed out like a terrified child in the backseat. As if *he* could die.

The man snatched the wheel an instant before they would have hit a dump truck head-on, and sent the car back into the correct lane. Still, cars around them slammed on brakes and swerved to get out of their way. "This would probably be easier if I knew how to drive, huh?"

Her eyes widened as she looked at the man beside her. "I hope you're joking."

"Not really," he said as he clipped the fender on a parked car.

Simone didn't know what horrified her most. The man beside her or what her insurance rates would be if he didn't stop hitting things.

"Watch out!" she screamed as he headed for another truck.

He swerved a heartbeat before it would have plowed into them.

By the time he turned into an alley and slammed on the brakes hard enough to put a bruise on her shoulder from the seat belt, she was ready to jump out of the car and take a chance on the road rather than die in a twisted heap of burning metal.

The man turned in the seat to look at her. With near perfect features, he was ruggedly handsome. Blue eyes showed intelligence, if not kindness. He had one muscular arm braced on the dash and the other on the seat. He would be gorgeous if he wasn't so frightening. "I have no idea what I'm doing. Given that, I think I should surrender this thing to someone who knows how to properly operate it."

Simone gulped for air as she tried to get her heart to stop pounding. She pried her grip loose from the door handle. "Who the hell are you?"

He glanced at the bracelet on his wrist, then snatched at it as if trying to jerk it off. "Xypher, and you are?"

"Pissed off. You wrecked my car, shoved me around, and are a complete and utter dickhead!"

"Dear God," he said dryly, "what a mouthful—your mom must have really wanted a son. Mind if I call you 'Pissed' for short? The rest of that is just too much to say every time I want your attention."

Jesse laughed from the backseat.

Simone glared at him.

Jesse at least had the good grace to look contrite. "Sorry, but you should be in my shoes. You two are hysterical."

"Careful, ghost-boy, or I'll summon a Daimon and feed you to it."

Simone was stunned. "You can hear him?"

Xypher gave her a blank stare before he replied dryly, "Can't you?"

"Yes. But no one else has ever heard him before."

"Guess you're not so special after all, huh?"

She screwed her face up at him. "You are so rude."

"No shit, human." He started tearing at the bracelet with his teeth.

She cringed at the sound of enamel on metal. She hated to hear teeth scrape like that. "What are you doing?"

He let out a frustrated sigh before he went back to pulling at the bracelet. "You have no idea what happened to us just now, do you?"

"Aside from being assaulted by you and a group of the damned, is there something else I should know?"

He held her arm up to show her the bracelet that matched his. "Yeah. Since both of us are wearing these I'm going to take a wild guess that they bind us together somehow. 'Cause, let's face it, the Daimons don't usually tag you before they bite. They're not Marlin Perkins out to study us."

Simone looked down at her arm as a bad feeling went through her. "What are you saying?" She actually knew, but she wanted to hear it from him before she was willing to believe it.

"I'm saying that if I were you, I wouldn't get too far away from me until we figure out what exactly these are and what they do. Knowing the gods as I do, I'm sure we're fucked somehow."

Knowing the gods . . .

Oh, this was going from bad to worse. "What

are you?" she asked, terrified of what answer he might give her.

His look was as cold as the wind outside. "Don't ask questions you don't really want answered."

"Um, guys . . ." Jesse said, interrupting them. "The Daimons have a car and they're coming after us."

Xypher cursed.

In the blink of an eye, Simone went from the passenger side to the driver's.

Xypher was now in her seat. "Can you get us out of here?"

She should probably question what had just happened, but given the fact that one of her best friends was a ghost and the other worked for immortal vampire slayers, she was used to the unusual on a daily basis. What mattered right now was getting free.

"Defensive Driving 101. Fasten your seat belt." She threw the car in reverse and headed for the Daimons, who quickly swerved to miss her. Simone did a quick K-turn in the center of the road and headed back toward the alley where they'd met.

"Nice work."

She was amazed that the surly Xypher was capable of giving her a compliment. "It pays to hang around the police. You pick up all kinds of useful things."

Jesse popped his head up in the front seat, between them. "They're still behind us."

"Not for long." Xypher rolled down the window and he pulled a gun out of his pants pocket. He opened fire on the car following them.

Simone's eyes widened as she heard the tire blow out. The car skidded sideways before it turned over in the street. "Nice shooting, Tex."

He pulled the mag out and replaced it with another one. "I have an unfair advantage. I can make the bullets go where I want them to. I took out the Daimons before I KO'd the car."

Simone cut into a small parking lot, then stopped again. She turned in the seat to face him. His cheeks were reddened from his exertion and the wind burn on his skin as he'd fired on the Daimons. The color made his eyes stand out even more.

He looked gorgeous and human, and yet . . .

"What exactly are you?"

Xypher didn't answer as he rubbed a hand over his brow. "We have to figure out these bracelets before it gets any darker. I don't like playing with unknown factors."

She gave him a droll stare. "You're not alone on Planet Ego. I, too, want to know what I'm dealing with, and right now, Psycho, you're the most crucial unknown factor in my world. So answer my question. What are you?"

The sneer was back on his face. "That's not so easily answered, human."

She turned the car off, pulled the keys out, and folded her arms over her chest. "Try."

Xypher ground his teeth as he fought the urge to kill her. After all, she was just another human, albeit a cute one. Human, nonetheless. Normally, he wouldn't have hesitated to put her out of his misery, but he had a really bad feeling about the bracelet on his arm. The fact that they both wore them probably meant their lives, if not actual souls, were linked together somehow. Which meant that if she died, there was probably a good bet that he would, too.

Dammit. She'd have to live until he figured this out.

He considered lying to her. But why bother? She'd seen the Daimons, some of his powers, and what the hell? There was a ghost in the backseat who appeared to be a friend of hers. The way she'd acted so far said that she was at least familiar with the supernatural.

What was a little more?

"How up are you on Greek mythology?" he asked her.

"Zeus is the king, right?"

Xypher snorted. "He thinks he is most days. Personally, I think he's a pompous ass who should be bitch-slapped by Hera at least once in his existence."

Simone winced as she realized that he was going to be somehow related to them . . . Yeah, her luck was improving by the minute. "So what has Zeus got to do with this?"

"Not much really. You're the one who brought him up."

She let out a tired breath of exasperation. "I'm getting a headache and you're still avoiding my question."

"Fine," he said simply. "I'm a Skotos."

She scowled at the unfamiliar word. "That means what? You have toe jam?"

He looked less than amused by her question. "No, human, it means I used to be a dream god."

Well, he was kind of dreamy . . .

Oh, no, Sim, you're not really buying into his baloney, are you? It seemed so far-fetched and yet the Dark-Hunters Tate worked for were an army of immortal warriors created by the goddess Artemis to protect mankind.

Yeah, it'd taken her a while to swallow that reality. And if she believed that Tate wasn't crazy and that the Daimons were real—because she'd seen them more times than she wanted to—then she had no choice except to buy this farm tale, too.

Taking a deep breath to brace herself for the rest of his story, she tensed. "And now you are?"

"The walking dead."

With images of the Daimons trying to eat her running through her head, Simone shot out of the car. All she could think of was escaping him before he made a meal out of her.

She didn't get very far.

Xypher flashed himself in front of her and caught her against his chest. "I told you not—"

She clipped him hard in the throat.

Cursing, he let go of her as he struggled to breathe.

Xypher glared at her as he imagined tearing her into bloody pieces. Angry beyond tolerance, he slung his hand out and pinned her to the wall behind her. His throat throbbing, he stalked toward her intending to make her pay for her attack.

He'd been hit enough in his life . . .

"Do that again," he growled between clenched teeth, "and, bracelet or no bracelet, I'll tear your head off and use it for a doorstop."

Simone felt fear crawling down her spine, but she wasn't about to let him see it. "What do you want with me?"

"Not a damn thing. All I want is an entrance into the Daimon hell so that I can visit and kill an old friend. You're just the poor sap who got caught in the crossfire."

He released her so fast that Simone almost fell. She caught herself and stood as tall as she could, but it was far from intimidating since he was a full head taller than her. "I don't like being threatened, lied to, or manipulated. You'd do well to remember that," she said.

He sneered at her bravado. "Or what you're going to snivel at me?"

Jesse started for him but before he could strike Xypher, Xypher turned and caught him by the throat. Throwing Jesse to the ground, he drew back to hit him, then caught himself before he completed the punch.

He moved away.

Jesse gaped at her as he pushed himself to his feet.

Simone was stunned. Though Jesse could move things, no one had ever been able to touch him before. "How can you touch him?"

Xypher crossed his arms over his chest. "I still have a lot of my god powers, but not all of them, and the ones I have keep coming and going without any predictability. No doubt courtesy of Hades and his sick sense of humor."

Jesse stared at her in disbelief. "I think we're going to have to believe him. No one's been able to touch me since the night I died."

Swallowing, Simone nodded her agreement. What Xypher had just done was impossible and unexplainable. "All right. Let's start over. You're a dream god with screwed-up powers who is out to kill someone. And these . . ." She held up her arm with the bracelet. "Are an unfortunate gift."

He nodded. "For all I know, these little Tinkertoys could explode and kill us. We've got to get them off."

You think? She bit back the sarcasm, sensing it wouldn't help the situation or his cranky mood. "Okay. I think I know someone who can help us."

"You?" He sneered. "*You* know someone." He laughed.

Oh, that offended her. "Hey, I happen to know a lot of people. Most of them are highly unusual."

"Yeah, and do any of them have a connection to a Greek god?"

"As a matter of fact they do." She raked him with a smug look. "They happen to work for Artemis."

He sobered instantly. "You know the Dark-Hunters?"

"Not personally, but I know a Squire."

"Take me to him."

Those words went over her like ice down a gown in the middle of the night. "You are one seriously bossy SOB. Who died and made you . . ."

Simone paused as she realized that if he was telling the truth, then the man really was a god. Which would answer her question. And it explained a lot about his ego and pushiness. "Never mind. Get in the car and let's find Tate. If you're right about these things exploding, then we need to hurry."

They were in the car instantly.

Simone shook her head to clear it as a foreign buzz whispered in her ears. "Wow. Can you take us to Tate's office like that?"

"Only if I've been to it first. I have to know

where I'm going to perfect it. Otherwise we could turn up in a wall or someplace foul."

Foul was bad. She definitely didn't want to do that. Implantation in a wall wouldn't be much better.

Jesse appeared in the backseat. "By the way, did you guys realize that Gloria vanished during the chase? I don't know if that's a good thing or a bad thing."

Sadness gripped her as she started the car. "I'm sure it's bad. But we'll worry about her after I talk to Tate. Unless you can find her in the nether plane, there's not a lot we can do about her for now."

Fear flashed in Jesse's brown eyes. "Yeah, right. Remember what happened the last time I did that? It's not an experience I want to rush back to."

Neither did she. Poor Jesse had almost gotten swallowed by a Daimon.

Simone headed toward Tate's office and picked up her phone from the console. She dialed his number to make sure he was there.

He answered on the fourth ring. "Hey, my love. I just got off the phone with the Squires."

She slid a glance to Xypher, who was sitting there looking grim and irritable. "That's great, but right now I have a really pressing problem."

"You find something?"

"More like something found me."

"What do you mean?" Tate asked, his voice full of fear.

Simone considered the best way to tell him what had happened. But she wasn't one to beat around the bush. Besides, if Tate worked for the Dark-Hunters, maybe he knew what a Dream-Hunter was. "While I was looking over things, a group of Daimons showed up and so did . . . a Skotos."

Tate laughed nervously. "You're shitting me, right?"

Xypher cocked a handsome brow at her as if he could hear her conversation.

"No," she said, dragging the word out, "and I take it you know what that is, then."

"Absolutely. Were you hurt?"

"Scuffed a bit." She turned left onto Canal. "But the point of this is the Daimons slapped something on my wrist and the Skotos', too. We don't know what it is and we need to find someone who does."

"You need an oracle." Tate made that sound so easy.

Simone shook her head. "Yeah, and we're just a little far from Delphi, hon."

"You don't have to go to Greece, boo. You know Julian Alexander, right?"

She frowned at the familiar name. "The hot classics professor?"

"Not that I personally consider him hot, but yeah."

She ignored his sarcasm. "You're not seriously telling me that he's an oracle who speaks to the gods?"

Tate laughed evilly. "Brace yourself, boo. He's the son of Aphrodite."

Of course he was . . . Why should anything in the world make sense? Dear Lord, it wasn't like she wasn't sitting beside one of the hottest men on the planet who was a god himself. Or that she had a goofy teenage ghost in her backseat mouthing the words to the Tears for Fears song "Everybody Wants to Rule the World."

It only made sense that the hottie in the classics department was a demigod, too . . .

"I just knew I wasn't going to like that answer," she muttered. "And to think, all this time I just thought he was a cute teacher."

"And all your students think you're eccentric for talking to yourself when they catch you having conversations with Jesse."

"Of course they do. Okay, how do I find him?"

"Let me give you his number."

Simone repeated the number to Jesse to help her remember it. Hanging up from Tate, she immediately called Julian.

He answered on the third ring.

"Dr. Alexander?"

"Yes?"

"I don't know if you remember me, but we've met at a couple of faculty functions. I'm Dr. Simone Dubois—"

"The ME and pathology professor . . . Yes, I remember you."

That was impressive since she was highly unremarkable. She was average height, average weight, with curly dark brown hair and hazel-brown eyes, and she normally wore beige and browns or a white lab coat. As a rule, she never stuck in people's memories. In fact, her senior high school paper had once voted her Most Likely to Be Forgotten . . . or Sat On By Mistake. The fact that Dr. Alexander remembered her gave her a bit of an unfounded thrill. "Good, 'cause I'm in a bit of a pickle with something."

"And that would be?" Even over the phone she could hear the reservation in his tone.

Xypher snatched the phone from her hand and started speaking to Julian in a language she couldn't even begin to identify. That being said, the smooth, lyrical quality of it was incredibly sexy. It was the kind of tone that could make a woman hot even if he were ordering pizza. And she hated the fact it was affecting her.

Good-looking or not, he was a jerk and the last thing any woman needed to do was feed his massive, pushy ego.

After a few minutes, he held the phone out to her. "He's going to give you directions to his house."

"Thanks," she said dryly. She took the phone from him. "Dr. Alexander?"

"Call me Julian."

She listened as he told her how to find his house. Luckily, it wasn't too far away.

It didn't take long to find the little bungalow off St. Charles. Simone had barely parked the car before Xypher flashed them to the porch. "You know, that's really obtrusive and disorienting."

"I really don't care." He knocked on the door.

Simone shook her head as Jesse joined her. Jesse looked about as pleased as she did.

Julian opened the door with a less-than-welcoming look. It never failed to shock her exactly how good-looking this man was. And she wasn't the only one to think so. His classes were always filled to the brim by female students who wanted nothing more than to stare at him. The fact he was one of the leading experts in the world about ancient civilizations was just a bonus.

The good doctor narrowed his eyes on Xypher as if he couldn't believe what he saw. "You have emotions."

Xypher curled his lip. "Not really. I only have one. Rage. Unless you count an insatiable need for vengeance. Then it's two."

Julian's scowl deepened. "How can you—"

"Look," Xypher snapped. "I don't have time for this. Get the bracelet off so that I can do what I have to do."

"He's extremely single-minded," Simone explained.

"Yeah, it shows." Julian stepped back. "Come in and let me see it."

Xypher literally shoved his arm in Julian's face. The man was truly obnoxious. "There."

"I suspect he might have been raised by apes," Simone said to Julian.

Julian gave a low laugh before he took Xypher's forearm and examined the bracelet while he stood in the doorway. "This isn't Greek."

Xypher scoffed. "Of course it is. I know the work of Hephaestus."

"So do I and this isn't it." Julian bent Xypher's arm so that he could see the lock. "I'm taking a shot in the dark here, but I think this is Atlantean in origin."

Xypher still looked less than convinced. "Are you sure?"

Julian nodded grimly. "Hephaestus is my step-father. I have trinkets from him all over my house . . . and experience with other items of his. Including handcuffs. The lock on this is definitely something else."

Simone wanted to groan in frustration. If Julian couldn't help them, who could? "Do you know what it does?"

"Not really, but if you can come in and get out of view of my neighbors, I can ask."

Xypher's eyes darkened dangerously.

"Don't even try," Julian said. "I've faced down a lot worse than a pissed-off Skotos."

Xypher gave him a menacing stare. "You have to sleep sometime."

"So do you."

Simone let out a sound of disgust. "Down, boys, down. Please, I just want to be free before I get testosterone poisoning."

Without another word, Julian led them into his house, toward the living room. Simone smiled at the sight of toys scattered about on the floor of the otherwise immaculately kept home. There were also pictures on the mantel of Julian with a dark-haired woman and kids—two boys and two girls. They appeared to be extremely happy.

"I didn't know you had children," she said, warmed by the sight.

He smiled proudly. "They're at a friend's house with their mom. I was trying to put together a syllabus for a new class while it was quiet and the baby wasn't trying to scribble all over my notes. Her older sister just taught her how to draw tulips and she's been putting them on everything."

Case in point, there were two bright pink tulips about toddler height on the wall behind him.

Simone could just imagine how hard it must be to think up interesting and beneficial class material while shuffling an insistent toddler. Personally, she hated coming up with new syllabi and that was without the addition of a . . . then again, she did have Jesse. She could actually relate to Julian's plight. "Sorry we're disturbing you."

"Don't worry about it," he said in a friendly tone. "If this is the worst interruption I have today, I'm doing remarkably well."

Then without another word to them, Julian tipped his head back and looked up at the ceiling. "Hey, Mom, you got a minute?"

Simone looked to the stairs, thinking his mother was in the house.

Apparently, she wasn't. A flash of light almost blinded her before an incredibly beautiful blond woman appeared in front of Julian. Thin and graceful while wearing a winter-white wool suit, his mother looked as stunned at Simone's presence as Simone was at hers.

Not to mention the fact that Julian's mother didn't look a day older than Julian. Holy cripes! There was a real live, breathing goddess in front of her! What would appear next? A dragon? Then again, if it were Brad Pitt, she'd be in business.

"What's going on?" Aphrodite asked.

Julian inclined his head behind her to where Xypher stood with his usual menacing glower. "We have a situation."

Aphrodite turned, then curled her lip. "You? What are you doing here? I thought you were dead."

"I am. Thanks. You look good for an old broad, too."

Aphrodite looked at him as if his words left a bad taste in her mouth.

Xypher ignored it as he held the bracelet up to her. "I'm here to get this off, or if not off, to at least find out what it is and what it does."

Simone wouldn't have thought the goddess could look any more repulsed and yet she pulled it off nicely. At least until she laughed.

"I swear by the river Styx, Xypher, I have never seen anyone make the gods madder than you. Whoever did you irritate for that?"

A muscle worked in Xypher's cheek. "Don't toy with me, Aphrodite. What is it?"

"It's a deamarkonian. A nice little trinket created by the Atlantean gods to kill the invincible. I didn't even know there were any left. Wherever did you find it?"

"I found it attached to my wrist. Now what exactly does it do?"

She made the most graceful shrug Simone had ever seen. "It binds the life forces of two entities together. You and"—she turned to Simone—"your little friend here. If one of you dies, the other dies. The Atlanteans used it as a way to kill a stronger person. You bind them to someone weak and you kill the weak in order to kill the strong. Simple."

Xypher cursed.

"Oh, but it gets even better," Aphrodite said, wrinkling her nose at him. "You have to stay near each other. If you wander too far afield, you'll both die."

Simone went still. "What?"

She nodded.

Xypher cursed again. "How far?"

"I have no idea. Guess we'll know when one of you crosses the boundary and you both die, huh?"

This time Xypher's curse was so foul it actually made Simone blush.

"I can't be stuck with you," he growled at her.

Her mouth dropped at his angry words. "Like you're my dream man come to life. Believe me, that sick feeling you have in your stomach is very much shared by me."

He narrowed his eyes on her, but she refused to back down. "Do you know of any way we can get this off?" he asked Aphrodite.

"Don't know."

By his expression, Simone could tell that wasn't the answer Xypher wanted.

"What do you mean, you don't know?" he said.

"What are you? Blind? I'm not Atlantean—that bracelet was designed to bring us down and that means the Atlantean gods who made it weren't real big on sharing its weaknesses with us. If you know someone tied to their dead pantheon, I suggest you try them." She turned toward Julian and her features softened. "I'll see you later, sweetie." She vanished.

"Aphrodite!" Xypher shouted at the ceiling. "Get your skinny ass back here!"

Simone scoffed. "I can't imagine why she wouldn't respond to that." She narrowed her gaze at Xypher. "Where did you go to charm school, anyway? Prison?"

He glared at her as if he could imagine his hands wrapped around her throat. That was okay by her since she currently held the same fantasy about choking him . . . preferably with one of the bracelets they were joined by.

Julian let out a tired breath as he put his hands on his hips. "I hope you're friends with Acheron. He's the only Atlantean I know of."

Xypher didn't looked overly thrilled by that prospect. "Give me his number."

Simone arched a brow at Xypher. "Can't you just call him out of thin air?"

Julian laughed. "Good luck. He's the only person I know who can be crankier than my mother or Xypher. You don't summon Acheron. You ask nicely."

"I'm so sick of the gods playing with my life," Xypher snarled as Julian handed him a piece of paper with a number scribbled on it.

A glimmer of something flashed in Julian's eyes. "I know the feeling. But sometimes salvation from them can come at the most unlikely time." His gaze went to Simone. "And from the most unlikely people."

Xypher rolled his eyes. "Don't sell me your bullshit. I'm on a countdown here. In twenty-two days I go back to hell. My only goal is to make sure that this time, I don't go alone."

"Then I wish you luck." Julian showed them to the door. "If you need anything else, let me know."

Simone thanked him before she led the way across the porch. She handed Xypher her cell phone as they walked to the car—she was actually surprised he didn't poof them back into it.

Then again, he was distracted. He didn't say a word. He merely took the phone and dialed the number with an irritable expression that was somehow inviting.

"Of course you're not answering . . ." he said in a guttural tone. Then in a more normal voice he said, "Acheron, it's Xypher. When you check messages, I need you to call me back at this number. I have a situation and I need you to contact me ASAP." He closed the phone and returned it to her.

Simone put it in her back pocket. "You think he'll be in touch?"

"Don't worry about it."

She pulled him to a stop on the walkway. "Do you have to be so surly over every question?"

"Do you have to be so damned perky? Was it too much to ask that I get chained to a depressed mute or one of those chicks who dresses in black and writes bad poetry?"

She'd never been more offended in her life. "What is wrong with you?"

His eyes flared in the darkness. "Be grateful, human, that you could never understand."

Understand what? That he was an asshole? There was no excuse in that.

"You know, you're not the only one with problems in this equation. I happen to have a life and a job. The last thing I need is to be pulling around a three-hundred-pound gorilla with a chip on his shoulder so big it's a wonder he's not hunchbacked from it."

"I don't weigh three hundred pounds."

She arched a single brow at his retort. "No denying the gorilla part?"

"No."

That took a lot of the bravado out of her. It was hard to get the upper hand when he seemed so content to be a monster.

"Um, Simone?" There was a note of fear in Jesse's voice.

She turned toward him. "Yes?"

"What is that?"

She looked to see what he was pointing at. Tall and lithe, it had eyes that were glowing red in the darkness.

And it was headed straight for them.

THREE

Xypher jerked her toward Jesse. "Both of you stay back."

Simone wasn't about to argue given the size of the creature headed toward them and the fact that his skin appeared to be boiling and smoking.

He was dressed in a flowing black cape that obscured everything but those creepy red eyes. He went for Xypher so fast, she could barely see it.

The two of them tore into each other.

Xypher flipped the demon, who rolled and shot a blast of fire at him. He deflected the fire, then flung his hand out as if to return it to Smokey the Demon.

It didn't work.

The demon laughed. "Poor Xypher. Having trouble?"

"At kicking your ass, Kaiaphas? Never."

The cloak vanished. In the darkness, the demon's boiling skin articulated into something that looked like leather. His face mutated into that of a gargoyle while the cotton of his clothes turned into sleek black armor that clung close to the muscular contours of his body. Still those eyes glowed like bright embers from a fire.

Kaiaphas pulled out a short sword and twirled it around his body before he lunged at Xypher who sidestepped the blade. A silver vambrace appeared on the arm that wasn't wearing the bracelet. Xypher used it to twist the blade out of the demon's hand. But before he could capture it, Kaiaphas caught it in his left hand and stabbed at him again.

Spinning around, Xypher shoved the demon. Kaiaphas staggered, then caught himself.

Kaiaphas laughed. "You've improved."

"Yeah, little boys grow up eventually." Xypher kicked at him, but Kaiaphas caught his leg and snatched it up.

Xypher turned a midair somersault to land on his feet. He ran at the demon and caught him about the waist. They fell back, still fighting.

Simone wanted to run, but remembered that so long as she wore the bracelet she couldn't go far without killing them both. "Find a weapon," she whispered loudly to Jesse as she started looking around for a tree limb or something she could use to help Xypher beat back the demon.

Suddenly Jesse cursed.

Simone turned to look at the combatants to see what had caused Jesse's reaction. Faster than she could blink, Kaiaphas twirled the sword in his hand and stabbed Xypher in the stomach so deep, the point of it came out his back.

Xypher gasped as blood pooled around the sword hilt and flowed over Kaiaphas' hand.

The demon laughed. "Apparently your skills didn't improve enough, eh?" He head-butted Xypher. The motion of it caused Xypher to stagger back. As he did so, the sword was jerked out of his body.

He fell to one knee on the ground while Kaiaphas lifted his sword for the coup de grâce.

Simone ground her teeth as she saw her mother and younger brother dying in her mind all over again. An unfounded rage consumed her so that she could no longer think rationally.

In that moment, the demon became the focus of twenty years of hopeless frustration with a justice system that had failed her and a rage so bitter, she could taste it.

Her only thought to save Xypher, Simone

grabbed the pepper spray from her coat pocket and ran at the demon. Shoving him back with all her strength, she held her breath and doused him with the spray.

Kaiaphas coughed and spat. His eyes flashing, he started for her.

Simone braced herself for his attack, intending to fight back with her bare hands. But before he reached her, something knocked him away.

A flash of blond hair confirmed it was Julian with a sword in his hand. He put himself between them and forced the demon away from her and Jesse.

While he engaged the demon, she ran to Xypher, who lay on the ground covered in blood. His face was pale as he visibly shook. Blood poured over his hands without slowing.

"Shh," Simone said, pulling his hand away so that she could see the jagged wound. "I've got you, Xypher. Don't worry." She glanced over her shoulder. "Jesse, pop the trunk and bring me my medical bag."

Jesse ran to the car while she examined the wound in Xypher's stomach. It looked gruesome. And the instant she touched it, he cursed. His nostrils flared and she was sure he'd hit her.

Fortunately for her, he passed out before he could make good on that unspoken threat.

She glanced up to see Julian engaged in an impressive swordfight. They moved so fast, all she could see was the sparks that flared whenever their blades met. The sound of metal on metal was deafening and drowned everything but their grunts and insults.

Then in one fluid motion, Julian dodged the demon and shoved him sideways before he stabbed him in the ribs.

Staggering back, the demon hissed, showing a full set of jagged teeth before he dissolved into the darkness. All that was left behind was the stench of sulfur and something that reminded her of treacle.

Julian cocked his head as if trying to sense something. He turned in her direction at the same time Jesse brought the bag to her. She focused on stanching Xypher's blood. It wasn't easy, especially since she was starting to get light-headed herself.

"You okay?" Jesse asked.

"I'm not really sure."

Julian knelt beside her. "We need to get him out of the public eye, if you take my meaning."

She certainly did. They'd been lucky no car had driven by during their fight . . . or worse, that a neighbor's dog hadn't needed walking. "I couldn't agree more."

A heartbeat later, they were inside Julian's house again, in an upstairs bedroom that was decorated in greens and cream and furnished with nice Victorian antiques.

She and Julian stood to the side of the queen-size bed while Xypher lay on top of it.

Jesse popped in a second later and wrinkled his nose. "That is one grody wound. It gotta hurt."

Julian grimaced as he saw the blood pouring out of Xypher's side.

Without a word, she ripped open Xypher's shirt. She sucked her breath in and remembered one of the advantages to her job. Decedents didn't bleed like this on the examination table. She hadn't tended a living patient since she'd been an intern in college.

Julian looked over her shoulder. "How's he doing?"

"That . . . thing, whatever it was, made a mess of him. The sword went all the way through his body."

Julian grimaced. "Yeah, wounds like that seriously hurt. Had a few myself back in the day."

She decided to let that remark pass without comment while she checked the blood flow as best she could. "I really need to take him to a hospital, but having worked in the ER for four years, I know the questions they'll ask that we can't answer."

"Hang on, I'll take you to one."

She opened her mouth to protest.

Julian held his hand up to silence her before she could even start. "It's a safe place, called Sanctuary.

The hospital ward was set up just for situations like this. It's a place where those who aren't quite human can go to for help. It'll have everything you need, and there won't be any questions about where either one of you came from."

That made her feel much better. "Good. 'Cause unless he starts healing by himself immediately, he needs surgery . . . quickly. Or he will die."

Death was a possibility she'd like to avoid.

Julian looked down at the blood-soaked bed and winced. "I should have taken you there before I messed up the comforter. It's what I get for trying to pass as a human all the time. Sometimes I forget my own powers."

The next thing she knew, they were in what appeared to be a doctor's office. The entire interior was made of steel, except for the white-tiled floors and white walls that were lined with glass-covered shelves of medicine. There was also a padded steel examining bed next to three trays covered with surgical and examination tools. As promised, it held everything needed to tend to Xypher.

Julian stood beside her, holding Xypher in his arms. No small feat since the man was a couple of inches taller than him.

"I'm so disoriented," Simone breathed as a wave of dizziness hit her. She put her arm out against the case closest to her to get her bearings.

Ignoring her, Julian bellowed, "Carson?"

A door on her left opened to reveal a tall, Native American man who glared at them. His long black hair was pulled back into a severe ponytail and his features were sharp, reminding her of a bird of prey. "Don't yell. I have extremely sensitive hearing."

"Sorry," Julian said quickly. "But we have a situation. Carson, meet Simone. Simone, meet Carson. He's a surgeon."

"Oh, thank God," she said, grateful there was another doctor here. "I only operate on the dead."

Carson didn't comment on that. Instead, his dark gaze went to Xypher. "And the guy bleeding would be . . . ?"

"A Dream-Hunter."

Carson's jaw dropped at Julian's answer. "They bleed on the human plane?"

"Apparently so and rather badly."

Carson gave a curt nod before he crossed the room to open a door behind them. "Bring him in here and put him on the table."

Julian didn't hesitate to obey.

Simone followed Julian into a bare operating room. Like the outer room, it was clean and sterile with steel furniture and large lamps over the surgical table. It looked like any operating room she'd ever seen and she was impressed with the quality of the state-of-the-art tools and monitors. In fact, she knew several hospitals that would kill to be this up-to-date.

While Julian placed Xypher on the table, she headed to the small room on her right where a prep sink waited so that she could scrub down.

Carson entered right behind her. "You look like you know what you're doing."

"I'm an ME and I thought you might need an assistant for surgery." She dried her hands on one of the green towels that were stacked on a table beside the sink.

He inclined his head before he began scrubbing his hands, too. "Good woman. My usual assistant is off today."

Julian came to the doorway. His clothes were covered in blood. "If neither of you needs me, I'm heading back to my house to do damage control on the bed . . . and pray none of my neighbors saw the major battle we had in the street with our friendly neighborhood demon."

Carson snorted. "Please, no more getting caught on videotape and God save us from Webcams. I swear I hate this modern age."

Simone ignored his caustic comment as she met Julian's gaze. "Good luck and thank you for all your help."

Julian smiled at her, then vanished while Carson wheeled a table of instruments back toward the other room.

"Don't we need a mask and scrubs?" Simone asked him.

He shook his head. "I wash my hands out of

habit. Basically your friend here should be immune to the typical germs that can kill a human. What will infect him would be things we couldn't protect against anyway."

"Oh." Simone moved to the opposite side of the table and helped to remove her temporary pressure bandage from Xypher's side. She was a bit surprised that Carson didn't remove Xypher's jeans, but he seemed content to leave him partially dressed.

Since she'd never operated on anyone, never mind someone who wasn't exactly human, she kept her backseat surgeon under wraps. Obviously the man knew what he was doing or Julian wouldn't have brought them here. Not to mention, no one would have paid for all this equipment unless they knew how to use it.

Right?

She hoped so. Stepping back, she watched as Carson opened him up and started working on the wound. She cringed at the damage done. His arteries and tissue were a nightmare.

Poor man . . . or whatever he was.

A twinge of guilt went through her as she considered the way he'd put himself between the demon and her. He'd taken the brunt of the fight—just like he'd done in the alley so that she wouldn't be harmed.

In spite of all his gruff bluster, he had heart and at least a basic code of decency. That realization softened her toward him. He actually wasn't that bad. And as she stared at him, a part of her was warmed by his consideration.

Carson reached for a clamp on the stainless steel tray. "What was he cut with?"

"A short sword."

He shook his head. "It looks more like a chain saw got him. Look at the damage here." He held the skin back so that she could get a full view.

Simone reached for another clamp to hand him since Xypher was bleeding so badly. Carson was right. It was awful. "I don't know if this helps or matters, but the man wielding the sword was some kind of demon."

"Do you know from what pantheon?"

This had to be the most screwed-up conversation she'd ever had. There weren't many people you could tell about a demon appearing in the street and then attacking you who would accept it with such a simple question. It should be interrupted with laughter.

And lots of alcohol.

"Uh, no. But Xypher called him Kaiaphas."

Carson cursed.

Simone looked up at the unexpected anger the name caused. "You know him?"

"Part Greek, part Sumerian, all pissed off. It's a wonder any of you survived. But the real question is, why did he attack you guys? It's not his normal style."

"What do you mean?"

"Kaiaphas is a doleodai. A bound demon. He can't act on his own, he has to be commanded by someone."

That was an interesting tidbit. Simone wanted to laugh at the absurdity of everything that had happened to her since lunch. "How on earth did I get caught up in this? All I wanted to do was check out a simple crime scene and go home. No . . . I take that back. All I wanted was to have a ham and cheese sandwich with an old friend. Now I've been dragged into the middle of some Greek-god conflict and it's not even dinnertime yet. I can't wait to see what happens next."

Carson smiled. "I've had those days."

"Sure you have."

"No, really. You should follow me around and document all the weirdness I get dragged into."

"Such as?"

He took the clamp from her hand. "Well, there was the time Marvin, our former mascot monkey, ran from his owner, Wren—he's a tiger that can take human form—and went upstairs to sleep with the dragon. Turns out our resident dragon is allergic to monkeys—who knew or could imagine that? Max broke out with a rash in areas I still cringe over, and if you mention the word 'monkey' to him to this day, he shoots fire at you. Then there was the time when . . . oh, I better not tell that. If Dev catches wind of it, he'll rip my heart out and eat it."

Simone stepped back at everything he was telling her. No . . . it couldn't be.

Could it?

"You have lycanthropes here?"

Pausing, he glanced up at her. "Aren't you a Squire?"

"No."

He sucked his breath in sharply and twisted his face up into a mask of aggravation. Growling, he reached for sutures. "You didn't know about any of what I just said until it came pouring out of my mouth, did you?"

"Nope."

He cursed again. "I can't believe I just did that. I assumed since you knew about Xypher and the demon, and Julian manifested you in here, that you knew everything about our world."

No, but she was getting a quick introduction that was becoming scarier by the minute. In all her conversations with Tate, he'd never once mentioned lycanthropes.

"Appears I do now," she said, trying to make Carson feel better about his slipup. "*Daily Inquisitor*, here I come . . . better yet, the local nut farm."

"Yeah, and I just broke nine hundred rules. What say we keep all of this between us?"

"Believe me, baby, I ain't talking. I value what little sanity I have left, and the last thing I want is to be in the middle of what I'm in the middle of.

Point me to the exit and Alice is out of the rabbit hole, back on earth, and happy to develop Alzheimer's over this entire incident. In fact, I'm not even sure I'm here. I'm thinking a Daimon konked me on the head and this is all one big hallucination brought on by severe blood loss."

"You ramble like that a lot?"

"Yes. I find it grounds me."

He laughed as he worked on Xypher.

Simone paused as she realized something. "We didn't give him anything to keep him knocked out. Shouldn't we do that?"

"Nah. It wouldn't do any good. Dream-Hunters are immune to those kinds of drugs."

"Really?"

He nodded, leaning closer for a better look at what he was doing. "They're gods. Normal human medicine doesn't work on them."

"Then why are we operating?"

"Because he's bleeding and unconscious . . . I've never seen a Dream-Hunter bleed before, especially not like this. But I figure if he bleeds, he could bleed out and die."

On one hand that made sense, but on another . . . "Gods can't die, right?"

"Sure they can. It just takes a lot and usually an immortal weapon of some kind, which I'm going to lay odds was in the hands of Kaiaphas when he attacked." He glanced up at her with a pointed stare. "Demons don't usually attack a god or anyone else unless they think they're going to kill them. It tends to piss off the target who then looks up ways to torture and kill the demon. Then it just gets messy as they go at each other. As a rule, the demon usually loses, especially when it's a god who's been angered, so demons tend to be a bit more circumspect than the usual predator. When they strike it's usually quick and fatal."

Simone let out a tired breath at the simple truth of that statement. She looked down at Xypher as he lay in a deceptively peaceful repose. His body was honed and lethal. A perfect specimen of male beauty.

Asleep like this, he looked like an angel, but then given his acerbic personality she could just imagine the list of people who might want him dead.

Including herself.

But to the point of calling out a demon to destroy him? That was harsh.

Poor Xypher.

She didn't speak any more while Carson cleaned, cauterized, and then stitched Xypher closed. By the time they were finished, Xypher was still unconscious, but sweating profusely. She put her hand to his whiskered cheek that was firm and, just as she suspected, feverish.

Feeling for him, she went to the sink to wash up and then wet a cloth with cold water. Hopefully this would help. She took the cloth to him and laid it across his brow and was struck again by his good looks. He really was an incredibly handsome man. But since he was a god, that was probably to be expected.

All she really knew about him was that he was a jerk . . . and that he'd twice saved her life.

She looked up at Carson who was in the washroom as she remembered the term Xypher had used to describe himself. "What exactly are Skotos?"

Carson dried his hands on a small hand towel before he walked back over to her. "Where did you hear that term?"

She held her hand out to Xypher. "He told me that's what he was."

Carson nodded. "In ancient Greece, they had sleep gods. Centuries ago, one of them thought it would be funny to play in the dreams of Zeus. The big guy didn't have a sense of humor about it so he ordered everyone possessing even a drop of their blood to either be killed or stripped of all emotions."

She remembered Julian pointing out that he was surprised that Xypher still had his emotions. "That was harsh."

"Yeah, well, Zeus isn't exactly known for his compassion." There was a note in his voice that said he had his own axe to grind with the god king.

Carson indicated Xypher with a tilt of his head. "After Zeus's curse, the Oneroi, or dream gods, were relegated to monitoring human sleep, and it was quickly discovered that while they were in a dream state, Zeus's ban didn't work. They could feel again. Terrified of being punished, the dream gods started policing themselves and making sure that they kept a check on their brethren. Even so, some of them started craving to emotions to the extent that they lost control of their appetite for it. Before long, they became dangerous to themselves and others."

"Like an addiction . . ."

"Exactly." He set the towel aside. "The dream gods who lose control and begin craving emotions are called Skoti or Skotos in the singular."

Personally, she liked the idea of it being toe jam better. But at least now she understood what he really was. "Xypher also said he was dead."

"Well, the theory goes that if the Skoti become too addicted, they'll be executed and sent to Tartarus for eternal punishment."

So that explained it. He'd been killed and then brought back. She wondered how that would be possible. Had he made a deal or something else?

It was scary to even contemplate.

Simone frowned as she noticed writing in a foreign script running down the length of Xypher's arm. Curious, she took the arm in her hands, amazed by the steely feel of his skin, as she studied the flowing letters. "Can you read this?"

Carson came to stand beside her. "No, sorry. It looks like Greek and I only know French, Cajun, English, some Creole, and gibberish."

She ran her hand over the dark red lettering, trying not to think about how strong the arm felt under her fingers. Why would he have it put here and what did it mean?

Releasing his arm, she looked up at Carson. "Do you know anything about Xypher himself?"

"No. Never saw or heard of him until you guys brought him here. There are several thousand Dream-Hunters and most of them shy away from the human plane, preferring to hide out in dreams." Carson paused. "You want to leave him here so you can go home?"

She looked down at her bracelet. "I wish I could, but I can't. Aphrodite said that so long as we both wear these"—she held it up to his view—"we're bound together. If we get too far apart we die."

"That sucks."

"Tell me about it."

He indicated the door behind him. "I have a more comfortable room for the two of you then. It'll give you a comfortable place to sit while he sleeps."

Simone cringed at the very thought of flashing

out again. "Please don't disintegrate me. I'm feeling nauseated from the back and forthing, and am getting a whole new respect for Kirk and Spock."

He laughed. "I understand." He clicked the brake off the gurney with the toe of his boot. "I'll wheel him over."

"A thousand blessings to you."

He paused to call for someone named Dev before he led her into an adjacent room that was furnished with antiques. The best of which was a king-size bed that had a bright red velvet spread. There were heavy drapes that made it very dark and yet strangely homey.

"Nice place," she said, running her hand over the top of a beautiful dressing table.

"Only the best for Mama."

"Mama?"

"Nicolette Peltier. She owns the place and everyone here calls her 'Mama.'"

Simone smiled. "That's so sweet. She must be really caring."

"She can be. She can also be a bear at times."

Simone smiled. "My mother was the same way."

"Um, yeah."

A handsome man in his mid-twenties with long curly blond hair pushed open the door. "Whatcha need, Doc?"

Carson indicated Xypher. "Help moving him. I don't want to jostle his side."

A stern frown creased Dev's brow as he saw Xypher on the gurney. "Who is he?"

"Dream-Hunter."

Dev looked stunned. "They bleed?"

"Looks like."

"Dang," Dev said under his breath before he helped Carson to lift Xypher from the gurney onto the bed. Once Xypher was situated, Dev glanced at her, then wheeled the gurney away without another word.

Simone wasn't sure what to make of him. "He's standoffish, isn't he?"

"Most of us are. Our survival hinges on secrecy."

"Which I have breached."

He nodded.

Simone wanted to let him know that she would never do anything to hurt them. Besides, who would believe her if she said there was a family of lyncanthropes calling New Orleans home? "Your secret really is safe with me, Carson. Believe me, keeping things to myself is a full-time occupation of mine. If the police department can trust me, so can you."

"I know. Otherwise we'd just kill you and devour your body parts."

She wasn't sure if he was kidding or not, but something about him said he was dead serious.

He indicated the door behind him with his

thumb. "If you need anything, I'll be outside at my desk. Just make yourself at home." He indicated a door to her left with a jerk of his chin. "The bathroom is in there."

"Thanks."

He closed the door.

Simone let out a long breath as exhaustion hit her. She was alone in a strange home—something she wasn't used to. "Where are you, Jesse? I don't like being alone." Their years of friendship had made solitude a rare thing. She was so used to him that when he was gone, she felt it like a physical ache.

Feeling a bit lost and overwhelmed, she moved to the bed to cover Xypher with the spread. He didn't look quite so fierce now, but there was still an aura to him that said he was lethal. She dropped her gaze to his hands and the scars that marred his knuckles. They were old and healed over, yet she could tell that they weren't caused by a single injury. They'd been opened up and scarred by many fights . . .

Yeah, there were times when her job told her way too much about a person. Not to mention there were numerous other scars marring his chest and arms. Strangely enough, the only scar on his face was a faint one at his right temple.

"Who are you, Xypher?"

"Sim?"

She smiled at the sound of Jesse's voice. He

reappeared right beside her. "Where have you been?"

"You guys left me," he said defensively. "Do you know how hard it is to trace a human through the ectoplasmic plane? No, you don't. And trust me, you don't want to learn. I'm just glad I found you this time and not the weird woman feeding Jell-O to her schnauzer."

Now, there was an image . . . "Ooookay. Sorry about that."

"You should be!" He narrowed his eyes on Xypher. "He doesn't look good. Is he going to live?"

"I think so."

"I would say damn shame except that until we find a way to free you, you'd die, too."

"Glad you remembered that small fact." She frowned as she looked at him and remembered his earlier tirade. "Ectoplasmic plane? What the devil is that?"

"It's jargon from those of us who are corporeally challenged. It's the great beyond where we bounce into each other like floundering atoms. It's really kind of gross—which is why I hang out with you. But only because you're less gross than they are."

Simone gaped at him and his criticism. "I beg your pardon. I'm not gross."

"Grody to the max. Gag me with a spoon. I've seen you in the mornings. You're not exactly well coiffed."

She rolled her eyes at the old eighties expressions. "I really hate you."

"Sure you do." He grinned like the Cheshire cat. "It explains why you were so worried about me."

He was way too astute at times. Simone huffed playfully at him before she turned back to Xypher.

It was a pity she knew so little about him and it made her wonder about his past. What had made him fight all the battles that had left such horrific scars on an otherwise beautiful body? "You think he has a reason to be so hostile?"

"Not really. I personally think he thrives on being an asshole. You know, there are a lot of those in the world."

It was true. She'd certainly met more than her fair share of them, too, and yet . . . There seemed to be something more. A person didn't hate to the extent that Xypher appeared to without having the ability to love to the same degree.

And his need to kill to the exclusion of all else spoke of extreme betrayal. The only person she'd ever really wanted to kill was whoever had taken her mother's life . . .

"There can never be hatred without love."

Jesse frowned. "What?"

"It's something my mother used to say."

He screwed his face up. "Oh, man, no . . . don't you dare."

"Dare what?"

"Get that weepy-eyed look like you're sympa-thizing with him." He made an irritated noise in the back of his throat. "You are such a bleeding heart. Hello? This is the man who has you bound to him while he's trying to descend into hell to kill someone. He doesn't care about your sensibilities. Don't you dare care about his."

Simone waved his tirade off. "Oh, hush, you grump. I don't even know him."

"And you better keep it that way."

She knew Jesse was right. Even so, there was a part of her that was drawn to Xypher even against her common sense. She wasn't even sure why. He just seemed lost somehow.

Oh, yeah, Mr. Badass temper was lost . . . Right. She *was* losing it.

"Have you heard from Gloria?" she asked Jesse, trying to distract herself.

He shook his head. "Not even a groan. I'm thinking the Daimons ate her."

Simone hated the very thought. No one deserved such a fate. "I hope not. She seemed really nice."

"I hear you." Jesse floated back toward the cur-tains.

Suddenly, someone knocked on the door.

"Come in," Simone called.

Carson entered the room carrying a small handsaw.

Simone took a step back, curious about his in-tentions. "What are you doing?"

He indicated her bracelet with the tip of the saw. "I was wondering if this might work to get that bracelet off."

She smiled in relief. For a second, she was afraid he was going to make good on his threat to silence her. "You are my favorite person on the planet right now. Yes, please try it."

Carson laughed as he moved to take her wrist into his hand. He paused a minute to examine the bracelet. "It looks like regular gold."

"Aphrodite said it was Atlantean. Something made by the gods."

He drew his breath in sharply. "Oh . . ." He pulled back.

"Is that bad?"

"Maybe. I don't know enough about them to even guess what trying to cut this off might do to you. For all I know, I could end the world."

She pulled her arm out of his grasp. "Please don't. There was a cliffhanger ending on *Dexter* last week and I have to see how it ends."

Her words seemed to surprise him. "You watch that?"

"Religiously. As an ME I'm morbidly fascinated by it."

"Given my job and life, that's a show I avoid as much as the Animal Planet network." He backed away from her. "I'll leave you two alone again."

He'd barely stepped through the door before

she heard the rumble of a deep voice behind her. "Where am I?"

"Wow," Jesse said from the bed. "The dead has risen . . . again."

Ignoring Jesse, she went to Xypher's side. His blue eyes were rimmed with red and bloodshot. His skin still had a grayish cast to it and by his shallow breathing she could tell he was in a lot of pain. "You're at Sanctuary."

He drew a deep breath, then grimaced. "I smell Were-Hunter."

"Were-Hunter?"

He shifted slightly under the blanket before he spoke again. "Lycanthrope."

"Oh." It actually made sense to her. Dark-Hunters hunted the Daimon vampires. Dream-Hunters hunted dreams and . . . well, it made her wonder what a Were-Hunter would hunt.

Yeah. She forced her thoughts away from that. "I think a Were-Hunter may have helped carry you in here."

Xypher tried to sit up, then hissed.

"Careful," she said, rushing toward him. She put her hands on his chest, then pulled back as an electrical shock went through her. She didn't know why, but touching his chest was extremely disconcerting, and it made her breathless. "You took a nasty stab straight through your body and Carson said we couldn't give you anything for the pain."

A tic worked in his jaw as he lay back on the

bed and pulled the cloth from his forehead. He stared at it as if it were an alien form wanting to suck his brains out.

"You were feverish" she explained.

His scowl deepened. "You did this?"

She couldn't understand his ire. It was as if her kindness truly ticked him off. "I thought I was doing something nice for you. Sorry."

"Why would you do something nice for me?"

"Because you were hurt and bleeding."

Still there was no reprieve in that cold, penetrating stare. "What do you care about that?"

"I went to medical school to help people. It's why I do what I do."

"Why?"

Never in her life had she met someone who had this much trouble accepting help. Dear Lord, what had they done to the poor man that something as simple as putting a cloth on his feverish brow made him this suspicious? "I'm sensing here that you have a problem with my being nice to you."

"Yeah," he said. "I do. People aren't nice. Especially not to me."

Something tugged deep inside her at those growled words. "Xypher—"

"I don't want your pity." He flung the cloth on the floor. "Or your kindness. Just stay out of my way and don't get killed until I find some way into Kalosis."

Wow. That just made her all warm and toasty inside. He was like an agitated porcupine in a balloon factory. "Why is it so important to you that you kill this person?"

Out of nowhere an image burned through her mind. It was Xypher. He was in a dark, dismal cave, hanging painfully by his arms. His black hair was matted with blood and dirt, and fell forward, over his face. Completely naked, his body was covered with bleeding wounds.

The agony in his eyes was searing. He tried to escape or fight, but there was nothing he could do. Blow after blow from a steel-barbed whip rained over his flesh, tearing open new wounds and spinning him about. The two skeletons who beat him didn't care what they hit so long as they caused him pain.

The more he bled, the more they laughed.

"Stop!" she cried, unable to bear it.

The images vanished as quickly as they'd begun.

Xypher gave her a look so cold it reached down inside her and made a part of her very soul freeze. "That is a ten-second glimpse of centuries of torture I have endured because of one person's cruelty. Any more questions?"

She couldn't breathe for the pain inside her. All she could do was shake her head. No wonder he was angry. It was hard to breathe past the lump in her throat.

"Yeah," she said after a brief pause. "I have

only one. Having given this person who betrayed you so much already, why would you give them your life, too?"

He laughed bitterly. "Let me explain how I got here, human. I did a favor for a goddess who talked Hades into making me human for one month. One. Single. Month. Now, having lived in Tartarus all these centuries, I've learned that Hades doesn't willingly let anyone go, especially not someone with my past. I'm headed back to hell, baby. No ifs, ands, or buts about it. The only undetermined factor left is whether or not I go alone, and I have no intention of doing that." His eyes burned into her an instant before he pushed himself up from the bed. "Where's my shirt?"

She couldn't believe the sight of him upright given the severity of that wound. How could he even move, especially since he hadn't had a drop of painkiller?

Then again, having seen what had been done to him in Tartarus, she figured he was probably so used to pain that it didn't faze him now. Even as badly as they'd torn into him, he'd still been trying to fight them. "You can't be moving around like that. You need to rest."

"Fuck rest," he snarled between his clenched teeth. "I have too much to do to lie in bed like some spoiled prince."

She put herself in front of him to keep him from leaving. "You're going to rip open your side."

"So what?"

"So what? Are you insane?" He had to be. "Have you any idea how much that will hurt?"

He gave her a dry, cold stare before he turned around to show her his back. "Yeah, I have a pretty damned good idea."

Simone covered her mouth as she stared at the horror of scars that marred the beauty of his skin. To say he'd been savaged was an understatement. She reached her hand out instinctively to touch him, but caught herself before she made contact.

Her hand hovered there, just above the marks. So close she could feel the heat rising from his feverish skin. The thought of his being beaten like that tore through her. What kind of monster could do such a thing?

The fact he'd suffered it alone with no one to tend him made her even more sick.

He turned back to face her. "Now where's my shirt?"

She had to clear her throat before she could answer him in a semihuman tone. "We cut it off you."

He looked away as if her answer had sent a wave of fury through him. "Thanks a lot."

Why was he so upset over a simple T-shirt? "We can go to your place and get another one."

"I don't have a place and I don't have another shirt."

Was he serious? "What do you mean?"

Xypher moved to stand before her. He looked down at her and smirked. "Why can't you follow this, human? I was let out of hell, not an amusement park. They don't exactly send you into the world with a wardrobe and wallet."

"But you've been here for a few days, right? Where have you been staying? How have you been eating?"

He didn't answer as he pushed his way past her.

It was then she knew what he refused to say. "You've been sleeping on the street, haven't you?"

"Who says I've been sleeping at all?" He opened the door.

Carson looked up from where he sat at a dark cherry desk as if expecting Xypher to intrude. He reached for a shirt that was folded on his desk and chucked it at Xypher. "You can have that one."

Xypher took the shirt without so much as a thank-you. He was pulling it over his head when Simone joined him in the room.

Her cell phone rang.

Simone pulled it out of her pocket and looked at the ID. It was coming in as a restricted call. She flipped it open. "Hello?"

The voice that answered was deep and incredibly sexy, and laced with a lilting accent that actually sent a chill down her spine. "This is Acheron Parthenopaeus returning Xypher's call. Could you please hand the phone to him?"

Yeah, but she really didn't want to. She'd much rather talk to this polite voice that was eerily soothing and peaceful. Reluctantly, she held it out to him. "It's Acheron."

In typical Xypher form, he yanked the phone from her hand. "Where the hell are you?"

Jesse leaned forward to whisper in her ear. "That would so make me want to help him. How about you?"

"Shh . . ." she said, stifling a smile at his honest words.

Xypher slammed the phone shut and handed it back to her. Another bright light flashed before a huge man manifested in front of them. Close to seven feet tall, he was lean with long black hair and an aura so lethal it made Xypher seem like a kitten.

He was wearing black Oakley sunglasses and a long, pirate-style coat over a black Misfits T-shirt. That being said, Johnny Depp had nothing on this man when it came to sheer sex appeal. Acheron oozed it from every pore.

He stood with his weight on one leg and had a black leather backpack slung casually over one shoulder. Simone frowned as she noticed his red-tinged black Dr. Martens combat boots that probably added two inches to his impressive height.

" 'Bout time," Xypher growled.

Acheron's only reaction was one perfectly shaped black eyebrow that arched over the frame of the sunglasses. "While I respect suicidal tendencies on most days, you'd do well to remember who you're addressing and, more to the point, what I can do to you. No one says you have to go back to Tartarus in one piece."

Xypher crossed his arms over his chest.

His mood lightening, Acheron turned toward her. "May I see your bracelet?"

Polite. Deadly. Gorgeous. Respectful. Sexy beyond human endurance. Oh, someone put a bow on this man, she definitely wanted to take him home. Swallowing as a shiver went down her spine, she did as he asked.

Acheron took her arm into his hands and held it up so that he could study the locked catch. After a moment, he released her arm and looked back at Xypher. "You want the good news first or the bad?"

"Does it really matter?"

One corner of Acheron's mouth turned up in a taunting grin. "Not to me . . . The bad news, I can't touch this. I mean I can, but you both will die if I tamper with it."

Xypher cursed. "Who the hell invented this?"

Acheron placed both hands on the shoulder strap of his backpack to anchor it over his jacket. "Archon, the king of the Atlantean gods. Trust me, he was a total prick."

Simone let out a breath she hadn't realized she

was holding. This wasn't looking particularly nice for them. "So what's the good news?"

"Somebody has a key to it and no, you won't wither and die because you have it on. In theory you can live for eternity bound together like this."

"But?" she asked.

Acheron inclined his head to her. "There's always a but involved, isn't there?"

Unfortunately. "And this but would be?"

"Whoever has the key won't be giving it up easily since it's in the hands of whoever summoned the bracelet, and I'm sure they didn't send it to you guys as a gag gift. But wait, there's more . . . the bracelets have a homing beacon in them."

Oh, she so didn't like the sound of that.

"You are shitting me," Xypher said in a tone so low and deadly it made her shiver.

"Not on your best day. Since the idea of the bracelets is to target an enemy and bring them down, they are equipped with everything your enemy needs to kill you. The key master will not only be able to find you no matter where you go, but whatever weakness either of you has will be laid bare before him . . . or her." Acheron glanced at Simone. "The Atlanteans played to win."

"Which is why they're all dead, right?" Xypher asked.

Acheron shrugged. "That's the food chain for you. Even those at the top are a meal for someone else. Sooner or later, we all get eaten by something."

Xypher turned his attention to her. "Look, the human didn't do anything to be in this mess. Is there anything you can do to extract her out of this?"

Simone was stunned that he'd even ask.

Acheron gave her a wistful nod. "I wish. Believe me, nothing pisses me off more than seeing an innocent suffer. The only way to get her free is to obtain the key and open the bracelet."

Xypher cursed again. "You know it's probably in Kalosis, right? Any chance you can fetch it?"

Acheron laughed. "I assure you if I went in there to do that, you'd have a lot worse problems on your hands than just killing Satara."

"Can you at least flush her out for me?"

Acheron scoffed. "Like she wouldn't see that coming? You she fears. Me she actively hates."

Xypher met Simone's gaze and held it. For the first time, she saw something inside him that appeared human. A small chip in that nastiness he seemed to wrap around himself like a cloak.

"But there is something I can do for you." Acheron reached out and touched Xypher's shoulder.

Xypher let out a gasp as his body illuminated. He threw his head back and cried out as if lightning were moving through him.

Simone cringed at the sight of him shaking.

After a minute, he lifted his shirt to show that his injury was gone. Not even a scar remained to mar his flawless eight-pack. "Thank you."

Acheron inclined his head, then looked past her, at Jesse. "You're her best defense. Anytime a demon comes near them, there's a small rift in the mortal plane. It feels like a tingle in your spine. You can give them a few seconds' warning before they're attacked."

Jesse appeared as stunned as she was. "How do you know I'm here?"

Acheron smiled. "I know lots of things."

Jesse grinned widely. "Man, I like hanging with these people. They see and hear me. You have no idea how refreshing this is."

Stepping closer to Simone, Acheron pulled a leather bracelet from his wrist and snapped it on her left arm. "This will give you the strength of a demon should one attack you. What it won't do is make you a better fighter and it won't keep you from dying. However, if you bash a demon on the head with something, I assure you they won't laugh at your attempts."

He leaned down to whisper in her ear. "There is something inside you, Simone, that scares you. You've hidden it your entire life, but you know it's there. Lurking and aching to be free. I know you run from it. Don't. It's the one thing in this that will save your life. Reach inside and embrace what you really are. When you're ready, you won't need my bracelet to help you."

And with that he vanished.

Her arm still tingled from where he'd touched it. She looked at Jesse. "What on earth was that?"

Jesse held his hands turned outward and shrugged.

Her gaze went past him to Xypher and there for a heartbeat she caught a glimpse of his vulnerability. There in his eyes was regret, sadness, and a pain so profound it made her breath catch. She wanted to reach out to him, but feared how violently he might react to such a gesture.

Carson cleared his throat. "I don't mean to be rude, guys, but I think it best you leave. The idea behind Sanctuary is to be a haven. The last thing we need is to have a demon bursting in here who isn't bound by our laws."

That evaporated all the emotions in Xypher's eyes except a grim determination. "Don't worry, I won't sully your pristine palace with my presence."

The next thing she knew, they were outside, standing on Ursulines Street. Luckily no one seemed to have seen them just pop in out of nowhere.

Jesse joined her. "I wish you'd stop doing that."

"*You* wish?" she asked. "Try being in my shoes. It's making me sick."

Xypher narrowed a threatening glare at her. "Life makes me sick, but notice, here I am. No one gave a damn what I thought about it before they brought me into it."

Simone hated to see them back to this. "Xypher, truce, please. I get it. You're bitter. You know, you're not the only one who feels shafted by the rod of life. Believe me. I was orphaned at age eleven and spent three years in a children's home before I was finally adopted. We're all survivors of a callous universe. The only buffer we have is other people."

He scoffed bitterly at her. "Gods, you're naïve. The only buffer we have is ourselves and how much pain we can tolerate before it finally breaks us."

Simone felt sorry for him if that was the best he could do. But then she remembered a time when she'd felt exactly like he did. Jesse was the only reason she'd kept herself together. She wasn't sure she'd have made it out of that dark hole she'd lived in after her parents' deaths without him.

It was obvious Xypher had never had another person to rely on. Not even a ghost.

Her throat tight in sympathetic pain, she started walking down Chartres Street. Her condo was over on Orleans, not too close, but not that bad a hike, either. The walk would be quicker than trying to get a cab.

And at this point, she couldn't even remember

where she'd left her car. Okay, not true, she'd left it at Julian's. But she just needed a few minutes at her place where everything was familiar. She needed something to ground her before the next round of lunacy assailed her.

As they neared the Hotel Provincial, she saw the way Xypher slowed down as a whiff of something good hit them. His gaze went longingly toward the Restaurant Stella. He didn't say a word, but then he didn't have to. His expression said it all.

"When was the last time you ate?"

He didn't answer.

Simone pulled him to a stop. "Xypher? Food. When was the last time you had some?"

"What do you care?"

It was then she understood what those four words meant when he said them. No one in his life had ever cared before. Why should she, a stranger?

"I'm going to get something to eat." She held the bracelet up for him. "I suggest you follow me." She headed for the small Mediterranean café across the street that would be much quicker than an upscale restaurant.

Xypher wanted to curse as he followed her. But the truth was, he was starving. It was another one of Hades' sadistic pleasures that Xypher could manifest weapons with nothing more than a thought—but not clothing, food, or money. Nor could he heal himself.

His stomach had been cramped with hunger even before Hades had dumped him here. For the last week he'd been eating things he didn't even want to think about in an effort to at least get his stomach to stop burning so badly.

Even so, he wasn't the kind of creature to take charity. No one had ever given him anything. He was used to it.

Damned if he was going to beg.

Simone paused at the entrance until a woman in a white shirt and black pants came forward.

"How many?"

"Two."

Xypher looked at Jesse, who grinned at him. "I'm never counted. But I'm always here."

The woman grabbed two menus and led them to a small table in a corner. Xypher didn't miss the way Simone very discreetly pulled a chair out for Jesse while making it appear she was using it for her jacket.

Ignoring Jesse, Xypher considered putting Simone over his shoulder and carrying her out of here. Honestly, he couldn't stand the thought of smelling all this food and not having any.

But then he was used to torture.

He sat down with his fury barely leashed. The woman handed him a menu and left. Xypher set it aside and stared out the window.

It was so strange to be back in the world after all this time. So many things had changed. Last time he was here, horses had been the best mode of transportation. There had been no electricity. Mankind had been afraid of the dark. Afraid of the dreams Xypher and his brethren gave them.

Now they mostly feared themselves and well they should.

Simone frowned as Xypher sat back, not even glancing at the menu. "Aren't you hungry?"

The look he sent her chilled her to her bones. "I don't have any money."

"Well, you don't think I'd eat and leave you to starve, do you?" The sad thing was, he most likely did.

She picked the menu up and held it toward him. "Order something or I'll order for you."

"Do you know what happened to the last person who took that tone with me?"

"Let me guess . . . Disembowelment. Probably painful. Definitely slow." She wagged her brows at him. "Lucky for me you can't kill me so long as I have the bracelet on." She gave him a smug smile. "I'm having the shrimp cocktail and blackened chicken Alfredo. What about you?"

For the first time, she saw a humble look about him as he pulled the menu toward him like a sullen child.

"Kindness makes you uncomfortable, doesn't it?"

He didn't respond as his gaze skimmed the menu.

She let out a tired breath before she exchanged a frustrated look with Jesse. She couldn't believe she had an easier time talking to ghosts than she did talking to a flesh-and-blood . . . something seated in front of her.

What had they done to him to make him so closed off from everyone?

Xypher wasn't sure what to order. Everything looked good and his stomach was burning. Not to mention he felt extremely awkward sitting here . . . like a civilized human.

No one had treated him like this. Ever.

He was a Phobatory Skotos. He'd spent his life making everyone around him tremble in fear as he gave them nightmares. Even the gods. He was evil incarnate. Even other Phobatory Skoti feared him.

And this woman had dared to order him around . . . She was actually quite pretty and more tempting than any woman should be while he had a goal so important. Until now, he hadn't thought about how long he'd been without a woman. But her gentle hazel eyes set him on fire.

"Are you having trouble deciding?"

He blinked at her question. "How do you do that?"

"Do what?"

"Talk to me like I'm normal."

She frowned at him. "Well, you don't make it exactly easy. But I remember a time when I was angry at the world, too. All I wanted was to lash out and make everyone around me as miserable and angry as I was. That . . . need burned like a fire inside and obliterated everything else. Then one day I realized that the only one I was really hurting was myself. I might piss off other people, but within a few hours they forgot me. I was the only one who lived in perpetual hell. So I made the decision to let the anger go and move on."

How easy she made it sound. But it wasn't that easy to just let go. "Yes, but you had a future to look forward to."

She shook her head. "It didn't feel like that at the time. You have to remember that I saw my brother killed when he was only seven years old." She clenched her teeth as the familiar pain lacerated her. "He thought he had a future, too, and in one blink of an eye it was gone. So were my mother and my father . . ."

Her pain reached out to him; it was something he could relate to. But what surprised him was the little twinge inside him, a part that actually . . . no, it wasn't caring. He wasn't capable of that. It was . . .

He couldn't place it.

"What happened?" he asked her.

She held her hand up. "I know I brought it up, but I really can't talk about this right now, okay? Just because it was a long time ago doesn't mean it doesn't hurt still. There are some pains that time doesn't numb."

"Then you understand me."

Simone froze at that simple statement from him as she realized she really did. No matter how many years it'd been, the agony of their death was still raw and fresh. "Yeah. I guess I do. And if yours is even a pittance of mine, then I'm really sorry."

Xypher looked away as those words touched a part of him that hadn't been touched in centuries. He didn't even know why. It was like they had a connection through their pain.

"Do you like seafood?"

How did she do that? Such a simple question and yet it touched him. It made him feel . . . he couldn't describe it. "I don't remember. I haven't been able to really taste food in centuries."

She laid her menu down on the table. "What have you been eating while you're here?"

"Whatever I could find."

Simone's heart clenched at his words. "We'll get you the gyro platter and oyster plate. Between the two of them, you should find something tasty."

Xypher didn't know what to say. Usually he was violent, wanting to lash out and hurt anyone around him, but sitting here like this . . .

He was calm and calm was something he hadn't tasted in so long he'd forgotten how it felt.

Glancing away, he was tormented by old memories. Even before his emotions had been stripped, he'd been angry and bitter. Lashing out at everyone around him. He'd been raised among

Sumerian demons, not humans or the gods on Olympus.

His mother's people had been harsh and unforgiving. And in the beginning, he'd welcomed Zeus' curse of feeling nothing at all.

Until Satara. She'd shown him other things. Laughter. Passion.

For a time, he'd even deluded himself that he loved her.

In retrospect, it was enough to make him laugh. What did the son of a demon and the god of nightmares know about love? His own parents had been incapable of it. Love wasn't in his genetic makeup.

But vengeance . . .

That was something he could sink his claws into.

A waitress came over, eyeing him as if she could sense his malevolent thoughts. She quickly turned her attention to Simone who ordered for him.

Xypher listened to the melodic accent that made Simone's voice seem softer and more gentle than any he'd ever heard before. Her dark brown hair hung in ringlets around her face while her hazel eyes reflected intelligence, curiosity, and an innate zest for life.

She wasn't as skinny as the waitress who was leaving them. Rather she was robust. Healthy.

And for the first time in centuries, he felt his body stirring with lust.

A mischievous glint sparkled before she took a sip of water, then spoke to him. "You're being quiet, which is making me nervous."

"How so?"

She looked at Jesse before she answered. "There's an old saying that the tiger lies low not out of fear but for better aim. It reminds me of you."

"It should."

She sighed as she cupped her glass in her hands. "You really like to scare people, don't you?"

"I was bred for it."

Jesse laughed. "Can I sign up for lessons? I feel really shafted that I didn't get to come back as a poltergeist." He held his hands up at Simone. "Ooo, I'm coming for you."

Simone laughed.

Jesse let out a sound of disgust. "See. Laughter. I want, just once, to induce actual fear."

Xypher cut a look to the ghost to remind him that he could reach out and hurt him. Jesse immediately shrank back.

Simone leaned her head against her hand as she watched him. "You don't have to do that, you know?"

"Do what?"

"Grimace and growl at everyone around you. Take a breath and relax."

"Relax?" Xypher was incredulous at her words. "You do know they're going to be coming for us? You let your guard down—you relax—you die. Trust me. I have firsthand experience with that."

"Yeah, you said you were dead. What happened?"

Xypher fell silent as her innocent question dragged him back to the fool he'd once been. "I was betrayed by the only person I made the mistake of trusting."

"I'm sorry."

"Don't be. I'd rather have died than lived an eternity with a lie."

"Well?" Satara asked as Kaiaphas materialized in front of her.

"He'll be dead soon."

She shrieked before she started pacing the small space that made up Stryker's office. "That's not good enough."

"Then I suggest you kill him."

"Don't you dare take that tone with me." She snatched up the bottle on Stryker's desk that held Kaiaphas's soul inside. She lightly tapped the side of it against the desk, not hard enough to shatter it, but hard enough to sound like it might. "In one flick of my wrist, I could end your existence."

She saw the shimmer of fear in his eyes, but to his credit, he didn't show any other concern over her threat. "Xypher was protected by a son of Aphrodite wielding the sword of Cronus. There was no way to defeat him and finish off Xypher."

Satara let out a disgusted breath. Relying on someone else was what had gotten her into this mess. Her only saving grace was the deamarkonian Stryker had given her. With that, Xypher could be found with little effort.

That was if the worthless demon before her was capable of it. "I want his head delivered to me, Kaiaphas. And if not his, I will take yours . . ."

He bowed low before her. "Your will be done, my mistress. My brother's head will be yours."

FOUR

Xypher had to struggle not to launch himself at the waitress as she brought food and snatch it out of her hands. The scent of it reached deep inside and literally made him ache for a taste of it. All he wanted was to tear into it like a rabid animal and it took all the restraint he had not to. But what amazed him more than the fact that he was able to stop himself was the reason why it was so important to him to behave.

He wasn't about to let anyone humiliate him again.

"*You're nothing but a mongrel. Uncouth. Uncivilized. Disgusting. Who could ever love a beast?*" Satara's words rang loud and clear in his head.

Simone sat across from him, eating daintily, primly. It was obvious manners had been bred into her and for some reason he couldn't even fathom, he didn't want her to judge him like the rest of the world had and find him an animal, too. Never once had he cared what anyone else thought of him.

Until now.

As if she could hear those thoughts, she reached across the table and placed one gentle hand on his arm, over the words he'd branded there. "I know you're starving, Xypher. You don't have to worry about your manners with me. Dig in."

Nothing had ever touched him so profoundly. Just as no one had ever looked more beautiful to him. The light in her hair, the way her hazel eyes flashed with an inner spirit that was intangible and electrifying. It baffled him.

He lashed out at her and she took it, just like he did in Tartarus. No matter what they did, no matter how hard they tried to break him, he stood strong against their best attacks. Just like her. Only her strength was innately good. She never sought to hurt anyone.

Not even him.

She was gentleness personified.

And because of that, he was more determined than ever not to give in to that rabid side of himself.

"I'm all right," he muttered, picking up his silverware.

Simone sat in silence while she watched Xypher's hand visibly shaking as he ate his lamb. There was no mistaking his hunger or his need to satiate it. She wasn't sure why he was fighting it when it was so obvious he wanted to tear into his food. In his shoes, she'd be ripping into it and shoving handfuls into her face.

Not him. It was as if he wanted to prove something. Like he needed to eat with good manners for some reason she couldn't even begin to guess at.

Shaking her head, she tried to focus on her own meal. Something that wasn't easy given the leashed power of him. He was compelling. The strength, the power. All she wanted to do was reach out and touch those perfect lips.

He was like watching a beautiful animal that was stalking its prey.

But the best part was when he tried to take a bite out of the oyster shell. The boyish confusion on his face was utterly charming.

Stifling a laugh, she got up and walked to his side of the table. "You don't bite into the oyster shell."

He scowled at her. "How do you eat it, then?"

"Let me show you." She took the oyster from his hand and picked up the small fork from beside his plate. "First you detach the meat and then you tip the shell to your lips and let it slide down, into your mouth. Then you swallow, but don't chew it."

"Why not?"

She stared at the oyster meat that appeared harmless enough, but she swore she could still taste the one time she'd mistakenly bitten into one. Nasty didn't come close to describing that taste. "Well, it's gritty and kind of gross. But if you really want to you can."

Xypher froze as he watched her put a dab of Tabasco sauce on the meat. The scent of her filled his head and reminded him that it'd been centuries since he last touched a woman . . .

Strange how in his rage and quest for vengeance, he hadn't even thought of that. Hadn't noticed any of the women he'd passed on the streets while searching for Daimons to take him into Kalosis.

Now that long-forgotten ache burned through him. He wanted to take her hand in his so that he could lick the pads of her fingers to taste the salt of her skin. To bury his face in the crook of her neck so that he could inhale her scent until it clung to his skin.

He didn't know why, but just the thought of her touching him in even the most careless way had him harder than he'd ever been before. And he longed to reach up and brush his hand through those chaotic curls that had defied her best efforts to tame them. He wondered what they'd feel like brushing against his chest while she made love to him. Were they as soft as they appeared?

Were her lips?

Would she welcome him into her body?

Xypher forced himself to look away from her and to squelch those thoughts. It wasn't his fate to have a woman like her touch him in that way. He was an animal and he knew it. He'd been left alone too long, had been cast out to find his own way. Tenderness was for humans. It wasn't for a renegade Skotos who was going to be taken back to hell in a few weeks.

Don't go soft. Don't let down your guard.

Sooner or later, he'd be back in Tartarus at the mercy of Hades. It'd taken centuries to harden himself so that he didn't feel the steel-barbed lashes so deeply when they beat him. Centuries of learning how to not fall for the cruel mind games that Hades played.

Comfort on this plane would only weaken him when he returned.

It would make hell even more biting. That was something he couldn't allow. It was bad enough. To soften his existence here . . .

No wonder Hades had agreed to let him loose for a month. The god of the Underworld had known exactly how much worse Xypher's punishment would be after he'd tasted freedom.

Bastard.

Curling his lip, he snatched the oyster from her hand. "I'm not an infant. I can feed myself."

Simone cocked her head irritably at his quick reversal. There for a moment, she'd almost thought that he was learning to be . . . well, nice.

She must have been hallucinating.

"Fine," she said, flinging out her hands. "Whatever."

Angered over his gruffness, she went back to her seat and finished her food in silence.

What was his deal? She'd never before met anyone so surly that they couldn't accept even a minimal amount of kindness. He reminded her of that awful Scott Murphy . . .

Her heart skipped a beat as she remembered the boy who'd been in her children's home with her when she was eleven. Hostile and feral, he'd barely been human.

At nine years old, he'd been taken away from his parents and then put into the revolving door of foster homes because no one could do anything with him. Finally, children's services had started sending him to various facilities that were equally quick to toss him out.

No one at the home where she'd stayed, including the staff, could stand him. He was always picking fights and mocking everyone, even Simone who'd tried to be his friend. He'd laughed at her, then bit her so hard, she'd needed stitches—she still had the scar on her left forearm. Because of that and other such tantrums and attacks, he'd spent all of his time being punished until he'd mysteriously vanished in the middle of the night.

His body had been found a few days later in the basement of the gym, still dressed in his pajamas. Apparently he'd gone there, alone, and slit his own wrists.

He'd only been eleven years old.

Simone had been sad enough over the horrible occurrence, but when she'd overheard two of the teachers talking later that day, that sadness had turned to all-out grief for the child who shouldn't have been reduced to ending his own life.

"It's a shame that boy ended up like that, but I guess given the trauma of his childhood, he didn't have any hope."

"Trauma?"

"Didn't you know? He was taken away from his parents because his mother was a crack addict and his father a drug dealer. Scott had his skull shattered one afternoon when he interrupted Daddy doing a deal because the poor thing was starving and dared to ask for a sandwich. That's when the state took him away. His dad's been trying to regain custody ever since. We'd just told Scott the day he vanished that his father was coming to take him home the next morning. Guess the poor kid would rather be dead than go back to whatever hell was waiting for him . . ."

In that one moment, Simone had learned a

valuable life lesson. *Judge no one until you know their circumstances.* No matter how awful they seemed, sometimes there was a valid reason for their behavior. Granted, some people were just mean and corrupt, but not always.

Many people were just in pain, and by acting out, they were only trying to protect themselves from being hurt more.

It was what she tried to teach her students. Anytime you entered a crime scene, the worst thing you could do for the decedent was to pass judgment on them. It clouded your professionalism and jaded your work. A medical examiner's job was to report without prejudice.

Personal views had no place in a morgue.

It was one thing to tell someone how to live their life and what decisions to make. It was another to be the person who had to do it and live with the consequences. Just because you would do something differently, it didn't mean they would. People rose and fell by their own life choices and experiences. The mistakes were theirs to make.

And as she thought about that, it made her curious over Xypher and his past. Why was he so defensive?

Who had hurt him?

"What are gods' childhoods like?"

Xypher looked up from his tabbouleh to meet a pair of the clearest, most innocent eyes he'd ever seen. "Excuse me?"

She didn't flinch at the causticity in his tone. "I was just wondering. I mean, mine was very typical until my family died. I rode my bike through the neighborhood, made mud pies, had tea parties with my friends and dolls, and fought with my brother over TV shows. What did you do?"

Like he would tell her that? It was none of her damned business. "What do you care?"

The friendliness on her face was washed away by a pained expression. "I really hate it when you ask that question . . . I care because you're a person I'm stuck with until we get the bracelets off and I'd like to know something about you. Who knows? There might even be someone in there buried under all that hostility that I can actually like."

His blood boiled to think about what she really wanted. "You won't get my weaknesses that easily, babe. I don't have any."

She gaped at him. "You equate childhood memories with weakness? Dear God, what did they do to you?"

He laughed bitterly at the memories of his past. Memories he tried so hard not to think about. But one of them was clearer than all the others. It was the only time in his life he'd allowed himself to be weak and it was an experience he would never again repeat.

"I was chained to a fence where they beat me down and then cut my heart out while I fought them. Even one-handed, I made my impact on those who killed me. Suffice it to say, I will never be that helpless again."

Simone wanted to weep at the horror he described. At the pain she saw in those clear, bright eyes. "You didn't deserve that."

"No kidding," he said between clenched teeth. "But deserving has nothing to do with anything. Life and death are what they are. They have mercy for no one."

Simone looked over at Jesse who wore the same aching expression she was sure was on her face. Xypher's words hit her hard as she remembered her mother and brother. They didn't deserve what had happened to them, either.

Not wanting to think about it, she didn't try to speak to him as he finished eating. It was just too hard to try and reach someone who obviously didn't want to be reached.

Once he was done, she tipped the waitress and headed back toward her condo.

They'd barely left the restaurant when Tate called.

"How'd it go with Julian?" he asked.

She glanced down at the bracelet on her arm. "Not really the way I wanted it to. We're still united."

"Man, I'm sorry."

"It could be worse, I suppose. He could be your serial killer."

The look Xypher gave her told her he could hear her conversation.

"Oh, damn, I have to take this call, boo. You guys be careful and I'll check in again later." Tate hung up before she could tell him good-bye.

Closing the phone, she saw Xypher rubbing his arm out of the corner of her eye. Even though he didn't say anything, both of his arms were covered with goose bumps. "You cold?"

He didn't respond.

"He's cold," Jesse said. "It's all over his aura, which I can see, even if you can't."

Xypher sent him a glare that should have set fire to him.

Simone paused as she considered where they could get clothes for him in the Quarter. Most of the places catered to women . . .

Or to goths.

A slow smile curved her lips. Yeah, with his caustic personality and height, goth would look really good on him.

Without a word, she cut down Dumaine to head to Decatur Street.

"What are you doing?" Xypher asked defensively.

"Getting you some clothes."

He pulled her to a stop on the sidewalk. "I don't need anything."

"Yes you do."

His handsome face turned to stone. "I'm not

taking your charity. I don't need anything from anyone."

She raked him with a cold stare. "And I'm not getting stuck for a month with a man who only has one shirt and one pair of pants when I'll be forced to smell you the entire time."

That took some of the fire out of his eyes.

Jesse scowled. "Hey, he's a god. Can't he just make clothes for himself?"

Xypher gave Jesse a quelling glare. "Hades is a bastard as I said earlier. My powers aren't intact. I can use them for defense. But not for food or clothing . . . or shelter." The last bit came out so low that she wasn't even sure she'd heard it.

The ashamed expression on his face told her that she hadn't been mistaken.

Why would Hades do that to him?

"C'mon," she said, tugging his hand gently. "You need clothing, especially a coat or jacket."

Xypher couldn't breathe at the gentleness of her fleeting touch that set fire to his entire being. It wasn't designed to hurt or to control. It was nothing more than a friendly touch any human might give to another.

He'd never been touched like that.

Awed by her kindness, he followed her into a store. Not that he was following per se. He never followed anyone. She only led because he didn't know where they were going.

As they entered the store, he paused at the sight

of a mannequin with a corset, short skirt, and striped leggings.

"Is something wrong?" Simone asked.

"I know a demon who dresses like this."

Her face lost color. "A demon?" she whispered.

Xypher nodded. "She travels with Acheron as his companion. Simi."

"Simi Parthenopaeus?"

Xypher was shocked by the exuberance of the clerk's voice. Short with jet-black hair, she stood on the opposite side of a glass counter filled with jewelry and goblets.

Simone frowned at the woman. "You know Simi?"

The dark-haired woman's smile widened. "Oh, yeah, we all know Simi and her sister. They clean us out every time they're in town. We love them. Are you a friend of theirs?"

Xypher bit back a snort. Friend . . . there was a word no one had ever applied to him before. But he couldn't exactly tell the woman that he was more an ally who once helped Acheron, Simi, and her sister hold off an army of demons and save the world.

"Yeah, we're friends."

"Oh, honey, then welcome to Roadkill. Any friend of the Parthenopaeuses is a friend of ours. What can I do for you?"

"We need to get him some clothes," Simone said. She pointed to a leather jacket high up on the wall. "Can we see that?"

The woman stepped out from around the counter to get it down.

She handed it to Xypher who shrugged it on. It was all he could do not to moan at how good the warm leather felt on his skin after being cold for all these days. The jacket was heavy, but he welcomed the weight of it.

It felt really, really good.

Simone smiled as she came up to him and adjusted it. Her hands brushed against his neck, making him instantly hard. "Very nice. Looks good on you. You like it?"

He didn't even know how to respond. "It's okay," he said, knowing that was incorrect. It was so much more than just okay. He wanted to hug her for the gift.

Simone stepped back as a strange wave of desire went through her and she didn't know why. Okay, maybe she did. Xypher looked hot in the black motorcycle jacket that was painted with an anarchy symbol on the left shoulder and the Misfits face on the back. She wanted to stroke the leather and feel the hard body underneath. He looked so dangerous and feral.

Which he really was.

It was all she could do not to purr.

"How many shirts you want?" Jesse asked.

Simone blinked before she stepped back, grateful for Jesse's interference. "At least a dozen."

"A dozen what?" The sales clerk stared at her.

Simone blushed as she realized the woman didn't know Jesse was standing beside her. "Sorry, I was thinking out loud."

"Ah. I thought you were speaking in code." The woman's gaze slid down Xypher's abdomen. "'Cause I'm sure he has a deadly dozen concealed."

Simone had no idea why, but a flash of jealousy went through her. How ridiculous was that? Yet when she corrected the woman, her tone was clipped by that stupid, unexpected emotion. "Eight, actually."

The clerk was impressed. "Really?"

She nodded.

"Damn, you're one lucky woman. Mine's only got a single, but I love him anyway."

Simone laughed.

Xypher didn't. "What are you two talking about?"

Simone patted Xypher on the arm. "Nothing, sweetie. Let's get you a couple of sweaters and some shirts and pants."

Jesse rolled his eyes. "They're ogling you, dude. Talking about your assets and the fact that you're nauseatingly ripped, which I would have been had I not bit the dust at seventeen." He puffed out his chest, trying to make himself look more muscular. "I'm forever trapped in my tall, gangly phase."

Xypher didn't comment on his appearance, he

was more perturbed by the women. "Are they supposed to do that?" he whispered to Jesse.

"Only if you're lucky . . . or if you're going to be." Jesse made strange clicking noises at him.

The clerk grimaced. "Are they supposed to do what?"

Simone cleared her throat. "Get his clothes. Yes, honey, they are." She leaned closer to him. "Ignore Jesse before they throw us in a padded room." She then gave Jesse a pointed stare.

"She's just jealous I can go into the dressing rooms and not be seen."

Simone mouthed the words "you are such a perv!"

"No I'm not. Perverted would be spying on you when you're bathing or changing clothes." He shuddered. "That's like spying on your sister. Gag me and leave me dead."

"I wish," Simone muttered under her breath.

Xypher was actually amused by their exchange. It took a couple of seconds for him to realize what the emotion he felt even was.

Amused. He'd never experienced it before, but it was good. His chest was light and his stomach tickled. There was no anger or intent to harm in their tones. They were merely bantering playfully and enjoying each other.

He liked watching them.

Simone gave Jesse another warning stare before he seriously got her in trouble. Though she loved him, she hated when he did this. She didn't like to ignore him, but she didn't want anyone to think her insane, either.

Turning away from Jesse so as not to encourage him, Simone followed the woman toward the back, then paused as she saw the shoes in the middle of the store on shelves attached to the walls. Most were pretty funky, including a pair of clear stilettos with nine-inch heels. But one pair of black biker boots with skulls and crossbones for buckles caught her eye.

A slow smile curved her lips as she knew the one person who could do them justice. "Xypher?"

"Yes?"

She pointed to the boots. "Would you wear those?"

The grin that question caused was absolutely wicked. And for once, it wasn't mocking. It was a look of pure pleasure and it warmed her all the way through. Damn, that man was gorgeous.

Clearing her throat, she called the clerk back to where they stood. "We'll take a pair of those."

The clerk laughed. "I just love it whenever friends of Simi come in. You guys shop like demons."

Simone cast a sideways glance at Xypher, who passed a guilty look to her. The woman was half right.

Before long, they'd picked out clothes, underwear, and accessories for Mr. Fine But Obnoxious. Simone had to bite back a whimper when she handed over her credit card. Even though she had a lot of money, it wasn't like her to spend it shopping, especially for a temporary guest. But she couldn't have him walking around for three weeks naked, either. Then again, he would be hot, but they'd both get arrested.

At least that was her thought until she caught an unguarded expression of joy on Xypher's face as he stroked the sleeve of his new jacket. It was obvious he'd never been given anything like it before.

Yeah, that made it worth it.

Smiling, she glanced toward the wall behind the clerk's head. A rack of scarves hung there. Her smile widened at one in particular. "Excuse me," she said to the clerk, "let me get that scarf behind the counter, too."

The clerk picked up the black one with a white skull and crossbones on it. "This one?"

"Yes, please."

As soon as it was rung up, Simone took it from the counter, pulled the tag off, and wrapped it around Xypher's neck.

"What are you doing?" The suspicion in his eyes actually burned her.

"It'll keep your neck warm outside."

Xypher didn't speak as she tucked the ends of the scarf in his jacket, then zipped it closed. It was such a tender gesture of caring that it brought a foreign ache to his chest. He didn't like the sensation of it. "I'm not a child."

She laughed. "Trust me, babe, that has not escaped my attention."

He frowned at her playful words. "Are you teasing me?"

"Yes."

Teasing . . . no one had ever done that before. At least not playfully. He looked at Jesse.

"Teee-zeeeen," Jesse said, elongating the word. "It means . . ." Scowling, he paused. "Well, hell, I don't know what it means. It's when someone, you know, teases you."

Grinding his teeth, Xypher popped him on the back of his head.

"Ow! Dang, I forgot you could do that." Jesse stepped closer to Simone.

When Xypher started to pursue him, Simone stepped between them and handed him the bags of clothes. "We're leaving now," she said in an exaggerated tone. "Thank the nice lady for her help."

The clerk laughed. "You're definitely welcome. You two have a good night."

Before Xypher could respond, Simone lightly pushed him toward the door. He followed after her grudgingly.

Was she insane for coming between them? He couldn't fathom anyone putting their life in danger for a ghost. Especially not a silly one like Jesse.

Simone paused outside to give them both a chiding glare. "You two are going to get me into so much trouble one day. Can you not behave?"

Jesse huffed. "He started it."

Simone held her hand up in frustration. "Not another word!"

Xypher turned and zapped Jesse so hard, his hair started smoking.

Simone grabbed his arm to protect Jesse, who was now whimpering.

Xypher's eyes flared as if he were about to fry her, too.

"Diplomatic immunity," she said, holding up the bracelet to remind him that he couldn't kill her so long as she wore it.

"You'd do well to remember that won't last forever."

"But it'll last long enough to get you to leave Jesse alone."

He growled threateningly. Luckily, though, he turned his back to Jesse and started down the sidewalk.

Relieved that she had them both quelled, Simone had barely taken a step when her phone rang again. "Hello?"

It was Tate.

"We've got another homicide . . . just like Gloria. Can you get your butt over here and take a look at it while the cops are still investigating the scene?"

"Of course. Where are you?"

She didn't hear his answer as two police cars went screaming by, headed toward the other side of the French Market. There was an urgency about them that set off her sixth sense.

"Oh, wait, let me guess," she said after they passed. "You're at North Peters."

"Heard that, huh?"

"To the depths of my now deaf soul." She watched the cars turn. "I think I'm only about four blocks from you. Be right there."

It didn't take them long to cut across the street and find the police . . . and a small crowd that had gathered to watch and comment or speculate. Simone pulled her wallet out of her back pocket to flash the first officer she reached. Even though she carried a purse, she always put her wallet in her back pocket—a force of habit after she'd had her purse stolen several years before.

He wrinkled his nose at her ID. "Meat Division. I don't envy you guys."

She smiled at him. "It's okay, I don't envy you, either. At least the people I take into custody don't try to kill me."

"Good point." He lifted the tape so that she could bend and go under it.

"He's with me," she said before he could stop Xypher.

"It's okay, Ryan," Tate shouted as he headed toward them. "We need them on this one."

"Whatever you say, Doc."

Simone stepped back to introduce them to each

other. "Tate, this is Xypher, my current paranormal dilemma."

Laughing, Tate offered his hand to Xypher. "I've never met a Dream-Hunter before."

Xypher shook it. "Sure you have. You just don't remember it," he said with an evil glint in his eye.

Tate shook his head. "That's not comforting."

"My kind seldom are." No missing the ominous tone in those words.

"Xypher is very much in the hair-raising scare'em crew," Simone explained.

Tate led them toward the victim who waited under a black tarp. "I can see that. And I'll make a note to stay on his good side. Last thing I need are any more nightmares in my sleep."

Simone couldn't agree more. "I think Xypher lives for nightmares."

Tate snorted. "In that case, he's going to feel right at home."

"Why?"

Tate indicated the body on the ground at their feet. "Just like Gloria. Same wounds. Same MO. No blood. Drained and dropped. Only difference is this one seemed to fight back."

"She must—"

"He," Tate corrected.

Simone frowned. That would debunk the serial killer idea. "He?"

Tate lifted the tarp to show her a Caucasian male in his mid-twenties who was lying faceup, staring blankly at nothing at all. His face was contorted, frozen by the horror that had taken his life.

Simone winced as a wave of sympathetic pain went through her. She hated this part of her job most. That feeling of seeing someone as a killer had left them. The sick dread that clamped her stomach tight. But the worst was the firsthand knowledge of how the family would react to this tragedy.

"We have to find this asshole and stop him," she said between clenched teeth.

"Yeah," Tate agreed.

Xypher set his bags down before he approached the body to examine it.

"Careful," Tate warned. "Don't touch the body. We don't want to destroy any evidence. We have to find the perp and bring him to justice immediately."

Xypher leaned over to carefully study the neck wound. "That's going to be hard."

"How so?"

"It's a demon kill."

"What?" she and Tate said simultaneously.

Xypher sat back on his haunches to look up at them. "A human didn't do this."

That didn't make any sense to her. "Daimons don't—"

"Not Daimon. *Demon*." Xypher indicated the

marks on the neck that were identical to Gloria's attack. "This is a Sumerian Dimme attack."

"Dimme?" Tate repeated. "What the hell is a Dimme?"

Xypher rose to his feet. "That's how I ended up here. I helped to fight them in Las Vegas. During the battle, one of the Dimme escaped and to my knowledge no one could find it. I think you just did."

Tate appeared as ill as Simone felt. "How the hell did it get here?"

Xypher shrugged. "There has to be something that called it here. An artifact, a person. Something. Otherwise it would have stayed close to the cocoon where its sisters are still trapped."

"Are you sure about that?" Tate asked.

"No, human. I don't know shit about this. I'm just rattling off randomness to confuse you."

Simone sighed. "I should have warned you about his sarcasm. It makes being around him a total joy."

Tate ignored her statement as he glanced around the dark street. "Can you find his ghost, Sim?"

"He hasn't popped in."

Xypher crossed his arms over his chest. "He won't have a ghost."

Simone cocked her head at his deadpan words. "What do you mean?"

"It's a Dimme kill. They usually suck everything

out of a human. Lock, stock, and barrel. And, for the record, you'll need to destroy the body since their kills reanimate a few hours after death."

Simone exchanged a sick look with Tate.

"Gloria," Tate whispered. "That's why her body got up."

Simone scowled as she thought about that. "Then why did we see Gloria's ghost?"

Xypher shrugged. "The Dimme must not have finished eating the soul. It happens sometimes. The soul gets trapped and eventually withers and dies."

Tate cursed. "So then how do we track and kill this thing?"

Xypher's expression was one of pure evil. "You don't. It tracks and kills you."

FIVE

Tate shivered before he led them a couple of steps away from the body and from where two detectives were talking. The last thing they needed was to have one of them overhear this particular discussion.

He gave Xypher a cutting grimace. "I'm getting all warm and fuzzy inside at the prospect of these demon things roaming the street, preying on us. Just how many of them are we talking anyway?"

Xypher was completely nonchalant about the terror they were facing. "There are seven of them in existence. Only one has escaped to the human realm."

Tate locked gazes with Simone. "I love the way he says 'human realm.'"

Yeah, so did she. "I don't know. I'm still stuck on the 'they hunt and kill us' part. And the 'dead walking.' I don't think I like that."

Tate snorted. "You and Nialls. I'm sure he's still having a swell time over it. Poor guy. No one's ever going to believe he's not crazy . . ." By the expression on his face it was obvious he was having a there-but-for-the-grace-of-God-go-I moment.

Shaking his head as if to clear it, Tate turned his attention back to Xypher. "What does the Dimme want? Why is it killing people?"

Xypher shrugged. "Basic demons are interesting in that they don't usually want anything. They just are. You get in the demon's way, you die. If it has to feed and you're on the menu, it eats you. Simple, really. They're not big on playing games or having ulterior motives."

Cursing, Tate moved them even farther away from the body as a photographer came forward to take pictures. "Things don't kill just to kill. That doesn't make any sense."

"Sure it does," Xypher said dryly. "Demons were created to be weapons or tools of various entities. You have the Charonte who served the Atlanteans . . . Actually, they were one of the few demon races that weren't always subservient. Until they were defeated and enslaved, they were the masters of the earth. Then there are the gallu, who were created to fight the Charonte, and the Dimme, who were made so that if the Sumerian pantheon was destroyed and its gallu with it, they would essentially eat the world and avenge their dead masters. It's what makes the solitary Dimme so dangerous. All she knows is how to kill." Xypher cast a meaningful glance toward the dead man on the ground.

Tate didn't appear to be digesting this news well. "Are there other demons in the world?"

Xypher nodded. "Every culture has its own set of demons. But the ones I mentioned are the ones you're dealing with over this matter." Xypher inclined his head toward the body. "It's possible a gallu attacked him. But generally the gallu are a little more circumspect. They know to dispose of the body after they kill it or they keep the body to use for some purpose—like a zombie. Such as to draw out an adversary or to troll for more victims. They learned a long time ago that a zombie usually returns to its family. If they follow the zombie back, they have more food."

Tate groaned as if that knowledge pained him. "You sure?"

"Unless they're renegades. Or neophytes. Which is what the Dimme would be. She would be lost in the modern world and would be trying to find her own kind. The Dimme and gallu have a hive mentality. They don't like to function independently. So whether it's gallu or Dimme, it's roaming the streets looking for others of its kind and food . . . which would be human in nature."

Again, Tate cursed. "How long has she been out?"

"A few weeks."

"And she's just now feeding?"

Xypher laughed bitterly. "She had to get here from Vegas. I imagine there are other victims along the way."

Tate exchanged a disgusted look with Simone. "So how is it you know so much about demons anyway?" he asked.

Xypher's eyes flared to a bright, flickering red. "I am one."

Tate took a step back, as did Simone.

Even Jesse.

"Um, Sim," Jesse said, stepping behind her. "He can do that freaky eye thing because he's a god, right? He's just screwing with us about being a demon . . . right?"

She wanted to believe that. It made sense . . .

But every instinct in her body told her that Xypher didn't have that kind of sense of humor.

Xypher's eyes faded back to that eerie blue. "My mother was a Sumerian demon whom my father seduced and I was raised with her people so I have a little more insight into the gallu than most."

Simone crossed herself. Was he serious? And yet she knew the truth. She just wanted to hear him say it in no uncertain terms. "You're a gallu?"

"Genetically speaking, yes. But I don't crave or live on blood. Well, my enemies notwithstanding."

He's a demon . . .

Simone didn't know why that was harder for her to accept than him being a Greek god, but it was. Probably because of the reputation demons had. The thought of being attached to one really didn't sit well with her.

She glanced at the body on the ground and shivered. Had Xypher ever done that to an innocent?

Was that why they'd killed him and sentenced him to Tartarus?

It was then it dawned on her exactly how little she knew about the creature she was now bound to. What he was capable of.

How had her life been put into his hands so callously?

Tate gestured toward the body. "Can you kill whatever did this?"

Xypher gave a subtle nod. "But why should I?"

Tate was aghast. "To stop innocent people from dying."

Xypher scoffed. "Innocent? That man on the ground was a rapist and a murderer. When you learn his identity, you're going to find that he got off light. I assure you, I would have done a lot worse to him."

"How do you know that?" Simone whispered.

He gave her a cold look that chilled her all the way to her soul. "Evil knows evil. It's how we find each other or, in the case of the Dimme, how you avoid being taken down by a more vicious opponent."

Jesse's eyes widened respectfully. "Wow. So you're like Satan's bloodhound?"

Xypher gave him a droll look. "Lucifer has his own demons he commands. I'm not one of them."

"Great history lesson on demons and their feeding habits." Tate slapped his hands together. "So, out of curiosity, how do I write up my report? Random demon slaying? Yeah. That's going to read real well." He turned to Simone. "You think I can get a job as a janitor with a medical degree?"

She patted his arm affectionately. "I wouldn't mention the degree. It would make you overqualified. But if it makes you feel any better, I don't think you'll need a job when they send you off to Mandeville."

"Thanks, Simone." His tone was as dry as the desert. "I'll remember that next time you ask me for a letter of recommendation."

"And I'll remember that when you apply to be a janitor at Tulane. See if I help you find work."

"Ow!" Tate groused. "You're vicious."

"Hey, Doc?" An older police officer approached them. "Homicide wants to know if you're ready to wrap up and move the body."

"Yeah, we're done." He lowered his voice so that only Simone and Xypher could hear. "Random demon slaying. Maybe I should just write it up as a mugging gone wrong." He paused and looked at Xypher. "You're sure about the cause of death?"

"When the body gets up in a few and tries to kill you, you'll have your answer."

Tate sighed heavily.

"What are you going to do?" Simone asked before he could withdraw.

Tate shrugged. "I don't know. I can't destroy the body. That's a lawsuit waiting to happen, followed by one major firing and public humiliation."

Xypher scratched his cheek before he spoke. "At the very least, sever the head. You'll thank me for it later."

Tate snorted. "You think 'oops' would cover that?" he asked Simone.

"Tate!" she snapped, horrified at the thought of it. "Our profession has a bad enough reputation. You can't do something like that or else we'll never live it down."

"I'm trying to be reasonable here. You know the ME test didn't exactly cover this. What do you tell your students about the odder elements of our job?"

"I don't. I merely tell them that there are some things that can't be explained."

"Yeah," Tate said with a nervous laugh, "this

definitely qualifies as inexplicable." He glanced back to Xypher. "Is there anything other than decapitation or absolute destruction that will keep the body down?"

"Quartering."

Tate rolled his eyes. "You're not helpful."

"I didn't bite him and create this situation. You asked a question and I answered it. If you want another answer, then ask a different question."

Tate scratched his brow with his middle finger. "I'm having visions of Shaun of the Dead appearing in my lab."

Simone laughed. "You mean Tate of the Dead."

"Exactly. And let us not forget that at the end of *Night of the Living Dead*, they shot the black man who survived the zombie attacks. Not a good precedent and I'm having a bad flashback here, Sim."

Shaking his head, Tate clapped his hands together and started away from them as if he were heading for his doom. "Okay, wish me luck . . . and much fire power—remember not to let the sheriff shoot me at dawn." He glanced back at the victim. "At least this time I know not to assign the body to someone else."

"*Bonne chance, mon ami.*"

"Yeah, thanks, Simone. I'd personally like to *bonne* your *chance* for this."

She stepped back as he left them and approached the body so that he could oversee the moving of it.

Simone looked away as she thought of Gloria

and wondered what had happened to her. Rubbing her arms, she whispered a silent prayer for the poor woman.

Jesse cocked his head as he studied her. "What's wrong, Sim?"

"Just thinking of Gloria. I wish I knew what happened to her. I hate that we lost her."

Xypher frowned. "Who was Gloria?"

Simone gave him an irritated look because he didn't know. "She was the other ghost who was there with the Daimons when you came crashing into my world."

"Oh, the blonde."

"Yes, the blonde."

Tate groaned as he returned to their group and caught that bit of their conversation. "Yeah . . . Speaking of, her family is due in any minute to claim her body. What am I supposed to tell them when we can't give the body over? Again, I don't think 'oops' will quite cover it."

"Hey!" the cop shouted. "Doc, I don't think this guy's dead. I just saw him move."

Simone paled at those words. Worse, she saw the decedent's foot moving herself. "Xypher, it's starting."

Before she could blink, he threw his hand out. An instant later, the entire body burst into flames.

The police officer shouted for help while several other cops scrambled for fire extinguishers.

She glared at Xypher. "Did you do that?"

He shrugged nonchalantly. "Sometimes my powers work. Sometimes they don't. Looks like this time they did. Yea, us."

Tate wrinkled his nose as he watched the police running around. "I'm not sure I should thank you for this or not . . . you think they'll believe there was some kind of gas in the body that made it move, then spontaneously combust?"

Simone let out an elongated breath as she silently wished him luck on that one. "If anyone can make it work, Tate, you can."

"Yeah, here's seeing you at the unemployment office soon." He left them to aid the officers in putting out the flames.

Simone watched them work as the true horror of it all sank in. "So that man really was eaten by a demon."

"You didn't think I made that up, did you?"

"No." She dragged the word out. "Not exactly, anyway." She frowned as she raked her gaze over that body that was made for sin up to those clear, breathtaking eyes. No one would ever guess Xypher was anything other than human, yet she knew better. "Are you really part demon?"

"Why would I lie?"

"I don't know. Sometimes people do, for no apparent reason."

"But I'm not human."

His being demonspawn at least explained some of his acerbic personality. It also excused it . . .

almost. Then again with him being a demon, she was lucky he was housebroken and not trying to scare everyone they met on the street.

I am bound to a demon . . . It sounded like a bad sci-fi movie.

Baffled, befuddled, and just plain confused, she went to get his bags where they'd left them on the ground. Right now, she just wanted to go home and get her bearings.

She led them away from the scene, toward her condo.

"Buck up, Sim," Jesse said cheerfully. "At least the demon didn't eat you."

"Yet, you mean."

Xypher took the packages from her hands. "Don't worry. I won't let you get hurt."

"Not unless it means you get a shot at your enemy, right? Then I'm fair game for death."

He didn't comment.

"All righty then," she said, trying to lighten the mood and not think about the fact that he would most likely sacrifice her to achieve his goal. "Let's make our way back safely, shall we?"

Xypher nodded as he tried not to think about the fact that he wasn't so sure he wouldn't protect her even at the expense of his vengeance. While he had demon blood in him, he wasn't completely heartless. Even at his worst, he had a code of ethics and those ethics would not allow Simone to get hurt in the crossfire.

Damn me for it.

Pausing, Jesse gave him a look that told him the ghost didn't think much about him. He was used to it. The Greek gods had given him the same look once they realized a Sumerian demon was genetically attached to their pantheon.

The moment Xypher had learned to infiltrate dreams and shown his god powers, Zeus had sent his minions out to drag him to Olympus in chains.

Even though Xypher was barely more than a child, Zeus had tried to kill him. But Poseidon had stopped his brother from making that mistake. "The Sumerians are looking for a reason to call out the Chthonians on us. You kill that boy and we'll all have to answer for it."

The Chthonians were essentially the gatekeepers of the universe. They made sure that the pantheons didn't war among each other since such things tended to lead to the ultimate destruction of the earth and everyone who called it home.

Zeus had curled his lip at his brother. "Then what would you have me do with him?"

"Strip his emotions and train him like the rest of Phobetor's brats. There's no longer anything to fear in an Oneroi. And once he's trained, we'll be able to use him to spy on the Sumerians for us."

And so Xypher's brutal training had begun.

Young and stupid, Xypher had actually thought his father would come to his rescue.

He hadn't. In fact, it'd been his father who'd helped to beat him and strip his emotions to prove his loyalty to Zeus. If Xypher had been a full demon, they wouldn't have been able to subjugate him. Unfortunately, he had too much of his father's blood in him for that.

They'd broken him on a hot summer's day when he'd decided it would be easier to give in to the training than to suffer any more abuse. All of his emotions had bled out of him until he was numb to everything. No taste, no smell. Nothing that could induce an emotion.

Honestly, he'd welcomed it. All the years of pain were gone. And at least the Greeks weren't quite as bloodthirsty as the demons. They hadn't made him fight for every morsel. Bleed for every comfort.

To be a demon meant to take and destroy. Food was only given to those who could kill for it.

I should have stayed an Oneroi.

Things had been so much simpler then. All he had to do was monitor the sleep of humans. Make sure other Skoti didn't fixate on one particular human too long. The gods permitted the Oneroi and Skoti to exist so long as they didn't disturb the balance of the universe or make the human host insane from their dreams.

Whenever the Skoti came too close to breaking those two laws, the Oneroi were sent in to either drive them away or kill them.

It'd been a cushy life.

Until Satara had come to him. A handmaiden to the goddess Artemis, she'd been as beautiful and alluring as any immortal. She'd summoned him into her dreams and there she'd shown him kindness and the softer emotions he'd never experienced before. They'd made love like they were on fire. Her every breath, every touch, had given him pleasure.

When she was with him, he felt alive . . .

Xypher cursed as he remembered the bitch. Sultry and seductive, she'd made him pay dearly for wanting to be something more than what he was.

It was a mistake he'd never make again.

"You okay?"

He blinked at Simone's soft voice that interrupted his thoughts. "Never better."

"Dang," Jesse said, leaning closer to Simone. "If that's his 'never better' it makes you wonder what 'never worse' looks like, huh?"

She glanced back over her shoulder. Xypher didn't know why, but there was something utterly charming about her expression and actions.

"Shh, Jesse, play nice. Remember, he can hurt you."

"Yeah, and I want to know right now who I can complain to about that. It just doesn't seem right."

Xypher narrowed his eyes on him. "How did you get to be a ghost, anyway? You annoy one person too many and they cut your throat?"

"Ha, ha," he said sarcastically. "No, it was a car wreck on a really rainy night as I was taking my girlfriend home from work. The last thing I heard was her telling me to go left at the light. So when the big bright light came, I went left and next thing I knew, I was trapped here on earth."

Xypher rolled his eyes. "That is the most pathetic thing I've ever heard."

Jesse snorted. "Really? The most pathetic thing I've ever heard was this half demon, half god who—"

"Jesse!" Simone snapped. "Again, I feel compelled to remind you that he can hit you and make it hurt. Bad."

That quelled the ghost a bit.

Xypher frowned as he watched the two of them. They were extremely comfortable together . . . like family. He'd never been that close to anyone or anything and it made him wonder what had happened to cause that bond between them. "How did you end up with Simone?"

Jesse laughed. "See, this is where you'd say something like, none of your damned business. But unlike you, I'm nicer than that."

Xypher narrowed his eyes.

An instant later, Jesse tripped as if someone had shoved him from behind.

He caught himself and turned to glare at Xypher. "Hey, Vader, keep your Jedi mind tricks to yourself. That hurt!"

"Yeah, and next time it'll hurt a lot worse. Now, how did you end up being the personal nuisance for Simone?"

"It was the night my mother and brother were killed," Simone said, her voice betraying a subtle note of sadness. "I was in the hospital, waiting for my dad to arrive, when Jesse came to me and told me not to cry."

Xypher hated to admit it, but it was a nice thing for Jesse to do. "How did they die? Car wreck?"

She shook her head before she wrapped her arms around herself as if to provide comfort or protection from the bad memory. "It was a robbery gone bad. We were coming back from a school play and Tony wanted one of those stupid candy ring pops for a treat. My mother pulled in to a convenience store to humor him. Since I was sleepy and didn't feel good, I stayed in the car while they went in. When they didn't come right back, I lifted myself up in the backseat to see what was taking so long. As soon as I did, I saw two men gunning them down by the counter. I was so scared, all I could do was cover my ears and crawl down behind the front seat to hide. The police found me there a few minutes later when they came. They had to take the seats out to get to me."

Xypher felt like shit. There was no other description. He saw the tears in her eyes and it made him angry that someone would do that to her.

When her gaze met his, the agony in those hazel eyes tore through him like a dagger. "Tony was only seven years old. How could someone open fire on a baby with his mother?"

Xypher looked away, unable to bear the pain and scrutiny he saw in her eyes. "I don't know."

"You're part demon. Can't you give me some insight into such evil?"

"No. As corrupt as I've been, I've never hurt a child and I never would."

Shifting the bags to one hand, Xypher pulled her to a stop. He wanted to comfort her, but he wasn't sure how. What did humans do for comfort?

Touch?

He reached out to place his hand on her cold, soft cheek. "I'm sorry for your loss, Simone." What surprised him most was that he actually meant it. He really did care.

Simone saw the hesitancy in Xypher's eyes. The uncertainty. If she didn't know better, she'd think he was afraid of touching her. She placed her hand over his and gave a light squeeze. "Thank you."

He inclined his head before he dropped his hand. "I didn't offend you by touching you, did I?"

"No."

Jesse made an odd choking noise. "Yeah, but you're both offending me with all this lovey-dovey crap. Get a room. No wait, don't. Separate rooms. Both of you!"

Simone shook her head. "Jesse, stop."

Jesse ignored her as he ran ahead. "Oh, look, we're home. Goody!"

Xypher stepped back as Simone pulled a set of keys out of her pants pocket. She stopped in front of a green steel door that opened into a short, narrow alley before it led to a large courtyard.

She swung the door open and stood back. "Jesse, lead the way while I lock up."

Xypher followed the ghost into the immaculate courtyard that held a couple of stainless steel barbecue grills and a black fountain.

"My condo is straight back." She passed by them and went to a brown door with the number 23 on it.

Xypher followed her into a small living room. The building was old, but her furniture was new. Decorated in tans and browns the apartment was neatly kept with nothing out of place.

She indicated the back of the house. "There are two bedrooms. Jesse? Will you sleep on the couch?"

He looked horrified by the mere suggestion. "No way! You're not giving him my room, are you?"

"You don't really sleep . . ."

"Well, yeah, but what if I get bored in the middle of the night?"

"You can haunt around the kitchen and living room."

He let out an aggravated squeak. "You make me do that and I'm going to stack furniture and reset your alarm clock."

"And I'll find an exorcist."

Jesse narrowed his gaze on her. "That would only work on a demon." He sent a pointed stare to Xypher.

"A psychic, then. I'll go to Madame Selene's shop in the Square and have her use a banishing spell on you."

"Oh, you would," Jesse accused. "Fine. Grump can sleep in my room, but he better not drool on my pillows. Or sleep naked. The last thing I need is to go blind from it."

"I don't drool."

Jesse appeared pleased by that. "Good. What about the naked part?"

"You're not my type, Jesse."

Jesse screamed before he took off running to the back of the house.

Simone rolled her eyes at Jesse's antics. He could be aggravating, but honestly, she couldn't imagine her life without him.

She pulled her coat off and hung it up, then waited for Xypher to do the same.

Once they were down to their shirts and jeans, she indicated the back of her condo with a tilt of her head. "Follow me and I'll show you the way." She led him toward the back and through the kitchen to where there were two bedrooms. "I'm on the right. Your temporary room is the one on the left."

There was a bathroom between them.

Xypher paused as he took in the small place she called home. It was nice and comfortable. Not overly posh, but the perfect size for a woman who lived alone. . . with a ghost.

She took him into Jesse's room which was painted blue. Xypher was fine with that, but there were posters of bands and movies from the 1980s plastered all over the walls. *Lost Boys*. Joan Jett. *Ferris Bueller's Day Off. The Damned. Flash Dance*. Wendy O. Williams. *The Terminator*. The Clash. Go-Go's. Bananarama. It was like a strange time capsule.

Three wooden crates designed for vinyl albums were stacked against the far wall and filled with LPs. On top was an old Pioneer stereo with a turntable. The dresser was scattered with odds and ends, including a Rubik's Cube, multisided dice, and Atari cartridges. It looked like a teenager's bedroom from 1987.

Xypher took a minute to let that seep into his consciousness. Most people who had a ghost force itself into their life wouldn't go to this much effort to make it feel at home. There was even an antiquated Apple computer on the desk by the crates, and an Atari hooked up to the TV.

"You love Jesse." It was an obvious statement given the room they were in.

"I do." Her eyes shone with sincerity and truth. "He stayed and looked out for me after my family was gone. He was like a big brother . . ." She tilted her head and smiled before she continued. "Now he's more like a younger one. But there's nothing I wouldn't do for him."

How he wished he had that kind of loyalty from someone. His problem was there was nothing anyone would do *for* him.

"You can put your clothes in here." She opened an empty drawer in the bureau.

Xypher set the bags down on the floor. "You know, this might not work."

"How so?"

"Your bedroom might be too far from this one. We may not be able to separate."

She sucked her breath in sharply. "I'd already forgotten about that stipulation. How will we know?"

Xypher stood back. "Start walking. When you hit a spot where you're gasping for breath, that should tell us our limitations."

"Oh, joy. I can't wait to be the guppy."

"Glub, glub, little fishy. Start walking."

Simone wasn't sure about this as she headed for the door, slowly. She walked through the doorway, into the hall. After a few steps, she was less afraid.

So far so good.

"This doesn't seem . . ." Her voice broke off as she choked. All of a sudden, she couldn't speak or move. Everything around her was getting dark. Frightening.

Out of nowhere, Xypher was there. He scooped her up in his arms and carried her to her bedroom and laid her on her bed. His face was red as he, too, struggled to breathe.

It took her several minutes before she could breathe normally again. Xypher stayed by her side, watching her with an expression that she would have called worried if the very idea of his concern for her wasn't ludicrous.

"That was scary," she said quietly once she could speak again. "How did you make it to me when you couldn't breathe, either?"

"Raw determination."

She placed her hand on his cheek where his whiskers teased her palm. How could a demon have moments of kindness and compassion? "Thank you."

He inclined his head to her. "Now we know how little space we have."

It was true. They had maybe fifteen to twenty feet before it killed them. "What are we going to do?"

Xypher considered their options . . . none of which were very good. He cleared his throat before he answered. "We're going to find some way to get you out of this."

"What if we can't?"

Then she was going to die with him when he killed Satara. And there wouldn't be any way to avoid it.

SIX

Simone jumped as the phone in her pocket rang, breaking the awkward silence between them. Pulling it out of her pocket, she answered it to find Julian on the other end.

"Sorry to bother you, Simone. But since my wife is back, we were wondering if you'd like us to return your car to you?"

"That would be fabulous. Are you sure it wouldn't be too much trouble?"

"Not at all. Just give me the address and we'll head over with it."

"Oh, wait, you don't have my car keys."

He gave a low laugh. "Trust me, it won't be a problem."

How could she forget she was talking to a demigod? "In that case, thank you very much."

Relieved to be getting her stuff back, Simone gave her address to him, then hung up. Finally something was going right. It was about ten hours too late, but maybe better late than never.

She pushed herself up from the bed. "I guess we need to bring the mattress from Jesse's bed and lay it on the floor for you."

Xypher stepped back to give her room to move around him. "Why would you do that?"

"So that you'll have a comfy place to sleep tonight."

His scowl deepened. "I don't need a mattress."

Was he serious? There was no way she was going to let a strange man sleep in her bed, especially not one who looked as good as him. She didn't trust either one of them to keep their hands to themselves. "You can't sleep on the floor. It's cold."

He arched a brow at her indignant tone. "I've been sleeping on ice-cold dirt for seven hundred years. At least your floors are clean and they don't have anything scurrying over them that'll bite me while I sleep."

Her heart ached at what he described. By his expression, she could tell he wasn't kidding or exaggerating. "What did you do that made them condemn you?"

He looked away.

Simone approached him slowly so that she could look up at him and touch his arm. She half expected him to curse and shove her away.

He didn't.

Xypher couldn't breathe as he stared into those curious hazel eyes that seared his soul. That touch, combined with those eyes, weakened him.

All he wanted to do was pull her into his arms and feel her soft comfort.

If only it were that simple. But it wasn't. His aches couldn't be relieved so easily. Too many centuries of abuse had left him hollow.

He let out a deep breath before he answered her question. "I let someone use me."

"Use you how?"

How could he explain Satara to someone who had no concept of a creature so devious and cold? There were times when not even he understood the nature of their complicated relationship. "She addicted me to her emotions and used that addiction to control me. I thought I loved her and I would have done anything to make her happy."

Simone cocked her head. "Anything, huh? So what did she ask you to do?"

He hesitated to tell her everything. There was no need in her knowing just what a monster he'd been. "I drove her enemies mad for her. Made them turn on each other and on their own families. They killed other people violently and then they killed themselves."

He winced at the memories that still haunted him. Men he'd goaded into fights for no other reason than to make Satara happy. "Believe me, I earned my damnation. I've never shirked from it. It's why I know that there's no way Hades will free me when this is over. The Fates won't allow it. But I shouldn't have to suffer alone in Tartarus. I may have done the deeds, but Satara commissioned them."

Simone tried to understand him and what he'd done. Why it had caused him to be condemned. But no matter how hard she tried, she couldn't reconcile him with someone worthy of being punished so severely. "You said demons were tools for others. Why were you held accountable for being true to your nature?"

"I'm not just a demon, Simone. I'm a god. What I did was unforgivable. I don't ask for any kind of salvation or for understanding."

No, he only asked for vengeance.

"What made you so unforgiving?"

The intensity of that stare singed her. It was empty and cold and at the same time it touched something inside her. "Be grateful that you have the luxury of asking me that question. Pray to whatever god you worship that you'll always be ignorant."

He pulled away from her and walked to her window.

Jesse drifted back into the room, making her wonder where he'd been for the last few minutes. Then again, Jesse didn't really like visitors in the house so maybe he'd taken a walk outside.

"Do you have any salt?" Xypher asked suddenly.

"Salt?" What a strange segue from their previous subject into an offbeat topic. What did salt have to do with anything?

He tested the lock on her window before he answered. "We need to spread it around the windows and doors, or anything else that leads outside."

"Why?"

"Salt is a pure substance. Incorruptible. No full-blooded demon can cross it."

Simone liked the sound of that, but she had one question. "You can, right?"

He nodded as he turned away from the window. "But Kaiaphas can't."

"Salt coming up!" Jesse ran for the kitchen.

Simone wasn't far behind him.

Xypher pulled up the rear as she got out her tub of salt. "It needs to be a high concentration."

"By all means, use whatever it takes." She handed the salt to him.

In no time, they had her condo prepped.

"God bless Morten's," she said, closing the spigot on top and returning the round container to her cabinet. "Who knew that could come in handy for anything other than cooking?"

A knock sounded on her door.

Simone's eyes widened as a stab of fear pierced her. "What are the odds that could be Kaiaphas?"

"Very slim. He doesn't knock."

"Oh." Feeling a little ridiculous over her question, she went to the door, only to have Xypher stop her by placing a hand on the door so that she couldn't open it.

"Careful of the salt when you open the door. If you wipe it away, it won't do us any good."

Good warning. "Thanks." She opened the door carefully to find Julian there.

"Hi," he said, smiling. "I left your car out front. I just wanted you to know."

She returned his smile. "Thank you so much for this . . . and for everything else. I really appreciate it."

"No problem." He looked past her to where Xypher stood. "Glad to see you up and about. We had a moment of fright when you went down. Nothing like a demon battle right after dusk to make you feel alive, right?"

"If you say so." Xypher held his hand out to Julian. "I appreciate your help."

Julian shook his hand. "Anytime . . . especially when the kids aren't around. Good night."

"Good night." Simone shut the door, then turned to face Xypher. She was amazed by what he'd done. It was so out of character for his demon self that she wanted to pinch him to be sure he hadn't been body-snatched. However, she wasn't feeling suicidal. "Did you actually thank him just now?"

"Yes. I know you find it hard to believe, but I am capable of it."

"Really?"

He looked baffled by her comment. "Why do you tease me?"

She shrugged. "You're rather teasable."

"Like a cobra," Jesse said snidely as he pretended to pet an invisible snake. "Here, reppie, reppie. Here, reppie, reppie. Ow!" He pulled his hand to his body and waved it. "He bit me!" Then he started frothing at the mouth and twitching before he fell on the ground. "He killed me."

Simone stepped over his spasming form. "You're so odd, Jesse."

He lifted his head to stare after her. "I'm not the one teasing the cobra, dude. That'd be you. Mr. Spicoli ordering pizza in Mr. Hand's class. Stop the madness, sister. Stop!"

Xypher took a step toward him and Jesse quickly pushed himself to his feet.

"I'm going to listen to Duran Duran albums. Later." Jesse vanished.

Simone rubbed her eyebrows in a slow circle before she moved her massage to her temples, trying to dispel some of the ache that had started in her head. She walked back to her bedroom to deposit her purse and keys on her dresser. "What a day this has been. Chased by a demon, threatened by lycanthropes, near-death experiences galore, mutilated bodies . . . I get giddy just thinking about what tomorrow might bring."

Xypher cast a sullen glare toward Jesse's room. "If we're lucky, a medium who'll help Jesse find that light and walk into it."

Simone gaped at his dry comment. "Oh, my God, was that a joke?" Laughing, she approached him. "Did *you* actually make an honest-to-goodness joke?"

Xypher was completely enchanted by the sound of her melodic laughter as she stepped in front of him. Her eyes glowed with warmth and humor. She was so vibrant and alive that he wanted to reach out and touch her.

No. He wanted to kiss her . . .

That knowledge tore through him. He was a Phobotory Skotos. They thrived on causing fear in others. But standing here, right now, looking at her, he wanted to strip her clothes off and taste every inch of her body until she came in his arms, screaming out his name.

He burned with a need so tight and fierce, it actually scared him. His body hardened to steel, begging him to pull her close and taste those tempting lips that teased, but never mocked him.

Simone was singed by the heat of Xypher's gaze. It was electrifying. Piercing. He was so feral and complex. So frightening, and at the same time she wanted to touch him. It was a compulsion like watching a caged wild animal you knew could shred you with its claws. Even so, it held so much beauty that all you could dream of was sinking your hand in its soft fur and feeling it purr against you.

But that wasn't the man in front of her. She wasn't sure if any woman could tame him long enough to pet that beautiful body. He didn't seem like he'd lower his defenses long enough to allow a woman to be intimate with him.

Simone could count on one hand the number of men she'd been with . . . and all of them she'd known a long time before dating them. Even longer before she'd welcomed them into her bed.

Never once had she met a man who tempted her like this. She actually wanted to pull him to her and strip him naked before tasting every succulent inch of him.

What was wrong with her?

He was obnoxious and rude. Terrifying and threatening.

And the sexiest thing on two legs.

His eyes darkened as he dipped his head toward hers. *Run, Simone, run . . .*

She couldn't. Instead, she opened her mouth to receive one of the hottest kisses she'd ever tasted. At first he didn't touch her. Just his lips sliding against hers, tasting and teasing.

A feral growl escaped him before he cupped

her face in his hands and deepened the kiss to an ecstatic level.

Xypher breathed the scent of her in, letting it wash over him. As their tongues swirled, he tasted her humanity, her spirit. Most of all, he tasted her passion. It set fire to his own, making him ache in places he didn't even know a man could ache. But the needful pain that surprised him most was the one in his condemned soul.

For the first time in centuries, he didn't feel like a demon.

He felt like a man.

This is how Satara got to you . . .

That thought washed over him like an ice bath. Gasping at the truth, he pulled away. Anger coiled through him that he would be so stupid again. And for what? A gentle touch? A fleeting moment of pleasure?

Idiot!

One moment of bliss wasn't worth an eternity in hell. And neither was Simone.

She was a human. No good could ever come of being with her. He belonged to the immortal world and she lived in this one with its rules and civility.

There was no way she'd ever understand who and what he was.

Simone couldn't breathe as she watched a multitude of emotions sweeping over Xypher's face. Confusion, remorse, torment, but the one that stung her was the bitter anger.

"What's wrong?"

"Stay away from me." His voice was a savage growl that reverberated through the room.

"You kissed *me,* not the other way around."

He laughed mockingly. "I never said I wasn't stupid. Obviously. If I'd had a brain, I wouldn't have fallen for the lies that got me damned." He turned and started to leave.

He cursed as he reached the doorway. "I can't even get away from you." Leaning his head back, he glared at the ceiling. "I hate you, Hades, you bastard." A muscle worked furiously in his jaw as he turned back toward her. "I'd rather they just beat me than to be stuck here like this."

Well, if that didn't sting her all the way to her core. How dare he! "I didn't realize I was such a nuisance to you."

"You're in my way, aren't you?"

She balled her hands into fists then raised them at him and flung her fingers out as if to hex him. "I wish you'd been the one who was mute. No, I take it back. I'm glad you're not mute. Because every time I start to think you're an okay guy or that I like you, you open that mouth of yours and remind me that you're not. So thank you. Now get out!" She pushed him through the door.

Xypher opened his mouth to speak, but before he could, she slammed the door shut in his face and locked it. Then she shoved her dresser over the opening, just to make sure he couldn't open the door.

Satisfied, she leaned against the dresser and folded her arms.

A light knock sounded on the door. "Simone?"

"Go. Away." She added a silent "jerk" to the end of that sentence.

"I can't. We'd die if I did."

"Then you can just stand there in the hallway until I calm down." It was immature, but even so it made her feel better. He deserved it.

You're so childish.

Perhaps, but sometimes immaturity was called for. This was one of those times.

Xypher raked a hand through his hair as he fought the urge to use his powers to disintegrate that door. He could feel her sense of satisfaction and it set off his ire even more.

Unable to let her have the last word, he manifested right in front of her.

She glared furiously. "No, you didn't!"

"You can't keep me out."

"You are such a dickhead." She put her hands up to force him back, but the instant she touched him, something inside him shattered.

He pulled her against him and kissed her with

every confused emotion he felt warring within him. Dizzy from it, he pinned her to the bureau she'd used to keep him out. Closing his eyes, he felt every inch of her body pressed against him. Her breasts were so soft against his chest. Her breath sweet and welcoming as her hipbone rubbed against the part of him that was swollen stiff and begging for the softest part of her body.

Simone couldn't think straight with him kissing her like this. His hands felt so good roaming her body as their tongues danced. She hadn't been held in so long . . . She'd almost forgotten the feel of strong arms around her. The scent of a man as his whiskers brushed her skin.

It was heaven.

And all she wanted to do was climb on top of him and ride him until they were both begging for mercy.

"Push me away, Simone," he said in her ear, his voice ragged.

"Is that what you want?"

"No," he growled. "I desperately want inside you. I want your scent on my skin as I taste every part of your body until I'm drunk from it."

She shivered. Right now, it was all she wanted, too. But they were strangers and he was a condemned demon.

Demon, Simone . . . demon.

Putting her hands on his shoulders, she pulled back. "I don't understand you."

Xypher bit back a caustic retort. In truth, he didn't understand himself, either. Any more than he understood why he wanted to be with her as badly as he did.

"*Would you die for me?*" Satara's voice taunted him from the past.

And so he had. He'd given his life for hers and she'd laughed while he died.

He hadn't been attracted to a woman since that day.

Until now.

He cupped Simone's face in his hand and tilted her chin until their eyes met. "If you loved someone, would you make them die for you?"

Confusion darkened her gaze. "What?"

"Answer the question. Yes or no. Would you make someone you love die for you?"

"My entire family is gone—both the one I was born into and the one that adopted me. I live in fear of losing anyone else I'm close to. Hell no, Xypher. I would *never* ask someone I loved to die for me."

The joy those words brought him was unbelievable. "Would you die for someone you loved?"

"Of course. Wouldn't you?"

Xypher stepped back as he remembered the day they'd dragged him down and killed him. Would he do it again?

He scoffed at the idea. "People aren't worth your life. It's a precious gift, and instead of cherishing it, they mock you for the sacrifice. Stop being naïve."

Simone flinched as she realized what he was saying. Someone he'd loved had betrayed him. No wonder he wanted revenge. "Not everyone squanders love, Xypher. My father didn't mock my mother when she died. He grieved more than anyone I've ever seen. So much so that he killed himself five months later."

She glanced to the photo on her desk of her with her mother, father, and brother. It'd been taken a month before their deaths. The happiness on their faces haunted her at times, and comforted her at others.

Tonight it comforted her.

"My father used to say that life is what you make it. Today is the first day of the rest of your life. You can't change the past, but the future isn't set in stone. You can effect a change there. Move forward not with hatred or love. Move forward with purpose."

He turned on her so fast that it made her gasp. "What did you say?"

She tried to remember. "That today is—"

"Not that. The last part."

It took her a second to remember. "Move forward?"

"Yes. Where did you hear that?"

"It was something my father always said. Does it mean something to you?"

He looked down at the writing on his arm. "It's an old saying among Sumerian demons. It's almost like a battle cry we use. I've never known a human to use it before."

She touched the intricate scroll she couldn't read. "Is that what's written here?"

"In part."

"And the rest?"

He pulled his arm away from her. "It's a reminder to me of what I've been through. A reminder to not fail until I've tasted blood."

"Xypher—"

"Simone!" Jesse's voice echoed in the room before he came running through the wall. "You've got to see this!" He snatched the cord for the blinds to lift them up.

Simone stumbled back into Xypher as chilling red eyes stared at her.

SEVEN

Xypher instinctively stepped between Simone and the window where Kaiaphas floated, glaring his hatred at them. Long black hair twisted around a repulsive face covered with boiling skin.

Screaming out, Kaiaphas tried to blast through the window, but the salt deflected the blast back toward him. He dodged it, then cursed.

He curled his lip at Xypher. "You don't really think something so simplistic will save you from me, do you?"

Xypher gave a low, evil laugh. "Am I blind or did it just kick your ass? Must suck to have something like salt assault you. Guess that's what happens when you're part slug."

Kaiaphas raised his hands as if he intended to blast the window again, but caught himself. "You can't stay inside there forever."

"True, but I can stay here long enough to ruin your best day."

Kaiaphas hissed at him. His gaze slid past Xypher to Simone, down to where Xypher had his hand protectively on her waist. "Fascinating . . . you've now progressed from frightening to protecting humans. If you really want to keep her safe, come outside and I'll take your life and let her live."

"That would work if we weren't wearing the bracelets Satara sent over. I die, she dies. Separate us and I might consider your offer."

Kaiaphas tsked. "Don't you trust me?"

Trust . . .

That single word took him back to his childhood. Barely more than a toddler, Xypher had been so hungry he would have done anything for food. The winter had been harsh, wiping out all the crops. Xypher had found a bit of bread cooling on a building ledge, but he hadn't been tall enough to reach it. He'd tried for an hour to find something to either stand on or knock down the loaf. But it continued to be out of his reach.

Frustrated, he'd cried and gone home, starving.

Kaiaphas had come to him. "What's wrong, brat?"

He'd foolishly told him about the bread.

"Tell me where it is and I'll share it with you."

"It's my bread!"

Kaiaphas had tsked at him. "Your bread will be eaten by a human. Isn't it better to have half a loaf than none at all? Trust me, brat. I'll share."

Xypher had agreed. After disclosing the location, he'd watched as Kaiaphas took the fresh bread and ate it while he cried. The worst part was, unlike him, the bastard didn't live on food. Kaiaphas needed blood. He'd eaten it just for meanness and nothing more. When Xypher had gone to his mother to complain, she'd backhanded him hard enough to bust his lip.

"If you're not demon enough to get it on your own, you don't deserve it." That had always been his mother. She'd nursed him on venom and hatred.

Trust was for a fool.

And he would never trust Kaiaphas again. "Not a bit. Give me the key, and once she's free, we'll fight."

"I don't have it."

Xypher gave him credit for not lying about it. "As I thought. No intention of carrying out our bargain. You never change, brother."

Kaiaphas charged the window. His face illuminated the entire pane. "I'm going to enjoy killing you."

Xypher walked slowly toward the window and grabbed the cord. "Give Mom my worst." He dropped the blinds.

Simone didn't know what stunned her most. The fact that she had one seriously ugly demon floating outside her window or that said ugly demon was the brother of the hot piece of cheese in front of her. "He's not really your brother, is he?"

"Can't you see the resemblance?"

"Since your skin doesn't boil and your eyes aren't normally bloodred, no."

"Neither are his. It's all affectation designed to scare humans. He's such a fucking rookie."

"You could do better?"

Before she could blink, he spun up toward her ceiling and transformed from a man into a black seeping shadow that filled half her room. Fangs shot out of his mouth as his eyes turned a sickly fluorescent yellow. Fire rippled over every inch of him.

Simone stumbled back.

"Yeah," he said, his voice demonic and terrifying. "I can do a lot better."

In a flash he was human again. "My father is Phobetor. The Greek god of nightmares. Kaiaphas's father was some flesh-eating demon that Ares used to set loose on his enemies for shits and giggles. My brother has no flair. No panache. Complete rookie poser who thinks a deep demon voice and some scary red eyes will make everyone wet their pants in fear."

His rant was oddly amusing. "Yeah, okay . . . that's some sibling rivalry you two have."

Xypher scoffed. "He doesn't rival me. Ever." A

muscle worked in his jaw. He tapped his thumb against his thigh as if he were contemplating something and not finding a satisfactory answer. "Satara knows he's not powerful enough to kill me. Why would she summon him after me, then?"

That seemed obvious to her. "To kill me since I'm the weaker of the two of us."

"No, there has to be more than that, and why only send one demon? She could summon more. Why hasn't she? Something's not right." He returned to the window and snatched open the blind.

Kaiaphas was gone.

"I need my full powers," Xypher snarled. He dropped the blind again.

"If you need an oracle—"

"No. I need something a lot more powerful than Julian."

That was an extremely frightening thought for her. "Given what I've seen today, I don't think I like the way that sounds."

"You're going to like it even less come tomorrow."

"Why?"

"Because tomorrow we're going to summon something so evil, it makes the earth itself weep."

Kaiaphas stood across the street, watching the window where he knew his brother was.

Waiting.

A gallu couldn't breach the salt restriction and a Daimon couldn't enter the apartment without an invitation. Damn the gods for their stupid rules. But for that, he'd already be inside, tearing them apart and appeasing Satara.

He cursed at the thought of having to face that bitch with failure. Of all his masters, she was the nastiest and that was truly saying something given the lowlifes he'd served in his lifetime.

Just once, couldn't the person summoning a demon be nice? Was that really too much to ask?

His thoughts turned back to his brother. "What are you planning, Xypher?"

That bastard was smarter than he'd given him credit for. Not to mention his skills had improved. But for Hades having weakened Xypher, he wasn't sure he'd have wounded him earlier . . .

Kaiaphas cursed as the slave band on his upper arm heated to a painful level. It was Satara summoning him.

If he had to listen to her mewling, pathetic . . .

He shot a blast at a car on the street and shattered the glass in it. An alarm began squalling so he shot it again. It faded into a broken gurgling noise.

If only it were Satara's head.

But that wasn't meant to be so long as she held his soul. A soul he'd traded for . . .

He didn't want to think about that. He'd made the deal and he would be bound to it throughout eternity.

Or would he?

A slow smile curled his lips as he considered an alternative. It was insidious, but it might work and it would solve both of his problems.

He cursed as the band blistered his skin. The cowardly bitch could wait until he was ready to face her. Shaking it off, he transformed himself into a human and headed down the street in search of a victim.

As he rounded a corner, he spotted a woman out walking her dog.

Perfect. Just what he needed . . .

The small brown canine started barking as soon as it caught a whiff of his inhuman essence.

Kaiaphas knelt down on the sidewalk. "Here, poochie, poochie."

The dog continued to snarl and bark.

He laughed before he blasted the animal into a ball of flames. The woman screamed and took off running.

She didn't get far.

Kaiaphas ran at her and swept her up into the air. His large, black wings fanned out as they soared above the homes. The human fought and cried, begging for his mercy.

As if he had any.

Holding her tight, he skimmed the landscape below until he found what he needed. A large, old oak tree. Completely isolated, it looked black in the night, shrouded by mist and stretching out toward the sky. In centuries past, mankind knew to take care of their trees and to guard them well from creatures like him.

How he loved the ignorance of the current generation.

An oak was a portal that could be used to summon the blackest of spirits. Kaiaphas smiled as he recalled the Englishman in Alton Towers who once chained the branches of his tree in an effort to thwart the evil it could conjure.

But evil would never be denied.

"Help me!" the human woman screamed.

"Oh, shut up," he snapped at the simpering human. For the cowardice alone she deserved to die.

"Please, let me go."

"Oh, I will, lovely. I'll let you go in just a moment." He dove for the tree.

As he swooped in, he took a moment to survey the area. There was nothing around him. No witnesses.

Good.

He landed a few feet away. Holding his sacrifice under one arm, he stalked toward the tree. The light of the full moon whispered through the bare branches. It was cold enough that he could see his breath in the air around him. He inhaled the crisp weight of it.

The woman struggled against him as he raised one arm to sever a single limb from the tree. He could hear the oak screaming as he cut through the wood. Loud. Strong.

Thank the gods it was healthy.

The limb landed at his feet.

"P-p-please."

"Shut up." He slung the woman against the tree so hard, she died on impact.

A human sacrifice wasn't necessary for what he intended but human blood was, and since he doubted the woman would have let him cut her without more whimpering and pleading, this sufficed. Using the claw from his right hand, he opened the human's throat and let her blood flow into the tree and soak the roots.

Then he opened up his own wrist as he chanted the ancient demonic words that would awaken the Primus Potis—the first power.

Before there was light in the world, there was darkness. Chaos.

And that power slept. Now it was time for it to reawaken and help him.

"I summon you forth with voice and blood. With the weight of the moon and the strength of the sacred wood. Oh darkness, come to me. So say the dark oh mote it be . . ."

As he chanted, the wind picked up speed. It whispered around him as ancient forces gathered to awaken the one he called.

Al-Baraka . . .

The tree began to shake as a black mist from the

earth rose to encircle it. Kaiaphas looked up to see a pair of glowing eyes—one vibrant earth green and the other dark earth brown—materialize in the center of the mist. The air swirled faster, rising up like a geyser that began to form the shape of a tall, lean man standing on a large limb.

Black hair rose up, tangling in the wind before it settled over broad shoulders. It was followed by a rippling white that formed a shirt, then black pants and a brown, stitched leather jacket. The last to form was a face that was as handsome as it was brutal.

A thin gold band encircled the man's throat and there at the base of his neck rested a stone as green as his inhuman right eye.

As quickly as it'd come, the wind stopped. The mist evaporated. Now the man and the tree stood out crisp and clear against the backdrop of night.

Those fierce duo-colored eyes seemed to penetrate Kaiaphas. Suddenly, something hard wrapped itself around his neck and squeezed it closed.

Choking, Kaiaphas fell to his knees.

"There now." The voice was deep and evil as Jaden jumped to the ground. He landed on his feet in front of Kaiaphas before he kicked him onto his back.

Unable to speak for the pressure still wrapped around his throat, Kaiaphas stared up into the very face of evil. Not human, not demon, not a god, Jaden was born of the first power.

Al-Baraka. He was the go-between for the higher powers and demonkind.

Jaden cocked his head as he studied the demon lying before him. "Kaiaphas . . ." He let the name roll off his tongue. In one heartbeat, he knew everything about the demon. His past and his questionable future. "Why have you awakened me?"

"I need your help."

Jaden laughed at the desperate plea. "Aye, you do. Tell me what you'll give for my services."

"Three unbaptized virgins."

He scowled at the demon. What was this? The Middle Ages? "Three?"

"Is it not enough?"

It depended on the virgins . . .

And their skills. In this day and age, virgins could be more talented than the sluts of the past.

"Perhaps." Jaden hissed as he felt his arm burn in response to the summons that constricted Kaiaphas's band. "You dare call me while your mistress summons you?"

"I—I—"

Jaden blasted him. "Go, you maggot. In one moon rising you'll have my answer."

The demon vanished instantly.

Jaden stood there in the cold stillness under the shelter of the oak, getting his bearings on this time and place. He lifted his head to smell the blood that tainted the air around him.

Turning, he saw the body of a woman in her late twenties. Her lifeless eyes stared in horror.

He went to her and knelt before her. "Sleep in peace, little one," he whispered, closing her eyes.

It was a most unnecessary death. Strike one against the demon.

Jaden paused as he caught something else in the wind. The tree was whispering to him, telling him what he needed to know. Kaiaphas wasn't the only one thinking of him.

There was another . . .

Xypher lay on the cold pine floor as he listened to Simone breathing. She'd fallen asleep about an hour ago while Jesse was in his room, playing records way too loud. He didn't know how Simone could sleep through the same Altered Images song playing over and over again, but unlike him, she seemed immune.

Of course, he'd gotten used to not sleeping. In Tartarus, part of his punishment was someone beating him every time he closed his eyes to rest.

"*Xypher . . .*"

He tensed at the whispered call. The voice was a deep baritone laced with a demon's sharp accent.

It was a voice he hadn't heard in centuries.

"Jaden?"

The demon lord appeared before the closed door in a crouched position.

"Salt?" Jaden laughed. He stood up, walked to the window and licked his finger. His smile was cold as he lifted the digit to his mouth and sampled the salt they'd put there. "I know you weren't trying to keep me out with this."

"I know better. How is that you're here?"

Jaden didn't answer as he walked to the bed where Simone continued to sleep, oblivious to the fact that one of the most powerful entities in existence was close enough to touch her. "She's pretty enough. Is she your offering?"

He had to bite back his fury. To snap at Jaden invited instant death. "No."

"That was a quick denial. Why do you seek me, demonspawn?"

As if he didn't already know. But that was one thing about Jaden, he always wanted you to speak your needs. "I was going to summon you tomorrow."

"In the daylight when I'm weak." He tsked. "What bargain do you wish this time?"

"I need my powers returned and I want the human protected."

Jaden arched a brow. He turned back toward Simone and brushed her face with his hand. "Human . . ."

Jealousy flared inside Xypher so that it was all he could do not to shove Jaden away from her. But that would be a fatal mistake, especially since he needed Jaden's cooperation.

"A Daimon bound us together and I can't do what I need to so long as we're joined. I need your help. I have to have my freedom and my powers unencumbered."

Jaden turned toward him. "My help comes at a premium price. You know that. You've already paid me once."

Xypher wanted to curse at the reminder.

"Was it worth it?" Jaden asked.

"I'm sure you know the answer."

"I warned you."

Indeed, he had. That was what stuck hardest in Xypher's craw. Jaden had told him at the time that such bargains seldom worked out.

If only he'd listened.

Jaden drew near him. "You know the law, Xypher. You have to barter something for my services."

"I have nothing to barter with."

"Then you're wasting my time." Jaden faded.

"Wait!" Xypher snapped. "Tell me what you'll accept."

Jaden solidified once more. His gaze went to the bed where Simone was.

Xypher's blood ran cold. "Not her."

"How badly do you want your revenge?"

"More than anything."

Jaden's gaze was harsh and unforgiving. "There

is an old woman in this city. Her name is Liza. She owns a doll shop on Royal Street. About her neck, she wears a green amulet. Bring it to me and I'll free you from those bracelets."

"What of my powers?"

"They'll be fully restored as soon as I have the amulet."

Xypher couldn't believe he'd take so little for his service. "Is that all?"

"Trust me, it's enough."

Relief coursed through him. Until Xypher remembered something else. "One more thing."

Jaden's eyes sparked as his fangs flashed in the darkness. "You ask much, demonspawn." But as quickly as it came, his temper fled. "But I'm feeling generous . . ."

"There's a spirit I need to find. Her life was ended by a gallu and her soul partially taken. Do you know where I can find her soul and body?"

"Of course."

"Will you tell me where?"

"The price?"

Xypher moved to the dresser where Simone had a pewter medieval-style goblet. He manifested a knife in his hand before he cut his arm and let it bleed into the cup. "You need to feed. I'll give you my blood." Since he was a demon and a demigod, Xypher's blood was a lot stronger than anything Jaden could find on the street.

Jaden licked his lips as his eyes darkened to

black. Xypher had been right, the creature was starving.

"Deal." Jaden's voice was husky from need.

Xypher handed him the cup.

Jaden took it and downed the contents with one gulp. A tiny bit of blood ran from the corner of his mouth. He wiped it with the tip of one finger before he licked it clean. "The blood of the damned. There's nothing sweeter."

"What of Gloria?"

He snapped his fingers, and her ghost instantly appeared by his side.

She frowned in confusion. "Where am I?"

Jaden caressed her cheek. "Safe, my sweet. Very safe."

"And her body?" Xypher asked. "It needs to be free from gallu control."

"I'll take care of it and leave it in the yard for you. Unless you want the stink of it in the house . . ."

"No, and don't leave it in the yard to scare the innocent neighbors. Can you put it back in the alley where she died?"

Jaden held the cup out to him. "That'll cost you a bit more."

Xypher ground his teeth before he complied.

Smiling, Jaden inhaled the scent of his blood before he again drank it.

"Ew!" Gloria said, wrinkling her face up. "That's disgusting."

Jaden gave her a cold smile. "So are sausage and escargot, but you ate your share of that, did you not, human?"

She didn't respond.

Jaden set the empty cup on Simone's nightstand. He ran his finger around the rim, gathering the leftover blood. He licked it from the pad of his finger before he spoke. "I'll be back tomorrow night. Have my amulet for me." He glanced toward Simone. "Otherwise you're going to be very sorry . . . and the woman even more so."

EIGHT

Simone woke up with an awful headache. She pulled the pillow off her head to find bright sunlight streaming in through her bedroom window. When had the blinds been opened?

"What time is it?" she whispered, rolling over to stare at her alarm clock. Seven twenty-five.

Why did it feel so much later?

Yawning, she paused as she caught sight of Xypher sleeping on the floor—he'd completely refused to sleep on Jesse's mattress, saying he was too used to hardness to want the comfort of it. Not to mention he'd pointed out that since his arrival in

New Orleans, he'd been sleeping sitting up in alley-ways with his back against the wall. Her floor was a step up for him. At least here he could stretch out.

The blanket she'd given him last night was still lying folded beneath the pillow. He hadn't touched them. Instead, he was lying on his side with one hand stretched out over his head and the other curled just under his chin.

A day's growth of beard dusted his cheeks. There was something so manly and yet boyish about him lying there like that . . . But as she stared at his lips and remembered the hot kiss he'd given her last night, it chased away any thought of him being boyish.

"Simone!"

She jumped as Jesse came running into the room. A slice of fear went through her. Had the demon found a way in? "What's wrong?"

He stopped beside the bed and stomped his foot. "Would you tell Gloria to stop whining about my music? I like Culture Club and Prince."

Simone frowned in confusion. "Gloria?"

"Yeah. She came back last night."

"How?"

He shrugged. "She said Xypher brought her back."

"How?" she repeated.

"I don't know, but could you have a talk with her? There's a reason I'm an only ghost in this house. I don't like sharing."

"Okay, tell her to come here."

"Gloria!" he shouted so loudly that Xypher jerked awake on the floor.

Gloria manifested in front of Simone. "If I hear 'Karma Chameleon' one more time, I swear I'm going to find Boy George and make him eat Jesse's record. What does red, gold, and green have to do with anything anyway?"

Jesse was offended. "It's a brilliant song! C'mon . . . 'Every day is like survival. You're my lover, not my rival.' What could be more meaningful than that?"

Xypher groaned as he lifted his head up from the floor to glare at the ghosts. "Someone please tell me that we're not seriously having a friggin' debate over the genius of 'Karma Chameleon' at seven o'clock in the morning?"

Simone laughed. "Afraid so, sweetie."

Xypher glared hostilely at the ghosts.

"How do you know about Boy George?" Jesse asked.

"I was in hell, Jesse. What do you think they used to torture me with? Bad pop songs."

Gloria gave Jesse a smug look. "Told you."

"It's a great song."

Xypher growled low in his throat. "Yeah, the first nine thousand times you hear it. After a while it gets trapped in your head until it makes you crazy . . . now you know why I'm so effing nasty all the time. For that alone, I take Gloria's side.

Now if you both don't go be quiet, I swear by the river Styx that I'm going to feed you to Daimons as soon as the sun sets."

The ghosts vanished instantly.

"Thank you," Simone said.

His response was to roll over onto his back and drape one muscular arm over his eyes.

Simone got up and knelt on the floor beside him. Lifting his arm, she waited until he opened his eyes and gave her a quizzical look. "Seriously, thank you. How did you find Gloria?"

"I'm not sure you want me to answer that. Remember not to look a gift horse in the mouth."

"Why did you do it?"

He shrugged. "You were worried about her."

"Is that the only reason?"

"What do you think? God knows I didn't want her here aggravating Jesse and waking my ass up at dawn."

She smiled at his surliness. "You're not a morning person, are you?"

"I'm a Dream-Hunter/demon. By my very nature I'm nocturnal. That big yellow ball in the sky offends me to the very core of my being."

Leaning over him, she gave him a hug. "Well, I personally like the mornings. Every one is a fresh start. My father always said that you should begin each day with purpose."

"My father always said that someone should

run Apollo and Helios over with their chariots . . . and throw Phaeton under them for good measure."

She laughed. "Your father wasn't a positive influence on you, was he?"

"Being the god of nightmares, he wasn't a warm fuzzy bunny. Unless you count Happy Bunny. Amazingly the two of them have a lot in common."

"How do you know about Happy Bunny?"

"What? You never walk around the French Quarter? There are Happy Bunny shirts hanging in almost every store. And I have to say that I've developed a fondness for that pissy rodent."

"Oh." He was right. Happy Bunny was everywhere.

His eyes darkened as he locked gazes with her. "And if you don't stop rubbing on me right now, Simone, I'm going to take that as an open invitation to go Skoti on you."

"Go Skoti?"

He rolled over with her, pinning her to the hard floor. Simone bit back a moan at how good he felt lying on top of her, and there was no denying what the hefty bulge against her hip was.

When he spoke, his voice was ragged and hoarse. "It's when Skoti slip into humans and have their way with them." He nuzzled her neck.

"I thought you were a nightmare Skotos."

Simone ran her hand over his muscular back, delighting in the feel of it and the weight of him.

It would be so easy to let him strip her bare . . . She could just imagine him inside her. The very thought made her wet.

"So I take it you had good dreams last night?" she whispered.

He jerked back from her. "I didn't dream . . ."

"I don't always dream, either."

"No. I'm a Dream-Hunter, Simone. It's what we do. Always." He looked dazed. "Why didn't I dream?"

"Maybe you didn't sleep deeply enough."

Xypher started to respond until she moved and brushed against his erection. All rational thought left him as he became totally focused on the fact he was lying on top of her.

And she wasn't wearing a bra . . .

Oh, this was torture. It'd been so many centuries since he'd last felt a woman like this. He could just imagine sliding himself into her body. See her head tilted back while he tongued her neck. He burned from wanting her . . .

Simone couldn't move as she caught the hot look in his eyes. This was it and she knew it. She was lost to him. How could she deny him after all he'd done to protect her?

"Simone!"

She jumped at Jesse's shrill call.

He popped into the room, then screamed like a girl. "I'm sorry. You two continue."

Xypher let out a low, evil growl as he hung his

head down and shook it over her. "I don't know about you, but that just killed my mood. The only thing to do more damage would be to see Jesse naked. That would probably make me impotent for eternity. I think we just found the perfect birth control."

Laughing, Simone rolled out from under him, stood up, and cocked her head as she saw her goblet on the nightstand. How had that happened? It was always on the dresser.

She went to move it back, then froze as she caught sight of what appeared to be dried blood in it.

"What on earth?" She glanced to Xypher who quickly looked away.

"Is this yours?"

He didn't answer.

Before she could pursue it, her phone rang. She picked it up and saw it was Tate. Flipping it open, she answered.

"We found Gloria's body."

She couldn't believe it. "Where?"

"In the alley where she died."

"You're kidding?"

"Nope. It was really weird. The police called a few minutes ago to let me know."

That was great, except for one tiny detail that made her stomach shrink. "Is she . . . moving?"

"Not at all. It's very strange, but I thought you'd like to know."

"Yeah, thanks. I know you're relieved." Simone hung up and turned to face Xypher. "They found Gloria's body again."

"That's good."

There was something extremely guarded about him. "You knew about it, didn't you?" She looked back at the goblet and wondered why someone would put blood in it. Besides her, there was only one other person in this house who could bleed. . . . "What did you do after I went to sleep?"

"Nothing."

"Xypher," she snapped from between clenched teeth. "Don't lie to me. I'm not stupid. I know blood when I see it. For Saint Peter's sake, I'm a pathologist. You know I can take that to my lab and get a DNA sample off it."

An angry tic beat against his jaw. "What do you want me to say, Simone? I summoned a demon lord and made a bargain with him?"

Yeah, right. "Would you be serious?"

"I am serious." His tone and face confirmed it even though she didn't want to believe it. "I had to feed him my blood to get Gloria and her body back for you—that was the price he demanded."

Simone was stunned by his words. No, it couldn't be, could it? "You're not kidding."

"Why else would there be blood in your goblet?"

Why else, indeed? After all, people waking up

to find blood in a cup next to their bed had to be a daily occurrence.

In the Twilight Zone.

"This can't be my life . . ." And yet why was she so surprised? One of her best friends was a ghost and the other worked for a group of immortal vampire slayers. So why wouldn't her pseudoboyfriend be able to conjure a demon lord and feed it blood?

"What next? You gonna tell me my new neighbor is a demon, and the dog down the street is a lycanthrope?"

He shook his head. "Now you know why I didn't want to tell you what happened. I knew it would only upset you."

"Yes, yes, it did. How would you feel if someone invited a demon lord into your bedroom while you slept and fed it blood from your favorite cup? I don't think you'd be all happy over that, do you?"

She glanced at her clock. It was just after eight. "And now I need to shower and get ready for work. Guess you have to follow me since I'll die if you don't and please try not to summon any more demon lords into my house while I'm naked, okay?" Damn, the ludicrousness of her life was beginning to know no boundaries.

Xypher's expression turned sullen. "Yeah, but I'll die if I do follow you and hear you naked in the shower."

Simone didn't know why, but that took a lot of the anger out of her. Probably because she was enjoying the idea of torturing him.

She patted his cheek affectionately. "There, there, baby, it'll be okay."

He looked down at where his erection made an impressive bulge in his pants. "Not really, it won't. You only say that 'cause you're not the one in pain. And here I thought I had a few weeks' reprieve from torture. You're working with Hades, aren't you? Go ahead. Admit it."

Simone gathered her clothes, then paused as something he'd said a minute ago seeped into her mind—*I had to feed him my blood to get Gloria and her body back for you.* Why would he do that? "Why did you get Gloria back?"

He turned around as if looking for something.

"Xypher?" She closed the distance between them. "Why?"

His expression sheepish, he shrugged. "You were upset over her. I didn't want you to be worried or blame yourself for her loss."

For the first time, she understood his incessant need to find out what her motivations had been for helping him. There were some acts of kindness that were so altruistic, they defied logic. To him, the simplest act was baffling.

To her, this one was.

"Why did you care?"

"I don't know."

Xypher ground his teeth. It wasn't true. He knew exactly why he'd done it. For once he'd put her feelings above his own, but to admit that . . . It was most likely more than he could do right now.

Even so, he'd sacrificed a part of himself to make her happy.

She lifted herself up to kiss him lightly on the lips. "Now you understand that kindness doesn't have to be motivated by anything except a desire to help someone else and make them feel better."

Xypher blinked as she withdrew. She was right. Never in his life had he done something to help someone just because. Even with Satara, he'd been out to get something. She'd send him to do her bidding, then would reward him, and he'd done what she asked purely to get those rewards from her. It was all done for selfishness.

But not this.

He hadn't expected Simone to even thank him for saving Gloria. For that matter, he hadn't intended to tell her what he'd done for her.

Why had he done it?

"Xypher?"

He glanced up to see her standing in the doorway.

"I need to shower. You have to follow so that I can."

"Sorry." He dutifully walked to the hallway.

She gave him a warm smile that touched his heart before she shut the door and left him to stand outside while she went about her business inside. He listened to her moving around and imagined what she'd look like naked with the water sliding over her body . . .

He shifted, trying to get some relief from his swollen cock, but it wasn't happening. Closing his eyes, he pictured himself in the shower with her. He could feel the heat of the water against his bare skin, see the contour of her back as she faced the spigot and washed her hair. Her eyes closed, she dipped her head to make sure her hair was completely wet. Gods, she was beautiful.

Needing to feel her, he leaned his front against her back and wrapped one arm around her waist.

"Xypher!"

The shriek of outrage jerked him away from his fantasy.

An instant later, the door was snatched open to reveal Simone in a clinging towel, glaring furiously at him. "What do you think you're doing?"

"I was just standing here."

"No you weren't. You were in the shower with me."

"No, I wa . . ."

Was he?

He barely bit back the smile before he made her angrier. Yes! His powers had been working. But that thought was followed by a sick feeling.

Ah, damn, had he known he was really in the shower with her, he'd have a copped a better feel.

She frowned at him. "You're not wet."

" 'Cause I was standing right here the entire time."

She narrowed her eyes suspiciously. "Are you sure about that?"

"Yes."

Doubt was heavy in her expression. "You're lying to me, aren't you?"

"Not intentionally."

"Xypher!"

He sputtered as he tried to find some way to calm her down. "I didn't know I could do that. I mean I knew I could do that before, but I didn't know it was actually working now until you screamed. I thought I was just imagining it. And don't give me that look . . . sorry?"

She growled at him before she slammed the door in his face. Two seconds later, she snatched it open again. "Stay out there! Don't you dare come back in here with those evil mind tricks." She shut the door.

Xypher wanted to whimper he was in so much pain from his erection. "Does it buy me any bonus points to note that you have a really nice-looking ass?"

She shrieked again.

"Dude! What are you doing?"

He turned to find Jesse behind him. His face was an expression of ultimate horror.

"I was just standing here."

Jesse let out a sound of disgust. "Let me explain something to you. When you've made a woman mad by spying on her, you don't fix it by telling her she has a nice backside. That'll just get you bitch-slapped."

Well, when it came to being bitch-slapped for something, he was sure Jesse was an expert. Maybe he should listen to him for once. "Then what do you do?"

"Simple, my brother. I am about to impart to you the sacred words my father gave to me. It's the five responses that will get you out of any female problem."

Yeah, right. This he had to hear. "And they are?"

Jesse held his hand up and ticked each one off on his fingers. "I don't know what you're talking about. I didn't do it. Baby, there's no one else in my world but you. Oops. And Jesus is Lord."

He understood the first four, but the last one seriously confused him. "Jesus is Lord?"

Jesse nodded. "A little sacrilegious, I know, but trust me. If a woman thinks you've found religion, it can get you out of all kinds of trouble. Not to mention, you can combine them. Such as—I don't know what you're talking about, I didn't do it, or Jesus is Lord, baby, you know there's no one else in my world but you. See, easy."

The door opened to show Simone glaring at both of them as if they deserved only to be mowed over and buried in the lawn.

Wanting to dispel her anger, Xypher decided to try Jesse's advice. "Oops, Jesus is Lord."

Jesse groaned out loud. "Oh, you're hopeless, and I'm out of here."

Simone scowled at him. "What on earth are you talking about?" Shaking her head, she mumbled a condemnation of all men before she headed to her room.

Completely baffled by the fact that it didn't work, Xypher followed her. "Why are you still angry at me?"

"You groped me in the shower."

"That wasn't a grope, trust me. Had I known I was in there with you, I'd have made it count."

She spun on him then with fury in her eyes. "You . . . you . . . ugh!"

"I didn't do . . ." He couldn't use that one because he had. "I don't know . . ." *No, moron, you do know what she's talking about. Telling her you don't will only make her angrier.* "Oops?"

"Oops? Is that your answer?"

"Baby, there's no one else in the world for me but you?"

"Yeah, right. I don't believe that one for a minute. What do you think? I fell off a turnip truck?"

"Honestly? All I was thinking about was how beautiful you are. How much I wanted to feel your skin against mine and how I've never been this attracted to a woman before."

She paused while brushing her hair. "Really?"

"Yes. Last night, I made a deal with a demon to make you happy. Do you think I did that lightly?"

Simone swallowed as she glanced at the goblet. And he'd done it to keep her from worrying— he'd helped her and Gloria and had expected no payment or reward for it whatsoever. "You bled for me." How many women could say that about the men in their lives? "I guess that's worth a little embarrassment on my end. Sorry I overreacted."

Smiling, he cupped her face in his hands before he kissed her. He pulled back and gave her a wicked grin. "Is it worth a little something more?"

She tilted her head. "You keep playing your cards right and it might be. But don't get any ideas and come prancing into my dreams. If you do, I might geld you there."

Grinding his teeth in unsated frustration, Xypher rubbed himself against her and took one long, deep breath in her hair. "Just remember that you're slowly killing me."

"There are cures for that."

"Yeah, you naked on the bed."

She gave him a playful grin. "Or you could take matters into your own hands."

He cupped her hand in his and pressed it against his swollen groin. "I'd much rather you take me into yours."

Simone swallowed at the large feel of him against her palm. He'd left the button on his jeans open and her thumb brushed up against the dark hairs that ran from his navel downward to vanish under his waistband. His breath fell against her face as his eyes pleaded with her for mercy.

He rubbed himself ever so slightly against her hand and shuddered.

"When was the last time you were with someone?" she asked.

"Centuries ago."

Her heart pounded at the thought . . .

The loneliness of that single statement tore through her. Centuries of not being touched. Centuries of abuse.

She looked down at the floor where he'd slept last night. He asked for nothing, and he expected to be rejected at every turn. To be abused and hurt.

This was a man who knew so little of kindness that even the simplest act of it baffled him. She remembered the torture he'd shown her, and it broke her heart to think of him having no comfort whatsoever.

She didn't want to be another person who took from him without giving. It was time that he saw that people didn't have to hurt him.

And before she could stop herself, she unzipped his pants.

Xypher cursed in pleasure as she took him into her hand. Her cool fingers slid from the tip of his cock, all the way down to the base before she cupped him. His head spinning, he tilted her head back to taste her mouth.

This was what he needed more than anything else. No woman had ever touched him so tenderly. His lovers in the past had always been demanding. His needs and pleasure were secondary to theirs.

But Simone didn't demand. She gave.

Always.

Simone burned as her desire tore through her, but this wasn't about her. Xypher had protected her, and she wanted to please him.

She pushed his jeans down his hips before she pulled back from his lips and knelt in front of him.

Xypher expected her to strip him, so when she took him into her mouth, it was all he could do not to cry out. Chills exploded all over his body as she gently tongued him. He ground his teeth against the exquisite torture as he remained perfectly still for her.

Her tongue licked and swirled while her hand stroked his sac. Nothing had ever felt better. He leaned forward to brace one arm against the bureau behind her and stared down at her while she pleasured him. Her dark brown curls bounced with each movement of her head.

But what struck him most was the relish on her face . . .

Simone moaned at how good he tasted. She could feel his muscles jerking and tightening as he fought himself. His breathing came in ragged gasps while he gently stroked her hair with one hand.

She could literally feel how much this meant to him. How much bliss she was giving him by doing this one simple act.

Then with one feral growl he came in her mouth.

Xypher went temporarily blind as unimagined pleasure ripped through him. He had to lean with both arms against the bureau to keep from falling. Staring down, he saw Simone look up at him with a hint of a smile on her lips.

"Are you okay?"

"No," he said raggedly. "I'm in ecstasy. I blew straight past okay the minute you touched me."

Laughing, she rose up in front of him, forcing him to push away from the bureau.

He gathered her into his arms and laid his forehead against the crook of her neck so that he could inhale the sweetness of her skin.

Simone closed her eyes as she wrapped her arms around his broad shoulders and held him close. He was so calm and gentle like this . . . a complete reversal of the snarling beast who'd shoved her into her car and then threatened her life.

She felt his hands on her thighs, lifting her skirt to her waist. His tongue toyed with her skin as he dipped one hand under the elastic of her panties to gently separate the folds of her body. The moment his fingers brushed her, she moaned and shivered.

Clinging to him, she leaned her head back as his

fingers swept and teased. When he slid one inside her, it was all she could do to remain standing.

He was extremely talented with this hands. Honestly, it'd been at least a year since she'd been with a man. She'd forgotten how good this felt.

"Come for me, Simone," Xypher whispered in her ear. "I want to see your pleasure."

Those words sent her over the edge. Unable to stand it, she bit her lip and cried out. Still, he continued to stroke and tease until he'd wrung the last bit of joy from her. Her breathing ragged, she wasn't sure how her shaking legs were supporting her.

"Thank you," he breathed in her ear.

"You don't have to thank me, Xypher."

"Trust me, for that, I do." He stroked her cheek with his fingers. "No one has ever taken mercy on me before. Why did you?"

"I know you're going to find this hard to believe, but for some reason I don't understand, I actually like you . . . most of the time."

He shook his head as if the mere thought were incomprehensible. "Well, you also love Jesse. Obviously your taste in men leaves a lot to be desired."

"Obviously." She smiled at him until her hall clock chimed the hour. That jolted her back to reality. "Now, if you don't mind, I have a class to teach in less than an hour so I need you to get ready to come with me."

He laughed deep in his throat. "Lady, right now you could tell me to throw myself under a bus to make you happy and I'd oblige you."

She joined his laughter. "Then it's a good thing I don't use my newfound powers for evil, huh?"

"For me, it is." He kissed her on the tip of her nose before he pulled his pants up and zipped them. He paused at the door to look back at her with a tender expression on his face that absolutely seared her. "You following?"

She nodded before she went with him to the bathroom.

"You know," he said, indicating the tub with his thumb, "I'm not bashful. If you want to come in, feel free."

Simone could still taste him on her lips as she considered his invitation. *Don't do it. You have a class to teach.* But before she could stop herself, she was in the bathroom with him, watching as he stripped himself bare.

She let her breath out slowly at the sight of all that tawny, muscular skin. It made her salivate.

He flashed her a devilish smile before he got into the tub. "You can join me anytime you want to."

And she did want to, that was the problem. "It's all right, I actually need you to hurry so that I won't be late." She turned her back away from the silhouette of him against the curtain and brushed her teeth. As she did so, a weird sensation went through her.

Again she felt as if something were watching her. Rinsing her mouth, she turned around. Xypher was busy showering, and there was no one else in the room.

"What is happening to me?"

"Simone?" Xypher asked.

She raised her voice to respond. "Nothing. I was just talking to myself."

He leaned out of the shower to check on her. "You sure?"

"Yeah. I just . . . do you have a feeling like we're being watched?"

"A feeling like how?"

She shrugged. "I don't know. It's like there's something else here."

He turned the water off. Opening the curtain, he reached for a towel. As nice a picture as he made, her concern was such that she barely noticed his wet body and that said it all for how creepy the sensation was. He wrapped the towel around his lean hips.

"When did it start?"

"A couple days ago. It's like something is crawling over my skin, and I don't know what it is." She let out a tired sigh. "Demons can't come out in daylight, right?"

"Daimons can't, but a demon can. They're just not as strong in the daylight."

"Oh, that sucks. What about you? Are you weaker?"

"Not like a typical demon. It's good sometimes to be a hybrid god."

Good for him, but not for her sanity. "Fine, then. Whatever it is, it's just watching me. It hasn't done anything so let's ignore it."

Xypher watched as she headed back to the bedroom. He followed after her, but he wasn't so quick to let it go. One thing he knew which he hadn't mentioned was that when something watched someone, it was seldom benign.

Rather, it was waiting to find the perfect time to pounce.

NINE

After having seen her teach her students, Xypher was even more impressed with Simone than he'd been before. "It's a good thing you're not a demon."

"Why?"

He took her satchel and books as she left the lab and carried them for her back to her office. "With your knowledge of human anatomy, you would be terrifying . . . and deadly."

She scoffed. "I'm harmless enough."

"Yeah, not from what I saw. I seem to recall you threw that Daimon to the ground and made him feel it. Where did you learn to do that by the way?"

"Self-defense classes. Tate insisted, and I agreed. If you're going to do my job, you need to be able to handle yourself around overbearing creatures."

He rolled his eyes at her obvious snipe at him. The strange thing was, he didn't really mind it. He was growing accustomed to her teasing and actually enjoyed it. "You know . . . Come to think of it, there are a couple of demons I'd like to see you dissect."

"If one of them is your brother, I concur. He's a nasty ogre."

"You have no idea. Just be grateful you weren't raised with him knocking you around. Blood-letting Mayhem should have been his middle name."

"Ouch, I'm sorry."

He shrugged. There was nothing really to say. Kaiaphas was a demon. Causing pain to those around him was his nature.

She unlocked her office, led him inside, then took the books from his hands and put them away. "You told me last night that we were going to summon something evil today. Not that I want to rush to my demise or anything, but are we still on for that?"

"No."

"No? Why? What happened?"

"The big evil showed up at your house last night, and I fed it my blood."

She passed a chiding look at him. "I really wish you'd stop joking abut that before I never sleep again."

He probably should, too, but for some reason he couldn't resist. "Well, the blood wasn't the only thing he wanted. He also requested that I do a favor for him."

Fearful doubt was etched on her brow as she turned toward him. "Requested?"

She was right to be fearful. With Jaden one never knew when a request from him could turn fatal. "Yeah, more like a request that can't be refused."

She crossed her arms over her chest. "And who is this Godfather-like character whose dubious request carries such weight?"

"He's called by many epitaphs. Al-Baraka—the Broker. Kalotar—the Summoner. Demon-Heart. Katadykari—the Damned. But as far as anyone knows, his real name is Jaden."

"And Jaden is a demon?"

Xypher hedged. "Not exactly sure."

She cocked her head as if trying to solve a puzzle no one had ever solved before. "How do you not know what he is?"

"Easy. Jaden isn't very trusting or talkative. We know how to summon him, and we know he draws powers from the primary source of the universe, but no one knows how he does it. Who, if anyone, he answers to or where he comes from or vanishes to. He's a total enigma."

"I'm confused. Why would anyone summon him, then?"

"Simple. Jaden can and will do anything without conscience, prejudice, or hesitation. And I do mean *anything*. If you're willing to pay his price and bear the consequences of the bargain, he can give you any dream you've ever had, no matter how impossible it may seem."

Simone scowled. "What is he? Satan?"

Xypher laughed evilly. "No. Lucifer deals with humans. Jaden barters with the source for demonikyn."

"Demonikyn?"

"Demon kith and kin. Humans and others can call him, but if you're not demonspawn, he won't answer. That being said, it takes both human and demon blood to summon him. Again, no one knows why."

She seemed to take that a lot better than he would have thought. "And he drinks blood?"

Xypher nodded.

"So does that make him a vampire?"

"He walks in daylight. But, like a demon, he's weaker then. He seems to have the powers of a god, but no followers. What would you call him?"

"I wouldn't call him anything that didn't make him deliriously happy."

Xypher smiled. "See, I knew you were a wise woman."

Simone wasn't so sure about that. This Jaden still

sounded an awful lot like the devil to her. The idea that he'd been in her house and drank Xypher's blood made her want to invite a priest in to cleanse it. "So what's this favor we have to do for him?"

"See a woman on Royal Street who works in a doll shop."

That hit her like a blow in the stomach. "You mean Liza?"

Xypher was aghast. "You know her?"

Simone nodded. "She's a longtime friend of mine and Tate's. I met her back when I was a kid. I love her store. It's really cool."

"Can we go now?"

She checked her watch. "I have an afternoon class so we should have time. Are you sure you're not going to hurt her?"

"Yes. Jaden wants a necklace she has. That's it. Once he has the necklace, he'll remove our bracelets."

Simone wasn't so sure about that. "And if Liza won't give it up?"

"She's your friend. You'll have to talk her out of it. Otherwise I *will* steal it."

Simone let out a sound of disgust. "You can't go around stealing things, Xypher. That's wrong."

"And I can't tell Jaden no once the bargain is set. For whatever reason, he wants this amulet. I promised it to him, and Jaden is one creature you don't renege on. Trust me, neither of us would live long enough to regret it. Why do you think I didn't go to him in the beginning to remove the bracelets? Jaden is always a last resort."

That didn't change one thing. She was Liza's friend. "Swear to me that Liza won't get hurt."

"You have my word, Simone. I won't hurt her."

Simone had a moment where she doubted him, but she quickly squelched it. Xypher had never been anything except honest with her every step of the way. She would trust him in this, but if he was wrong . . .

Jaden would be the least of his problems.

She grabbed her purse and led him back to the hallway.

Xypher tried not to think about what the amulet could be that Jaden would make such a bargain to have it. Normally the demon wanting the deal made an offering, and Jaden either accepted or rejected it.

For Jaden to pick the payment . . .

It set off every alarm inside him, but to have his powers completely restored and to remove these bracelets made it worth it. At least he hoped. For all he knew, the amulet could unleash the Atlantean Destroyer, the Dimme, or any one of numerous disasters.

You should have asked for clarification.

Yeah, right. Like Jaden would have answered. The entity answered nothing. No one who valued their existence questioned him.

Simone got into her car and waited for Xypher

to join her. He was being strangely quiet, which concerned her. "What aren't you telling me?"

"That we could be ending the world by doing this."

"Is that humor?"

"God, I hope so."

Not sure if she should encourage him or not, she drove over to Liza's shop. Since the road was closed this time of day to traffic, she parked on Toulouse, and they walked two blocks down Royal until they reached the Dream Dolls Boutique. The picture window was filled with the reproduction antique baby dolls and custom-made Barbies that Liza designed.

Simone's foster mother had brought her here for Christmas the first year they'd adopted her and bought her the porcelain doll that she still kept on her dresser at home. Even now Simone remembered the way Liza had looked the day they first met. Liza's hair had been dark back then, her eyes shining with warmth and kindness.

"What a beautiful little girl you are. Pick out a doll, baby, and we'll make its eyes look just like yours."

Liza had fed her cookies and tea while she made good on that promise. There for an afternoon, Simone had felt like the queen of the universe. It was a feeling Liza always managed to duplicate every time Simone visited.

Smiling, she pushed open the teal-blue door and entered the store.

There was a young woman with blond hair standing behind the glass counter that was filled with doll clothes and pieces.

"Hi, there," Simone greeted. "Is Liza around?"

Before the woman could respond, Simone heard a happy cry from the back room.

"Simone, my china doll! How have you been?" Liza came out from behind the curtain and approached her with a giant smile.

Simone hugged her close. "It's been too long since I was last here."

"Don't I know it." Liza pulled back. She looked at Xypher, and the smile faded from her face. "You're unnatural." Her voice was barely a whisper when she said those words.

Xypher held his hands up. "I'm not here to hurt you."

Liza's eyes darkened with suspicion as she stepped back and turned toward the girl behind the counter. "Beth? Why don't you take your lunch break, sweetie?"

Beth looked up with a frown. "It's kind of early. You sure?"

"Yes, please. I've got the store."

Beth set down the doll sweater she'd been folding. "Okay. You want me to bring you something back from the deli?"

"A chicken salad sandwich. Make sure to get the money out of the register."

Beth smiled as she complied. "One Liza special coming up. I'll see you in a few."

Liza waited until the girl was gone before she spoke again. For once, there was all-out hostility in her eyes as she looked at Xypher. "You reek of death."

Simone gaped. "How do you know he's died?"

"She's an oracle, like Julian," Xypher explained. "She can sense the fact that I defy normal existence."

Liza nodded. "And you can't have what you're here for. I won't let you."

"If you know what I need, then you know why I need it. You also know I can take it from you, and there's nothing you can do to stop me."

Simone put herself between Xypher and Liza. "But I can and I won't let you hurt her."

This wasn't the tender Xypher who teased her. This was the same Xypher who'd shoved her into her car. "Noble. Stupid, but noble." His lethal gaze went over her shoulder to Liza. "If I don't get it, Simone is the one who'll pay the price. Jaden said so."

Liza glared at him. "Why would you make a deal with the devil?" No sooner had the words left her lips than her eyes widened with understanding.

"Exactly."

Simone scowled. "What?"

"Nothing," they said in unison.

Liza hesitated before she pulled the green amulet out from under her shirt and lifted it over her head. "My family has protected this from evil for nine generations. I can't believe that after all this time, I'm the one who's handing it over to a demon." She closed her fingers around it. "Do you know what this does?"

Xypher shook his head.

"You put it over the heart of a god and it paralyzes him . . . or her."

Xypher scowled at her words. "Why would Jaden want that?"

"He obviously has a god he wants to immobilize. The question is which one and why."

Yeah. That was the question. Depending on the god, that could put a major rift in the universe. "Will it affect demons?"

"No. Which is a damn shame."

"Why?" Simone asked.

"Because there are four of them currently waiting for you outside my store."

TEN

Simone turned around to look out the shop windows. Sure enough, there were four men who appeared ready to fight outside on the sidewalk, staring in. Though to be honest, they didn't look like demons to her. Tall and lean, they were rather handsome. Dressed in jeans and leather jackets, they had sunglasses to shield their eyes and didn't appear any older than their late twenties, early thirties.

"Maybe they're customers."

Liza snorted. "For a doll store? Yes, I can just

see them now . . . I'll take the frilly pink baby doll." She patted Simone's shoulder. "No, hon. They're not customers. They're demons being repelled by the salt I use to keep the riffraff out of my shop." She let out a long sigh before she moved to her counter. She put on her glasses, then pulled out a small weapon that looked like a hand-sized crossbow. "You know how to use this?" she asked Xypher.

"Absolutely."

"Good. Give me back the amulet for safekeeping."

He obliged without another word.

Liza put it around her neck. "Now, wait here a second. There's something else you can use."

Simone was shocked. She'd known Liza was a Squire and a little odd, but she was seeing a whole new side to the tiny woman. Liza was fearless.

A second later, Liza returned with a gold broadsword. "This one's easy to use. The pointy end goes into their body."

"Thanks," he said dryly. "I'd hate to get that confused."

"Yes, you would, sweetie. Now, go kick some demon ass."

Simone arched a brow at that. "You know, the police station is only a couple of blocks down. Isn't this dangerous? What if they see the fight?"

Xypher snorted. "They won't live long enough to call it in."

Simone was horrified by his dry tone. "You can't kill them, Xypher."

"I won't have to. Demons will do it for me. Now, if you'll move closer to the door, I've got some fighting to do."

Simone followed him to the entrance and held her breath as he walked out into the street to face them.

The tallest demon moved forward. His brown hair was laced with blond highlights. He had a goatee and crystal blue eyes. Dressed in a pair of jeans and a brown leather jacket, he'd look like just another guy on the street to any casual observer. As would the other three. Like the tall one, they were handsome and dressed the same as anyone you'd see in public. It sent a chill down her spine to realize that such evil could exist without drawing attention to itself.

How many times had she sat beside a demon and not known it?

Xypher swept the group with a look that said he didn't consider them much of a threat. If only she could be so confident.

"Kaiaphas," he greeted, surprising her with the fact that the tallest one was his brother. Wow, without the boiling skin, the demon was rather prime. "I see you finally made some friends. You must have learned to use a toothbrush at last. You know it's the whole up and down, back and forth that confuses people . . . or demons."

One of the demons opened his mouth and displayed two rows of serrated teeth.

Xypher curled his lip. "You really should see a dentist about that. I hear they can do wonders these days."

"Kill him," Kaiaphas snarled.

Xypher caught the first one with an upper cut of the sword. It sliced through his stomach. But before he could withdraw it, one of the other demons tackled him to the ground.

Simone hissed as she saw Xypher hit the sidewalk. "I can't watch this and do nothing."

"You can't fight a demon, Simone," Liza said. "You've no idea how strong they are. The best thing we can do as humans is stay out of it and let them fight. Don't become Xypher's weakness."

Liza's words reminded her of Acheron. She looked down at her wrist where she still wore the leather band. "Actually, I think I can."

Before Liza could stop her, she ran out to the street and shoved the demon away from Xypher. The moment she touched him, something went through her like an electrical current. The demon went flying, literally. He hit the building so hard that it jarred loose the masonry.

"Holy crud," she breathed, amazed at what

she'd done. Acheron had been right. She had super-human powers.

"Simone!"

She jerked around to see Kaiaphas rushing her. She caught his arm and flipped him to the ground. Unfortunately, he didn't stay there. He sprang to his feet and delivered a staggering kick to her ribs. Simone hissed from the pain of it.

He bit her arm, then backhanded her. She tasted blood. All of a sudden, Xypher was there. He caught his brother and slugged him so hard, the force of the blow lifted Kaiaphas off his feet.

Simone felt so strange . . .

Her vision dimmed, and everything went hazy. Another demon came at her, but to her, he appeared to be moving in slow motion. He started to hit her. She dodged it, then elbowed him hard in the back.

He spun around and sank his teeth into her arm.

She screamed as unbelievable pain tore through her.

"No!" Xypher shouted, rushing to her side.

She couldn't really understand or see anything after that. Everything was a blur. She heard someone screaming out in pain, and the next thing she knew she was in the doll shop again.

"Oh, no," Liza was whimpering. "No, no, no. What are we going to do?"

Xypher couldn't breathe as he saw the bite marks

on her skin. Unlike a Daimon, who couldn't convert humans into vampires, the gallu could. Because he was part demon, he was immune from their infected saliva.

Simone wasn't.

Something hit the window, shattering it. "What's the matter, Xypher? You tired of playing with us?"

He rose to attack, but Liza pulled him back.

"Simone needs us. Leave them be."

That was easier said than done, but in the end, he complied. Killing Kaiaphas could wait. Simone couldn't. Not to mention that so long as she was down, he couldn't go outside without killing them both.

He raked an angry hand through his hair as he tried to think of something to save her. Dammit, if he'd just been able to get to Jaden with the amulet, this wouldn't have been a problem. Simone would have been free to live her life without him, and he'd be off to kill Satara.

Now she could very well end up a gallu zombie, and it'd be all his fault. "What can we do?"

Liza pulled a cell phone from her pocket. "I'm calling Acheron. If anyone has a solution . . ."

"Maybe I should call Jaden."

"No!" Liza said, her eyes snapping fury at him. "I refuse to have that creature here. He's more a threat than the gallu are, and I'm not willing to pay his prices."

She was right.

Xypher nodded. "Call the Atlantean and I'll call Jesse." In the event they failed to save her, Simone would want Jesse here, and Jesse would want to be with her. The only reason the ghost wasn't here already was because he didn't like attending Simone's classes. Being dead, he didn't like hearing about autopsies or seeing other decedents.

Xypher pulled Simone's phone out of her pocket and called her house. As soon as the answering machine picked up, he spoke as calmly as possible. "Jesse, it's Xypher. I think . . ." He couldn't bear to say it, but he had no choice. "Simone's hurt. Bad. You need to come to Liza's store immediately."

The ghost was there before he could hang up.

Jesse's face paled as he saw her lying on the floor, writhing in pain. "What the hell happened?"

"Demon attack."

Jesse's eyes flared as he ran for Xypher's throat.

Xypher caught him and threw him to the ground. "Don't push it, boy. I'm in the mood to seriously mutilate someone, and since I can't reach my brother, you might prove a worthy substitute."

"Don't," Simone gasped, reaching out to touch Xypher's leg. "Please, don't hurt him."

All his anger fled. The last thing he wanted was to hurt her in any way.

They both leaned over her.

"I'm here, Sim," Jesse said, his eyes tearing. "You're going to be okay. You hear me?"

She stared at him in disbelief. "I can see the auras you talk about, Jesse. Yours is white. It's beautiful . . . like you."

Jesse sniffed. "Remember, stay away from the light. Go left, Sim. Left at the light. I'll be right here waiting for you to run away from it."

"She's not dying, Jesse." Xypher swallowed as pain hit him hard. Dying would be easier. Kinder. "She's turning into a demon."

"What?!"

"You heard me."

Jesse growled in a voice that was almost demonic. "Do something!"

"Don't you think I would if I could? I wouldn't wish this on my worst . . . Oh, hell, yeah I would, but I'd never wish it on Simone."

Simone shivered on the floor. "Why am I so cold?"

The demon blood was infecting hers, lowering her heartbeat . . .

Xypher took her arm in his hand and rubbed her skin, trying to warm her. "Just breathe slowly. Don't take any deep breaths." At least he hoped that was true.

Suddenly, he felt a presence behind him. It was one of absolute power.

Acheron.

Xypher looked over his shoulder to see him standing there, watching them. "I hope you have something to say that I want to hear."

Acheron snorted. "Ironically no one ever wants to hear what I have to say about anything. They usually argue with me to the point I want to put them through a wall. Hopefully you won't be so dense."

"I'm not in the mood, Acheron. Tell me what to do to save her."

Acheron moved forward to kneel on one knee beside Jesse. His swirling silver eyes glowed in the dim light. "How do you feel?" he asked her.

Simone's teeth chattered incessantly. "Sick."

He glanced up at Liza who was standing off to the side. "You might want to get a bucket or something in case she hurls."

She went to find one.

"Is that all you're going to do?" Xypher growled.

Acheron shrugged. "You want the good news or the bad?"

Anger tore through him so ferociously that he wanted to slice open the Atlantean's throat. "Don't play that game with me, Acheron. Tell me what I need to know."

He was unfazed by Xypher's threat. "Nice tone. We should rent you out to record Halloween albums."

Xypher had to force himself not to attack.

"Relax," Acheron said quietly. "She's not really converting."

Was he insane? Of course she was converting. She was pale and trembling. Her brow was damp with sweat . . . "Look at her! She's not exactly baking cookies."

"Yeah, but this isn't a human mutating, either."

Cold dread went through Xypher. If she wasn't mutating, then what was happening to her? "What do you mean?"

Acheron glanced over to Jesse. "Haven't you noticed that she's not like other women? That strange things are attracted to her?"

Simone moaned slightly.

"I'm not strange," Jesse said defensively. "But, yeah. She has always known things. Seen things that she shouldn't have. We just thought she was psychic."

Acheron shook his head. "No. She was always much more than that."

"Acheron," Xypher interrupted. "Tell me what's going on."

Acheron took a deep breath before he answered. "She's half demon, Xypher. Like you."

Xypher's jaw dropped at his words. It wasn't possible . . .

"The hell she is," Jesse said, his voice breaking. "There's nothing demonic about her."

Acheron held her wrist up so that Xypher could see the demon bite. "Smell her blood, and you'll know the truth. There's no mistaking that scent."

Still, Xypher refused to believe it. "How could she be demon and not know it?"

"Her parents were protecting her from the truth." Acheron pulled off the bracelet that he'd given her. "This is nothing but simple leather. The whole reason I gave it to her was to let her think that her powers were coming from something other than herself. The truth is, she's as powerful as any demon you'll ever meet."

"Why didn't you tell us that yesterday?"

"Because her father gave up his life to keep her roots a secret from everyone, including her. To make sure that she was hidden from all the people and creatures who would use her or threaten her. Who am I to undo such a sacrifice?"

"Xypher?" Simone breathed. "I'm scared."

Acheron took her other hand. "Don't be. Your powers are being unlocked. That's all that's happening. I know it hurts and it's frightening and shocking. But don't fight it. Just take deep breaths, and let the power flow through you."

That only made Xypher angrier. "It's easy for

you to say. You have no idea what she's going through."

Acheron gave a bitter laugh. "Yeah, unlike you, I know exactly how she feels. I was human when my god powers were unlocked. Trust me, it wasn't pretty, and neither will this be."

That took the anger out of him. "What can I do?"

"Don't leave her alone. She's going to need someone to show her how to use her demon senses. You grew up with your powers, but you know how they differ from normal human functionality. You're the best teacher she could have."

Xypher cursed at the thought of having someone be dependent on him. He wasn't reliable. He didn't know how to function that way. It scared him that he might corrupt her or harm her because of his own ignorance. She needed a better teacher than him. All he knew was pain and betrayal. How to use his powers to harm others. That wasn't Simone. She was kindness.

How could an animal like him teach her what she needed to know?

But he would never admit that to anyone.

"I have my own agenda here, Acheron. I can't be tied down to her."

"You have three weeks to achieve it. For once, Xypher, think of someone other than yourself."

He curled his lip at Acheron's words. He was

thinking of someone else, but again, he'd never admit that out loud. "Thinking of someone else is what got me damned. It's a mistake I don't want to repeat."

Those silver eyes burned with an ancient wisdom. "You know sometimes it's by repeating our mistakes that we realize what went wrong the first time. Knowing that, we're able to fix the mistake and move past it."

Xypher scoffed at that. "Right, and the definition of basic stupidity is to keep doing the same thing over and over again while expecting a different result. I'm not stupid."

"I didn't say to keep doing it." Acheron glanced down to Xypher's arm where his vow was branded. "Move forward with purpose. Examine what went wrong and correct that one mistake."

Why did everything keep coming back to that one phrase?

Move forward with purpose . . .

"Help her, Xypher. Right now she needs you more than you need to kill Satara." And with that, he vanished.

Xypher sat on the floor with Ash's words ringing in his head. There was truth there, but the need for vengeance was so strong . . .

Then he remembered the way Simone had touched him earlier that morning when she'd taken mercy on his pain. She'd asked for nothing from him in return.

Nothing.

Xypher gathered her in his arms and held her close. "I'm here for you, Simone."

Simone could barely understand those words as her body continued to burn. Everything around her felt amplified. The colors, the scents, the sounds . . .

She experienced the world in a whole new way.

"How's she doing?" Liza's voice seemed to come from a long way away.

Type O positive. That's what Liza's blood type was. She also had a slight murmur in her heart.

And Jesse . . .

She knew his weaknesses, too. She could smell and taste them, and a tiny part of her wanted to exploit those weaknesses. That scared her more than anything else. "What does it mean to be a demon, Xypher?"

"You're not a demon."

She lifted her arm and stared at her hand. It looked like her hand and yet she felt as if she could crush steel with it. Could she? "I feel so powerful."

"It's an illusion."

Was it? It seemed real enough. The thought had barely completed itself before she felt her stomach heave. She grabbed the pail from Liza and emptied the contents of her stomach into it.

When she was finished, she no longer felt so

strong. She felt weak and worthless. "I want to go home."

Xypher nodded. He paused to look at Liza. "Can I have the amulet back? I still have to hand it over to Jaden or he'll have my ass."

The reluctance showed in her eyes as she removed it one more time. "I hope this isn't a mistake."

"Me, too," he concurred.

After putting it in his pocket, Xypher pulled Simone against his chest, and the next thing she knew, she was home, in her bed. He was still beside her. "You should rest."

"Will you hold me?"

Xypher wanted to curse the tenderness those words stirred inside him. He should ignore her and his conscience.

If only he could.

Instead, he lay down beside her on the bed and pulled her close. "Get some rest."

She snuggled against him before she closed her eyes and did what he suggested. It didn't take her long to fall into a deep, restful sleep.

Lying here with her like this, he almost felt human. How ridiculous was that? They were two demons now lying together. He glanced at the photo of her parents and wondered what had brought them together that they'd tried to live an average human life.

In the picture, they looked like any other family. No one would ever have guessed the secret they hid.

It was a secret that might yet cost their daughter her life.

ELEVEN

At dusk, Xypher paced the small condo, wondering if he was making a mistake by staying with Simone. For all he knew, his presence here was an even greater threat to her than leaving would be.

He felt the air stirring an instant before Jaden appeared. His unholy eyes were a particularly vibrant shade of green and brown.

"You have it." It was a statement of fact, as if he could sense the amulet.

Xypher pulled it out of his pocket and held it in his hand. No larger than the size of a quarter, it looked like a piece of green turquoise with delicate silver scrollwork around it. It seemed so harmless. It was hard to imagine this object bringing down a god, but then, salt was a completely innocuous substance while being powerful enough to ward off an army of demons. "I have it."

Jaden extended one hand and waited.

Xypher dropped the amulet into his palm.

Taking a deep breath, Jaden closed his hand and held it reverently. When he opened his eyes, they were bloodred. "Thank you."

The gold bracelet fell open and hit the floor at Xypher's feet. "How did you do that?"

He scoffed. "As if I'd explain the source of my powers to you, demon. Merely be grateful that you have fulfilled your part of the bargain."

Xypher could feel his powers growing with each word Jaden spoke. This was what he needed. What he had to have.

Leaning his head back, Xypher laughed. For the first time in centuries, he felt like the god he was. And with those powers came sudden clarity.

"You knew about Simone's parentage . . ."

Jaden shrugged. "Of course I did. Who do you think her father bargained with for her protection? I took his soul in exchange for binding her powers from her and the rest of the world."

A shiver went down his spine. "You betrayed him by allowing her to be converted."

Red licked the irises of Jaden's eyes as he glared at him. "I betrayed nothing. She exposed herself.

By being bitten, she undid her father's bargain. I told her father at the time the drawbacks of my shield. He never thought she'd come into contact with other demons."

Poor bastard. He should have known his daughter would find mischief.

Then again, had it not been for Xypher, her secret would have been safe forever. He had no one to blame for her current situation except himself and he hated himself for his part in her conversion.

"What of her mother?" he asked Jaden. "Was she a demon, too?"

"She was human."

That baffled him. Humans and demons seldom ever interacted in anything other than a combative situation that almost always resulted in the death of the human. "How did they end up together?"

Jaden placed the amulet in his pocket. "Simone's mother was an unfortunate mistake. Palackas, Simone's father, was a bound demon who stumbled across her one night while he was carrying out an order for his master. One thing led to another . . . He inserted part A into slot B, and he fell in love with her, but as to be expected, his master refused to release him. Rather than come to me, he ran for freedom to be with her. His master called out the hounds to hunt him down, and either return him or kill him. They hunted him for years until they found his scent here in New Orleans. Because Simone's mother and brother held the scent of the father, they found them and killed them instead of him by accident."

"Why did Simone live?"

"Unlike her brother who inherited all of his mother's humanity, she had her father's demon genes in her. Enough that her blood held its own unique scent apart from her father's. The Skili weren't authorized to slay anyone except her father and so she was spared."

"But they killed her mother and brother."

Jaden snorted. "Have you ever met a Skili? Just because they look human doesn't mean they have a brain. They're dogs. All they smell is blood and genetics. They thought the two of them were her father. Palackas's master was pleased since he thought their deaths would bring Palackas home again."

But it hadn't. The poor man must have been lost after their deaths and stricken not only with grief but guilt. And fear that his daughter would soon join his wife and son.

The Skili were an elite tracking force that was sent out to destroy any demon who violated their laws. Part human, part bloodhound, they had no will of their own. All they did was track and kill. If Palackas hadn't known why Simone had escaped, he'd have been terrified of the Skili finding her next.

"Did her father know why they didn't kill her?"

"He didn't ask."

"You mean you didn't tell him."

Jaden shrugged nonchalantly. "He summoned me for a bargain. Who am I to dissuade a demon when he offers me his soul?" He gave Xypher a pointed look.

Xypher cursed as he remembered the bargain he, himself, had made with the demon lord.

"My father killed himself."

Xypher turned at the sound of Simone's quiet voice. She stood in the doorway behind him, holding on to it with a grip so tight he could see her knuckles turning white. Her wan face worried him.

Jaden took no mercy on her. "He killed himself to protect you, child, and to appease his master. Even if he'd gone back to his master at that point, his master would have ordered his execution. He'd been gone too long from his bindings. Plus there was still the matter of you to worry over. The last thing your father wanted was for you to be captured and turned into a slave, too. So he took his fate into his own hands and used his life force to seal our bargain."

"You bastard!" Simone ran at him.

Xypher caught her to his side and held her in place. "Don't, Simone."

"He let my father die!"

Xypher could feel the anguish of her cry, but it changed nothing. "You can't attack him, Simone. He'll kill you."

One corner of Jaden's mouth quirked up. "And I'll enjoy every minute of your dying."

She lunged again. "You're a monster."

"I can be. But I prefer the term . . . 'broker.' "

Growling, she fought against Xypher's hold. "Get out!"

Jaden tsked. "And to think I've always heard how wonderful Southern hospitality is. Guess that's only for humans." His eyes faded back to their normal color. "Our bargain is met, Xypher."

Jaden tapped his shoulder twice with his fist, gave a short, mocking bow, and vanished.

Simone turned on him. "Why didn't you let me scratch his eyes out?"

"Because he would have ripped your head off before you got near him."

She shook her head in disbelief. "You're a god. How powerful can he be in comparison?"

"Powerful enough to kill me and you with nothing more than a thought."

Simone paused as she realized he wasn't kidding. "I don't understand."

"The universe has order, Simone. At the end of the day, we all answer to someone. While gods are all-powerful, we have limitations. A creature like Jaden can kill us and absorb our powers for himself."

"Then why doesn't he?"

"My guess is he, too, has limitations on what he can and can't do."

"Set by whom?"

"That's the question, isn't it? I don't know the answer, and I don't know anyone who does."

She wiped at the corner of her eye as she left him to look at the photographs of her family on her mantel. "Do you think my father knew and understood what he was doing when he summoned Jaden?"

"Probably. Most demons do. Even though we're raised aware of the fact that he's our bogeyman, Jaden usually explains the drawbacks of a bargain to those who make it. I may not like him, but as a rule, he is fair and impartial . . . even when he's being intolerant."

Simone turned to face him. "He didn't tell you about the amulet and what it did."

She had a point. Jaden had hidden that knowledge from him. "No, he didn't, which tells me it must be important to him on a personal level."

Simone barely heard those words. Honestly, she didn't care about Jaden and his desires or wants. What mattered was the fact that her family had died.

And he'd played a part in it.

I'm a demon . . .

Those words kept chasing themselves around in her head. How could this have happened? How could she not have known? Suspected something . . .

"There's a special fire inside you, angel," her father had once said. *"One day you'll understand it."*

Was this what he'd meant?

She looked at Xypher, needing answers she doubted she'd ever have. "Why would my father have killed himself? Wouldn't he have been better off protecting me while alive?"

"I'm sure he was thinking of the fact that he hadn't been able to protect your mother or brother."

"I needed my father!"

Xypher flinched. The pain in her voice tore through him. He'd never wanted to comfort anyone before, but right now, he'd give anything to ease the anguish he saw in her hazel eyes.

He gathered her in his arms and held her close. "I know."

She shook her head against his chest. "Do you know how hurt I was that Jesse came to me and not my family? Over the years I've seen hundreds of ghosts. But never my mother or father. Never my brother. Didn't they love me enough to at least say good-bye?"

His gut tightened in sympathy for her pain. "Of course they did, Simone. How could they not? Your father died to protect you. That is real, true love."

"Then why haven't they ever come to me?"

"I don't know. I don't. Maybe they couldn't."

"Because they didn't care."

"I'm sure that's not it."

Simone wanted to believe that, but it was hard.

And in all these years, she'd never shared that with anyone. She'd always kept it bottled up where it incinerated her soul. Squeezing her eyes shut, she forced herself to stop these thoughts. They were counterproductive.

What was done was done.

Surely Xypher was right and they would have come to her had they been able. But there was still that part of herself that doubted. That part of her that felt as if no one had ever loved her.

At least Xypher was here.

Their bracelets were gone. He could leave any-time he wanted to, but so far he hadn't.

Her stomach jerked from her nerves and grief. She pulled back, afraid of the sensation. "I still feel sick. How long is this going to last?"

"Until you get used to your powers. I imagine."

She didn't like the sound of that. She wanted something concrete she could put her hands on. Something tangible. "I can hear your heartbeat. Jesse is in his room with Gloria, showing her how to play Atari. My neighbor on the right is fighting with his wife over the phone, and my newest one, the woman on the left, is hungry. How do I know all that?"

"It's your powers. You'll be able to sense other people in a way you've never imagined."

"Will I hear their thoughts?"

He gave her a kind smile. "Only if they think out loud. But you will be able to sense the emotions people struggle to hide. That will tell you more about people than anything else."

"Will this massive headache ever ease?"

"Eventually."

Nodding, she looked down and touched his wrist where the bracelet used to be. "You're free of me now."

"I know."

"Then why are you still here?"

Xypher hesitated. It was something he wondered about himself. But he couldn't leave her. She was vulnerable and alone, and having been there himself, he couldn't bring himself to abandon her. "You need help."

"I can manage on my own. I always have."

"I've no doubt you can. But you helped me when I needed it. I'm returning that favor."

Simone leaned her head against his shoulder, truly grateful for his support. "Thank you, Xypher."

"No problem."

She rubbed his arm as the entire events of the day played out in her mind. "Because I'm a demon now, is Jaden over me?"

"No. So long as you own your soul and you don't barter it, no one has power over you."

She pulled back to look at him. "What if someone takes my soul?"

"No one can take your soul without your consent. Souls don't work that way."

She was glad to know that. Being a demon was scary enough, the idea of losing her soul was even more terrifying. God, she had so much to learn. It was like being born all over again. There was so much about herself that she didn't understand.

She wanted to learn the depth of her powers and what part Jaden played in the universe.

"I have a question . . . If Jaden is so powerful, couldn't you make a bargain with him to kill Satara?"

Xypher brushed the hair back from her face. "Jaden doesn't work that way. He won't actively do anything. Rather, he provides the means for each of us to carry out our desires. If you need more power, he finds it. If you seek an amulet or device, then you call him. As he would say, he's a means to an end, not a lapdog."

"Why didn't you have him open one of the portals to her, then?"

"He refused me when I asked it of him."

"Refused you? Why?"

"Since Kalosis is controlled by the goddess Apollymi, I guess his powers wouldn't work there. But I don't know. It could be something as simple as he didn't like what I bartered with. Jaden can be extremely capricious at times."

"That doesn't seem right."

"Tell me about it." He looked around. "Now, I don't know about you, but I'm hungry."

She smiled. "Famished." Suddenly that smile

faded. "I'm not going to be drinking blood now, am I?"

"I hope not. If you are, we're going to have to learn how to bleed Jesse."

Jaden flashed back to the tree where he'd first been summoned. As expected, Kaiaphas was waiting for him.

"Greetings, my lord," the demon said, bowing.

Jaden would give him kudos for knowing when to grovel. But kudos wouldn't save his ass. "You attacked your brother in the open today."

"My mistress demanded it."

Jaden slung his hand out and pinned the worthless bastard to the tree. "And by doing so, you undid a bargain I made. Do you know what that makes me?"

"No, my lord."

"A liar. And that is one thing I've never been." Jaden wanted blood over what had happened today. Palackas had given his life in vain and that sent Jaden to a level of pissed off he didn't like to function in.

But it wasn't his place to demand satisfaction over the demon's death. Frustrated, he released Kaiaphas and let him fall back to the ground. "I don't want your virgins. You can keep them."

"What then, my lord? Name your price and I will deliver it to you."

"There's a Dimme in this town. Bring me her heart."

"Is that all?"

"Trust me, it's enough."

Kaiaphas blinked as Jaden vanished from his sight . . .

A Dimme. That was easier said than done. First, they were brutal and rumored to be invincible. He wasn't sure if he had the powers to even look at one.

Licking his lips, he remembered his fight earlier that day. The woman . . .

Her blood had held the Dimme in it. He was sure of it.

Perhaps if he delivered her heart to Jaden, that would suffice. After all, wasn't one Dimme as good as another?

Yes.

Snapping his fingers, he went back to Kalosis to round up a sortie for his next attack. Simone was a medical examiner . . .

Smiling, he thought of one way to definitely get her out of her house.

TWELVE

Simone was still trying to get her bearings as she moved back to her bedroom, but it was hard. Everything seemed so amplified now. Every noise pierced her head. The lights were incredibly bright, and she could hear Xypher's heartbeat competing with hers. It was all very disconcerting.

Xypher was by her side, and she was holding on to him. She needed his strong arm to steady herself. But the smell of his skin was haunting. It also made her hungry for a taste of him in a way she'd never wanted a man before. It was almost like there was another part of herself. One that was braver, more seductive . . .

More hungry.

"Simone!"

She looked up as Jesse came running into the room through the wall.

"You're up! You're up!" He ran at her like an exuberant puppy.

In the past when he did that, he'd run right through her. Today, he slammed into her so hard, she stumbled.

"What the . . . ?"

Xypher gave her a look that was half amused, half evil. "Bonus round for your new powers. Now you can bitch-slap him when he gets on your nerves."

"I can touch Jesse?" She breathed the words, trying to fully understand them.

Turning, she met Jesse's shocked gaze. In all these years, they'd never been able to touch. Her hand trembling, she lifted it to place her fingers against his cold cheek.

It was solid.

Jesse was real to her. She could touch him . . .

Tears welled in his eyes as he laid his hand over hers. Gasping as her own emotions overwhelmed her, Simone pulled him into her arms and held him close. "I can touch you!"

Xypher crossed his arms over his chest as emotion pierced his heart like a knife. He had no reason to be jealous of a punk kid ghost and yet the way she held onto him . . .

He wanted to rip Jesse's head off.

"I wish I could have held you like this when you were little," Jesse breathed. "All those times you cried, all I could do was watch and try to cheer you up by making faces."

"I know, Jesse. I know."

Xypher hated to admit it, but it was actually touching the way they embraced each other, and he realized that the jealousy he felt wasn't because another man was holding Simone. It was the love the two of them had for each other.

They *were* a family.

Through thick and thin. No matter what, these two had stood by each other and would do so for eternity. There would never be betrayal. No treachery. They only wanted to love and help one another.

No one had ever loved him like that. And they never would.

Not once had he been touched by a loving hand. Suddenly, he felt like an intruder. Worse, he didn't feel worthy to witness something this pristine.

Aching inside, he turned away and headed for the kitchen.

Simone felt the air stirring. She looked past

Jesse to see Xypher leaving the room. There was an aura of such sadness around him that it made her hurt for him.

She pulled back from Jesse.

"Is something wrong?" Jesse asked.

"I'm not sure." She let go of his hand to follow Xypher and see what had happened.

"Xypher?"

He paused by the counter to look at her. His handsome features were stoic, but she could feel his turmoil inside.

"Are you all right?"

He nodded. "Fine. I just didn't want to watch the two of you slobbering all over each other. It was ruining my appetite."

If only she believed that. Now she understood what he'd meant earlier about her powers. Such incongruity between what she felt and saw was extremely disconcerting.

She moved closer to him. "Why are you hurting inside?"

"I'm not hurt, I'm hungry. You really should learn to tell the difference." He indicated the fridge over his shoulder with his thumb. "Isn't it lunchtime?"

She shook her head as she realized he was changing the subject. Something had made him uncomfortable, and rather than deal with it, he wanted food.

Fine, she could cope with that. But she wasn't

fooled by his actions. "I have some tuna salad left. We could make sandwiches."

"That'll work."

Simone pulled out the bread. "Why don't you grab the tub out of the fridge for me? It's in the clear container with the white lid."

Jesse joined them while she counted out the slices of bread. "Did you know Gloria was studying to become a psychologist?"

Simone smiled. "Nope, how would I know that?"

"True, you've been off doing stuff with Xypher . . . getting turned into a demon and all. Gloria's actually a really neat person once she quits mocking my music."

Simone was bemused by his sudden change of heart toward Gloria. "I mock your music, too, Jesse."

"Yeah, but you'll also dance to it with me." He struck a Michael Jackson pose. " 'Just beat it, beat it, beat it.' " Without thinking, he bumped into her.

"Jesse!" she said playfully, "I'm trying to make lunch."

"All right, but later, 'we gonna wake me up before you go go' and 'walk like an Egyptian.' "

Simone groaned and smiled at the same time.

Jesse blew her a kiss. "Now I'm off to see my woman." He drifted to the back of the house.

Simone laughed at him, especially since Gloria

had now become his 'woman.' "Jesse," she said playfully. "You're not old enough to date, boy!"

"I'm older than you. And at least I'm not dating a cradle robber who outdates me by countless centuries." The disembodied voice echoed in the kitchen.

"But remember that now I can smack your head . . ."

"Point taken, now leave me alone. We're comparing ectoplasm."

She didn't want to touch that one with a thirty-foot cattle prod. Shaking her head, she went back to making sandwiches.

Xypher handed her the tuna salad. "What's it like?"

"What?"

"To have someone who knows you that well? Someone you can tease around with and share inside jokes. I've seen people do it in dreams, but never up close before. There's a warmth inside you whenever Jesse's around. Even when he annoys you, it pleases you on another level."

Simone paused to look up at him. Poor Xypher, to have no idea what friendship meant. "It's good. There's a lot to be said for having people around you who aren't trying to tear you down. People who know how to laugh and who aren't jealous. Unfortunately, those relationships are sometimes hard to find."

"Sometimes they're impossible."

She nodded. "People are complicated. Emotions are complicated. Explain to me how you can both love and hate someone at the same time."

"*Odi et Amo.*"

She frowned. "What?"

"It's an ancient Latin poem written by Catullus. 'I Love and I Hate.' It talks about that very thing. He wrote it for a woman he both adored and despised."

"Yeah, see? That's just wrong, isn't it? Shouldn't you love or hate, but not both at the same time?"

"But you and Jesse don't hate each other."

"No, we never have. And for that I'm grateful. It's not easy living with someone day in and day out without wanting to strangle them. But Jesse, he never really annoys me." She sliced the sandwiches and put them on plates.

Xypher watched the way her hands moved while she worked. There was so much grace to her. So much beauty. He'd always been clumsy. But not her.

As she reached for a bag of potato chips, her phone rang. She glanced at it before she answered. "Hey, Tate. What's up?" She handed the potato chips to Xypher. "All right, we'll be right there." She shut the phone.

"Another murder?" He didn't really have to ask since he'd heard their discussion through the phone.

She nodded. "How many people will a Dimme kill?"

"Honestly? She's been remarkably circumspect."

Simone was aghast. "How can you say that? This is the third body."

Xypher shrugged. "They were created to be indiscriminate killers. The fact that there're not bodies piling up everywhere is a miracle."

"Are you sure it's a Dimme, then?"

"The guy who died—I'd bet my life on it. Gloria . . . maybe, maybe not."

Simone considered that. If the Dimme hadn't killed Gloria, then who did? No, it had to be the same killer. She didn't want to even consider the fact that there might be more of them out there. "We need to get to the latest victim. Grab the sandwiches and we'll eat them in the car."

He did, and they quickly grabbed their coats and left the house. Simone cursed as she realized she didn't have a car . . .

They'd left it on Toulouse when they'd gone to Liza's store.

She was turning toward Xypher when she caught something strange on the wind. It was a light musky scent . . . Unfamiliar to her. Lifting her head, she inhaled deeply trying to identify it, then cringed at what she'd done. "I'm not part dog now, am I?"

Xypher laughed. "No, but your olfactory

glands, like everything else, are more sensitive. You can smell in a wider spectrum than you've ever known before. For that reason, you might want to avoid Bourbon Street."

"Thanks. There for a minute, I was afraid I was going to turn into some kind of crotch-sniffing lunatic."

He sucked his breath in sharply. "You know that's the quickest hard-on I think I've ever gotten."

Simone paused as she realized that she could actually feel that painful heaviness in his groin.

"Yes," he said, his voice an octave deeper. "That's normal, too."

"I'm not sure I'm liking this newfound me."

"Trust me, baby. You're going to like demon sex a whole lot more than human. I can show you things that will make your head spin like Linda Blair."

She gave him an indignant look. "That's not the way to get into my pants, Xypher. Ew! Bad imagery."

Before Xypher could answer, the scent intensified. Simone turned to see a tall, blond man in his early twenties coming toward them. Something about his features reminded her of Dev from Sanctuary.

"Lycanthrope." The word came out as a low growl.

Xypher nodded. "Demons have an unnatural dislike for each other. It can be overcome, but it's not easy. Were-Hunters are an offshoot from their Daimon cousins, which is why you're feeling that burst of adrenaline that makes you want to attack him. It's your instinct providing you with an extra boost in the event you have to fight."

The man stopped as he caught sight of them. He cocked his head as if he could sense them the same way they could sense him.

"Peltier?" Xypher called.

He came over to them slowly, sizing them up with each step. "Kyle. I'm their youngest."

Xypher narrowed his gaze on him. "What are you doing here?"

"I was visiting a friend."

Xypher wasn't so sure about that. But then, suspicion was his middle name. "You're a Katagari in human form during daylight hours . . . how is that—" He stopped as he understood.

The Katagaria were animals who could take human form. During the daylight, they, especially while they were as young as this whelp, were relegated to their animal forms until the sun set.

Kyle Peltier was more than what he seemed.

"It was nice meeting you, Kyle," Xypher said curtly. "Give Carson our best."

"Will do," Kyle said before he headed across the street to where a Ninja motorcycle waited. He hopped on and took off without looking back.

"What aren't you telling me?" Simone asked.

"I'm not sure. It's a strange feeling . . ." But he couldn't place it. Truthfully, it felt like the Dimme, but that didn't make sense. If the Dimme was anything like her gallu cousins, she'd be looking for a dark place to rest during daylight hours. Not out here in open housing and she definitely wouldn't be near a Katagari.

As soon as the Dimme caught that scent, she'd be running.

He shook his head to clear it. He had to be imagining things.

Pushing those thoughts aside, he turned to Simone. "Okay, I have all my powers intact. I don't know where we're going, but you do, right?"

"Yes."

Good. He was about to show her how to transport through the cosmos with her powers. Hopefully, they wouldn't end up in Alaska. "Think of the place we're going. Picture it perfectly in your mind."

She did.

Xypher wrapped his arms around her and closed his eyes. An instant later, they were in the shadows of an alleyway. He heard the police talking among themselves, saw the photographer and Tate moving around a covered body.

He glanced around to make sure they wouldn't be seen before he solidified them.

A slow smile spread over her face. "Will I be able to do that on my own?"

"Most of it you'll be able to do. But it will take a lot of practice. And be careful doing it. Sometimes your clothes don't follow with you."

Her face paled. "That would be unbelievably bad."

"For you, yes. For me? I'm all for skinny-flashing." He raked her with a hot stare that actually lit her blood.

But she wouldn't let him know that.

Grinning wickedly, he handed her a sandwich, then headed toward Tate who looked up at them from the body.

Tate frowned at their food. "Eating at a crime scene?"

Grimacing at the blood spatter on the walls around them and the gore on the street, she handed her sandwich back to Xypher. "I'm not."

Tate gaped. "Wow, you're finally squeamish. I never knew you had it in you."

Simone was surprised, too. She'd always prided herself on not getting sick at a crime scene. But the smell of dried blood was rank in her nostrils. The color of it was a deeper shade than normal. It was almost like she could taste the blood and that made her extremely queasy.

Xypher on the other hand appeared completely unaffected.

"So what do we have?" she asked, taking deep breaths so that she wouldn't undignify herself.

Tate let out a long, tired breath. "Well, his head is missing so I don't think we have to worry about him getting up and walking around again. This isn't Sleepy Hollow."

Xypher frowned. "Sleepy Hollow?"

Simone shook her head. "A famous story about a headless horseman who chased victims."

"That's sick."

Simone arched a brow at him. "This from a demon who's eating at a crime scene?"

"I'm hungry. You should be grateful I'm eating the sandwich and not chowing down on someone's blood. I can do that, you know."

"Yeah," Tate said slowly. "Let's try to avoid freaking out any more civil servants."

Simone tried to focus. "What are the deets?"

"We're not sure. It looks like a fight of some kind ensued and obviously our guy here lost."

Xypher moved around the scene while they spoke.

Simone watched the way Xypher studied the blood patterns as if he could picture the exact way the fight had played out. When he neared the body, one of the officers shooed him away.

She approached slowly. "What are you thinking?"

"I want to see the body."

She went over and uncovered it, then flinched as the smell hit her full force. Damn, she was never going to get used to these new senses.

Xypher nodded before he finished off the sandwich. "It's what I thought."

He was so nonchalant. The least he could do was share what he knew. "Which is?"

"Trophy kill."

Simone exchanged a puzzled look with Tate. She didn't like the sound of that in the least. "What do you mean, 'trophy kill'?"

"The body is a message from one demon clan to another. 'Don't fuck with us.'"

Tate shook his head in denial. "Whoa, whoa, whoa, what are you talking about?"

Xypher indicated the body with his thumb. "You better autopsy him yourself, Tate, 'cause he isn't human and a regular human is going to freak when they open up his body and find that his internal organs aren't where and what they're supposed to be. He's a Charonte . . ." He glanced back at the body. "Or was a Charonte."

Tate held his hands up in frustration. "What the hell's a Charonte?"

"A. Demon," Xypher said as if he were talking to an imbecile.

"Are you sure?" Tate asked.

"Yes. Gallu don't die like that. When a gallu demon dies, it disintegrates like a Daimon. Daimons disintegrate like a Daimon. Humans who are killed by gallu become zombielike creatures." He pointed back to the body under the tarp. "And Charontes die like humans. Their bodies stay intact for burial."

Tate scowled. "But how do you know he's Charonte and not a human?"

"His skin is blue."

This time Tate scoffed out loud. "Humans turn blue when they die."

"Their skin doesn't marble when it goes blue."

That took some of the steam out of Tate. "I assumed it was body paint."

"No, it's genetic paint that he was born with and runs all the way through his entire epidermal layer. Mr. Charonte obviously strayed into the wrong place." He pointed up to the walls around them where blood was splattered as high as twenty feet from the ground. "I give him credit, he fought well. You can smell his blood and those of his attackers."

"Plural?" Tate asked.

Xypher nodded. "Three of them. I'd say they ambushed him and left him so that he'd be found and the rest of his clan would see the body and be afraid. Or depending on what breed of Charonte, his clan will attack and start an all-out war between them."

Tate let out a long breath before he glanced at Simone. "Man, he's like having one of those trackers from the Old West movies in the thirties. What else do you know, Tonto?"

"Well, let me tell you what I didn't know."

"And that is?"

"That there were any Charontes left in the human world. So going back to the trophy kill . . . Why? Who did the gallu want to see this?"

A chill went down Simone's spine. "Maybe it's a message to us."

"No. They'd be terrorizing us. This"—he again gestured to the large amount of blood—"was over territory." He looked back at Tate. "You guys have a Charonte clan living here and now you have a gallu one. And if something isn't done, New Orleans is about to get caught in the crossfire."

"And it's not even three yet," Tate said bitterly. "Makes me want to go home, crawl into bed with my wife, and just wait it out, doesn't it?"

"Not really," Xypher said. "Makes me wish I'd been here to fight it out with them. I'd like to tear into some gallu hide."

Simone ignored that. "So we're looking for a hungry Dimme and a clan of Charontes."

"Yes."

Even though she didn't like the concept of it, Simone nodded. "Any idea where the Charontes might be hanging out?"

"Offhand, I'd say someplace not too far away."

Tate cocked his head. "Why would you say that?"

"Well, if you're going to send a message to someone, you don't leave the message in a place where they won't see it. You put it somewhere obvious." He looked around at the buildings surrounding them. "Which means the Charontes would be near here."

Another chill crawled down Simone's spine. "How dangerous are these Charontes?"

Xypher shrugged. "Depends on how socialized they've become and how angry they are. Obviously, they've been hiding here under your noses without anyone knowing it."

Tate scoffed. "Well, it is New Orleans. Lot of freaky shit happens here."

An officer approached them. "We've looked everywhere for the poor guy's head. We think whoever killed him must have taken it. You thinking voodoo, Doc?"

"I'm thinking something, Sam. I'm done with the body. Wrap it up as soon as you guys have what you need and I'll finish up at the lab."

"Okay."

Tate walked over to them. "Thanks for the help. I'm going to fabricate paperwork as usual. If you guys come up with something else, let me know."

Simone turned toward Xypher, who was pacing around. The wind whipped at his hair, dragging it down into his eyes. The demon inside her was now even more attracted to him than the woman in her had been. There was a new sensual side to her that hadn't been there before.

It allowed her to understand him so much better. The power inside her was hungry, but she didn't know for what. It was like a physical ache.

As if he sensed her thoughts, he turned in her direction. The intensity of his gaze scorched her.

And it was then she smelled the same thing he did . . .

Before she could move, Xypher was there, moving faster than anyone could see. "Your eyes are red," he whispered, putting himself between her and the officers who were still investigating the scene.

She went cold at his words. "What?"

"Your eyes have changed. You need to recognize when it happens so that you can prevent it."

"How bad do they look?"

He looked down at her. Instead of blue, his irises were white, rimmed in red. "They look like this."

She cringed. "What can I do?"

His eyes went back to blue. "Act like you have something in one eye, and I'll walk you away from the humans."

Bowing her head, she closed her eyes and rubbed the right one. "I don't like this, Xypher."

"I know. But you'll get used to the physical cues and then you'll have more control over the demon part of yourself."

She winced at that. "I don't want to be a demon."

"Neither did I, but we can't help who or what our fathers impregnate, can we?"

His words were harsh and they stung her. "My father loved my mother," she said defensively.

He scoffed at her. "You've seen what the gallu look like in their demon form. It makes you wonder what kind of woman could be attracted to that."

Still Simone wanted to defend her parents. She'd loved them completely. "They met at a bar when my mom was in college."

He frowned. "What?"

"That's what my mom told me once. She was working as a waitress when my dad came in and they started talking."

Xypher paused as he remembered what Jaden had told him about her parents. "He must have been there scoping out his victim. It's a wonder he didn't kill your mother while he was at it."

"My mother said it was love at first sight. As soon as she saw him, she knew he was different from other men . . . It makes me wonder if she ever knew exactly how different he was. Do you think he told her he was part demon?"

"I don't know, Simone. You would think, but that was one hell of a secret. I can easily see why he wouldn't tell her."

So could she. For that matter, how would she ever tell someone what she was? Who, other than Tate and Xypher, would ever believe her?

He stopped her on the sidewalk. "Look at me."

"Are my eyes better?"

He nodded. "Just stay on top of your emotions, and that'll help."

She swallowed. He made that sound so much easier than it was. Dear Lord, what if she did this during class? They'd never believe it was instantaneous special effects. "I'm scared of this, Xypher. If anyone finds out I'm a demon, I'll lose everything."

He put his hands on her arms and squeezed them comfortingly. "You'll be okay. I promise. But can you imagine the fear your father must have had when he decided to be with your mother? He had to abandon everything and everyone he knew. To throw off his shackles like he did . . . That must have been strong love indeed."

"What do you mean?"

"Your father was a bound demon, Simone, with a master he served. When that happens, your master owns you completely until you fulfill whatever indenture contract he holds over you. If you escape that bond before you fulfill that contract, it's a death sentence. Your father knew that and still he ran."

"To be with my mother."

Xypher nodded. He couldn't imagine what her

father had been thinking or what kind of contract he'd run from. It was . . .

He paused as a scent filled his nostrils. He inhaled deeply before his eyes flashed to red.

"What is it, Xypher?"

"Charonte."

THIRTEEN

Simone and Xypher turned and there on the street behind them stood three extremely tall, well-built men. One was lean with jet-black hair that was short in back, but longer in front where it fell over his eyes. The other two were auburn haired and built like weight lifters. But for the orangelike scent of their skin and their strangely glowing eyes, they would have appeared human.

The dark-haired one drew closer. *"Misafy . . ."* he hissed dangerously as he raked them with a hostile glare. "What brings you here?"

Simone leaned closer to Xypher. "Did he just insult us?"

"Depends on whether or not being called 'half-blood' offends you." He locked gazes with the Charonte. "I saw what the gallu did to one of your people. I was looking for you to find out why."

The Charonte moved closer to them with an impressively lethal gait.

"Xedrix," the one on her left said in warning. "We know nothing of them or their powers."

Xedrix ignored him as he drew closer to Simone. Leaning down, he took a deep breath in her hair.

Xypher shoved him back.

Xedrix's eyes flashed dangerously as he refused to back off. "Katika?" he asked Xypher.

"Yes."

Xedrix went down on one knee before her.

Completely baffled by what had happened, Simone looked to Xypher for an explanation. "Katika? What is that?"

The demon rose up. "You are his owner."

Both of her brows shot up in surprise. *She* owned Xypher? In what alternate universe would that ever happen? "I am?"

Xypher gave her a look of warning not to say anything else before he turned his attention back to Xedrix. "*Pieryol akati.* We come without war. Neither of us has an alliance with the gallu."

Xedrix scoffed. "No? You reek of our worst enemies. Greek and gallu. And you expect me to believe that you mean us no harm?"

The demon on Simone's right stepped forward. "My brother lies dead. I say we kill the male to retaliate."

Xedrix cast a glare that was malevolent enough to be felt over his shoulder at the demon who had spoken. "You know the laws of our people. He's owned by one who hasn't declared herself our enemy."

"I will not serve a human-gallu *misafy*!"

Xedrix threw his hand out and the demon came flying toward him to land in his fist. "You have forgotten yourself, Tyris. The female comes to talk peace, we will listen. We may be brutal but we are not savage." He looked back at Xypher before he released Tyris. "One war like move from you and, Katika or not, we will kill you."

Xypher folded his hands together and held them up to his eyes for the Charonte to see. "No war so long as my Katika isn't threatened."

"Then we have an accord." Xedrix stepped aside and swung his arm out so that they could pass. *"Pieryol akati."*

Simone scowled. "What does that mean?"

"Peace is our journey, my lady." Xedrix fell in behind her. "If you'll follow Tyris."

Tyris led them toward the building on the left where a small door opened on the other side of a Dumpster.

Simone blinked from the heavy darkness as they entered what appeared to be the backstage area of a club. Everything back here was painted black, including the floor. Gathered black curtains separated the area where they stood from a stage that had the sign CLUB VAMPYRE hanging above it.

The irony wasn't lost on her. "Nice name."

Xedrix's eyes flashed red in the dark. "I may not be human, my lady. It doesn't mean I don't know sarcasm when I hear it."

"Sorry."

As Xedrix led them to the other side of the curtain, Simone gasped. There were at least two dozen more Charonte, and unlike Xedrix and his two companions, these looked like demons. With horns coming out of their heads, their skin was a myriad of colors, usually two per creature, that were marbled in such way as to actually be attractive. Their eyes ran from yellow to white to red or black. Likewise their hair colors ranged from black to brown or auburn. Large, brightly colored wings jutted out of their backs, giving them a strange angelic appearance that was belied by their fangs and battle-honed physiques.

Simone stepped back and bumped into Xypher,

who appeared to find what they were walking into totally copasetic. "I think I left my keys outside."

"Relax," Xypher said, wrapping his arm around her waist to keep her from running. "You're not the one in danger."

"How you figure?"

He indicated the group with a tilt of his chin. "By nature the Charonte are an extremely matriarchal race. The males are always subservient to females, which is why I told them you were my owner. That's the world they understand. And luckily for us, the males usually aren't as warring in nature as their females are."

"Really?"

He nodded. "Since there's no female present, I'm thinking we're relatively safe. Unlike a female Charonte, the males will only attack when ordered to or threatened." One corner of his mouth lifted. "Word to the wise, don't threaten them. I'm good, but they seriously outnumber me right now."

"Don't worry. I'm not about to taunt the entire pride in its den."

Xypher released her. "Where is your Katika?" he asked Xedrix.

Xedrix crossed his arms over his chest. "We are without."

"Did she die?"

He shook his head. "We are Dikomai."

"Male warriors," Xypher whispered in Simone's ear so that she'd understand.

"A few human years back our Katika was under attack. There was a Greek"—he spat the word out as if it were the most disgusting thing he could imagine—"god who sought to release her from her captivity. She sent us to protect her child and to fight the Greeks who wanted to harm him. We came and we fought. Many of us died and before we few survivors could return home, the portal closed, locking us here in this realm."

Tyris curled his lip. "And now we're being assaulted by the gallu. May they all burn and perish in the ashes of a dragon's scaly ass."

"Ooookay," Simone breathed, but she had to give them credit, it was a good curse to give someone you didn't like. The imagery said it all.

"Why are the gallu attacking you?" Xypher asked.

The males refused to answer.

Xypher shook his head at them. So, they knew, they just weren't willing to share it with him. Perfect. Just perfect. "Let me try this again. What do you have that they want?"

The males moved to stand shoulder to shoulder with their arms crossed. A unified wall of staunch machismo.

Simone shook her head at the sight. "Is it just me or is anyone else getting a case of testosterone poisoning?"

Xypher grimaced. "What?"

She held her hand out. "Look at them. Ready

to fight to the death rather than answer a simple question . . . you know there's only one thing I can think of that would make men, especially those who are from a highly matriarchal society, willing to lay down their lives without speaking."

"And that would be?"

"A woman."

Xypher paused as he realized that she was right. It would be the one thing that they'd die to protect.

But who was it?

"Where's the female?" Xypher asked.

Xedrix stepped forward to glare at them. "Get out!"

"It's all right, Xedrix." The voice was gentle and quiet, and framed with the most lilting song-like tone. "I'm not afraid of them."

The male demons began parting as a tiny figure pressed through their center.

When she finally broke through, Simone gasped at the fragile beauty dressed in jeans and a large green sweater—it was the same woman who'd moved into a condo near hers a few weeks back.

Barely five feet tall, she looked like one of the china dolls Liza made. Her skin and lips were so pale as to be luminescent. Long, silvery white hair flowed around her tiny, yet voluptuous body. The only color she had was her silver-gray eyes that glowed against a thick fringe of jet-black lashes.

She couldn't look more harmless or beautiful.

But the newly awakened demon powers inside Simone sensed the lethal capabilities of the tiny woman.

This was the gallu Dimme.

"I'm called Kerryna."

Xypher put himself between Simone and the Dimme. "The gallu and Charonte are vicious enemies. How is it they protect you?"

Kerryna held her hand out to Xedrix who went down on one knee by her side before he clasped it and held it against his heart.

Warmth spread through Simone as she realized that the two of them were in love.

But that didn't change the fact that Kerryna had killed Gloria and others—

"No, I didn't."

Simone blinked at Kerryna's soft words. "What?"

"I didn't kill Gloria. I've only killed two men since I was freed, and I assure you, they both deserved what happened to them. Even you would have ended their lives."

Xypher shook his head in disbelief. "I'm really confused. I was there when you broke out of your cocoon in Nevada."

Kerryna nodded. "I remember you and the god

Sin and his woman, Katra. The other god, Zakar, chased me for days on end until I was able to finally escape him and hide. He is a persistent beast. And it was hard. I knew nothing of this world or its people and their languages."

Xypher could understand. Parts of it eluded him even with his god powers and having been here to help Katra and Sin. "Why did you come to New Orleans?"

She indicated Simone with a tilt of her head. "We are cousins. Her father was the brother to mine. It is my nature to need my family with me, but once I met her, I knew she wasn't ready to accept herself or me. Her powers had been bound. Her scent hidden. She believed herself human and I thought it best to leave her with that delusion."

"You know," Simone said, stepping around Xypher, "for an indiscriminate killer, she's remarkably lucid and thoughtful."

Kerryna smiled. "Out of fear, my sisters and I were locked away so fast that no one bothered to learn anything about us. While we are born of the gallu, we are not gallu. The goddess Ishtar gave us the gift of compassion and understanding. I think she knew what was to happen and wanted to make sure that we didn't destroy the world as our creator intended. That being said, should all of us be freed, I don't know what will happen. Two of my sisters are not so kind or caring. They do crave blood above all things."

Xedrix stood up and draped a protective arm around her shoulders. She lifted her hand to stroke his forearm affectionately. He held her back to his front while he glared his mistrust at them. "The gallu want to take her and use her. That I won't allow."

Kerryna leaned back against him. "They kill to draw me out."

Simone sighed. "You know, the more I learn about the gallu, the less I like them and the more I really hate sharing a genetic link with them."

Kerryna nodded her agreement. "The males are hard to take at times. Unlike the Charonte, they're domineering and cruel. To them women are only breeders or food."

Simone cast a meaningful look at Xypher over her shoulder.

He was completely unrepentant. "I can't help it if I resemble them. We're all creatures of our birth. But at least I listen from time to time."

It was true. He did, and that made him semitolerable. She smiled up at him. "Well, what can I say? You are, after all, a god."

The only clue she had that he was amused was a very subtle softening around his eyes. Not that she blamed him. When surrounded by a warrior class of demons, it was probably good not to show any kind of humor.

Which reminded her of how important this was. "All right, we still have the gallu out there killing innocent people . . . and demons. How do we stop it?"

Xedrix rubbed his cheek against Kerryna's hair. "We've been trying to find a way, but as of yet there's nothing we've thought of. So long as we have Kerryna, they won't even discuss a truce."

"I won't go back to them. All of the gallu are disgusting." She looked at Xypher and blushed beautifully. "No offense."

"It's all right. I'm used to insults." Xypher cast a glance at Simone, who sputtered.

"I don't insult you . . . much."

Xypher didn't respond. Instead he narrowed his eyes at Xedrix. "You know, I just thought of something . . . you can open a bolt-hole down to Kalosis."

Xedrix shook his head. "We've tried. For some reason, we're not able to do it."

Xypher tsked at the demon. "You're lying, Xedrix. I smell it."

"We refuse to go back," Tyris said angrily as he stepped forward. "We were slaves there. Xedrix served as the Destroyer's pet. She treated him like a simpleton. I won't be at her mercy for another day. It was a godsend that we escaped when we did. Better to die here as free agents than to return to what we were."

Simone scowled at Xypher. "The Destroyer?"

"An ancient Atlantean goddess named Apollymi. She was imprisoned in Kalosis by her husband eleven thousand years ago."

Simone wondered what the goddess had done to merit that sentence. "Nice, and you want to go visit her, huh?"

"No, I don't. I want to kill Satara."

At the mention of Satara's name, more than half of the demons made disgusted noises.

"Kill that bitch!"

"Feed her to the Destroyer."

"Rip out both their throats."

Simone was impressed by the venom. It appeared Satara and the Destroyer could both benefit from a seminar on how to make friends and influence people, or in this case, demons. "Wow, this Kalosis sounds like a rival for Disney World. Sign me up for the next trip."

"I would, but apparently a ride down there's a lot harder to come by than a spare Hannah Montana ticket in a middle school."

Simone laughed. "Nice, timely reference."

"You can thank Jesse for it. He has a crush on Hannah." Xypher met Xedrix's gaze. "What will it take for me to talk one of you into opening that portal?"

"There's nothing."

Xypher looked at Kerryna, and Simone knew exactly what he was thinking.

Xedrix pulled her behind him and stiffened.

"Don't worry," Xypher said. "I wasn't thinking that. I would never threaten your woman. I was only considering how wrong I was about her."

Simone arched a brow. "Were you really?"

The offense on his face was deep. "Not you, too?"

"I'm sorry. You're right, I know better. But the way you looked at her . . . in my defense, it was spooky."

Grimacing at her, Xypher turned his attention back to the Charonte. "I know there has to be some way we can help each other. Think about it. I need to get inside Kalosis."

Xypher duplicated his earlier gesture of clasping his hands together and holding them up. *"Pieryol akati."*

Xedrix inclined his head to him before he repeated the words.

Xypher pulled her toward the door, but before they went far, Kerryna stopped them.

"We are family," she said softly to Simone. She took the small red stone necklace from around her neck and placed it in Simone's palm. "If you need me, take the crystal in your hand and call my name. I will come immediately."

"Thank you."

Kerryna hugged her close. "There is strength inside you, Simone. Our bloodline was one of the strongest of the gallu. Never forget that."

"I'll remember."

Kerryna patted her hand. "I will work on Xedrix for you," she said softly to Xypher. "If revenge is truly what you want, I'll find some way for you to have it."

With that, she left them and rejoined Xedrix.

Simone turned to Xypher. "Not even dinnertime and it's been an interesting day. I'm kind of afraid to see what the next hour will bring. How about you?"

"Any minute I'm not being beaten with a barbed whip is a great one in my opinion."

Her stomach shrank at his dry tone and the reminder of the world he'd left behind. If Xedrix thought his was bad, he should try Xypher's. "Do you really have to go back to that?"

"If I thought there was a way to avoid it, believe me, I would. But I've already been sentenced. And you can't run from a god."

"What if I talked to Hades?"

He laughed. "Hades isn't going to listen to you. All we can do is take the time I have and try to expel the gallu so that you'll be safe when I'm gone."

When I'm gone . . .

Those words tore through her and brought a wave of pain so severe it actually took her breath. How could he have come to mean so much to her so quickly?

And yet there was no denying what she felt. She didn't want him to leave. Ever.

Don't think about it.

She would find a way to settle this. A way for it to end without costing Xypher his freedom. She had to.

The alternative was wholly unacceptable to her.

FOURTEEN

Simone canceled her afternoon class. Between her powers, which were still making her ill, and all the chaos of attacking demons and her body going out of control without notice, she thought it might be the safest thing for her students. The last thing they needed to see was their professor's eyes turn bright red.

Or worse, have one of them eaten by a gallu. The administration might take some issue with that.

So would the poor student.

In the meantime, she was learning certain things

about herself and her new powers. Xypher had moved the furniture around in her living room so that he could show her specific moves to fight the gallu and make them cry. Her favorite to date was gross, but highly effective.

Acid spit.

She scratched the back of her neck as she looked at the metal cup she'd just destroyed. "I feel like the alien in the space movies."

Xypher gave her a hot once-over before he pressed himself against her and breathed in her ear. "Lucky for me, you're much better looking."

She smiled at the compliment as her entire body heated from his touch.

"Ooooo!" Jesse said as he came skating sideways into the room. "Someone moved furniture. This is great!"

Before Simone could speak, the Clash "Should I Stay or Should I Go" started playing. "Jesse . . ."

He started dancing like a chicken. "Oh, c'mon, Sim. It's the Clash. You gotta dance." He took her hand and spun her about.

Laughing, she shook her head and then joined his famous Chicken Neck Dance thing that they did, usually when no one else was around.

Gloria squealed in delight before she joined them.

Xypher stood back, watching the three of them with a stern frown. Never in all his existence had he seen anything so strange. They went from a chicken line dance to robots to something that looked like the twist—if you had some sort of spinal injury. And then they began do-si-doing. The song didn't last long before it went into "Boys Don't Cry, I Wanna Be a Cowboy."

Jesse pointed one finger and then another at him and pretended to shoot him as he sang to the song.

Xypher scratched his cheek. "All of you have lost your mind."

Simone laughed. "C'mon, Ted," she said, using the name of the cowboy in the song. "Dance with us."

"I have never in my entire, long existence danced."

"And I've never been able to hear someone else's heartbeat from three feet away until today, either." She grabbed his arms and tugged him toward the group. "Dance with me, Xypher. No one here will laugh at you for it. Trust me, if we don't mock Jesse for his lack of grace, we'd never mock you."

He felt completely ridiculous for all of ten seconds. But moving in unison with Simone while her eyes sparkled made him forget about the fact he probably looked like a jackass.

The music segued into Tina Turner, "Better Be Good to Me."

"Monkey dance!" Jesse shouted.

Xypher exchanged a puzzled look with Gloria, who was as lost as he was.

Simone came to rest at his side and showed him how to raise one hand at a time in time to the music. "Now shake your tail like a monkey . . . It's a monkey dance."

Xypher laughed, and for the first time in his life, it wasn't bitter or mocking. It was a real, honest-to-goodness, from-the-depth-of-his-stomach laugh that warmed him from the inside out. Dear gods, he was enjoying himself. Really enjoying himself.

He'd never, ever done this before.

So this was what real fun felt like. No wonder people sought it out. Fun was incredible.

Minutes and songs flew by as they just enjoyed being together, acting completely stupid. Simone twirled around, laughing, then collapsed on the couch.

"Oh, I'm getting old. I can't keep up."

Jesse and Gloria kept dancing while Xypher went to sit next to her on the couch.

"You okay?"

She laughed. "Hot and sweaty. You?"

"Same. You guys do this a lot?"

She smiled as she watched Jesse and Gloria dancing together. "About once a week. But we don't usually move the furniture first."

Xypher brushed a stray piece of hair back from her face, but the moment he touched her, he realized he'd made a mistake. A wave of heat scorched his groin.

Growling at the ferocity of the sudden desire, he leaned over and captured her lips with his.

Simone moaned softly at the taste of Xypher. Her heart raced even faster as she buried her hand in his thick, black hair and let the strands twine themselves around her fingers. His whiskers grazed her skin, making her burn with need. Closing her eyes, she imagined being in bed with him . . . naked.

No sooner had that thought shot through her mind, than she was in her bed with him, completely bare.

"Oh, my God," she breathed, pulling back as a wave of dizziness went through her.

With an evil glint in his eyes, Xypher laughed. "I think I like the fact that you don't have control over your powers. As long as you don't flash us into public naked, I'm good with it."

Pulling her sheet tight against her bare body, she squeaked in indignation. "I can't believe I just did this."

"Don't be embarrassed." He snuggled closer to her before he nibbled the corner of her mouth.

Simone hesitated. Part of her wanted to bolt from the bed, but the other part was absolutely eager for this. They'd been through so much already. More than that, he'd touched her heart and life in ways no man ever had before.

Smiling at him, she placed her hand against his whiskered cheek. His blue eyes were beguiling.

She saw the need and the heat of his passion there, but he wasn't pushing her. He was waiting to make sure it was okay.

That alone broke her last bit of resistance.

She rolled into his arms and kissed him.

Xypher trembled with the relief that tore through him at her actions. She'd come to him.

Unable to stand it, he kissed her fiercely as he rolled to his back and draped her over his chest. He hissed at how good her breasts felt against his bare chest. At of the sensation of her naked legs sliding against his.

"Hey, Sim, what—"The words broke off into a horrified shriek that sounded more like a little girl than a teenage boy. Jesse ran through the wall to escape.

"Next time, knock," Xypher called after him.

Jesse said something, but it was muffled by the stereo.

Simone didn't let it faze her. She'd see to Jesse later. Right now, she only wanted to be with Xypher. There was something about him that captivated her.

Once more, he rolled over with her, pinning her to the bed. "You are so beautiful," he growled, nipping at her lips before he buried his face against her neck. He kissed a blazing trail over her skin to her breasts.

Simone arched her back and held him close as she raked one hand down his back to feel his muscles flex. She was absolutely dizzy from the sensation of his lips on her flesh. From the warm, masculine scent of his body.

He looked up from her breast before he moved lower, to her stomach and then lower still.

Xypher took his time tasting her as he dipped his right hand to gently probe the delicate folds of her body. She gasped and jerked in response. Smiling at that, he circled her, delighting in how wet she already was. His own body was on fire at the thought of taking her. But he didn't want this over that fast.

He wanted to savor her.

With that thought foremost in his mind, he spread her legs wide before he moved his hand away and ran his tongue down her cleft.

Simone whimpered in delight as she buried her hand in Xypher's hair. His tongue worked magic on her. She didn't know why but this was something more than just sex. Something about being here with him . . .

She needed this. It was like he touched more than just her body. He touched her heart. Her soul. And she wanted him to feel the same way.

Xypher nuzzled her, letting the scent of her body mark his. Grinding his teeth, he laid his head on her stomach and just enjoyed the sensation of her hands in his hair. She was so gentle with him. So sweet. He'd never thought to touch another woman like this. To have her touch him.

This was so much better than any dream he'd ever had. Here for a moment, he could pretend he belonged to someone. That he mattered to her. It was stupid, he knew. They were strangers. Jesse was her family, not him. He'd be gone in a few weeks and she'd go on with her life while he returned to hell.

But here for a moment, he was with her.

"Will you miss me?" As soon as the words left his lips, he wished he could recall them.

"Of course I'll miss you, Xypher. I don't want you to leave."

Those words branded themselves into his heart. Did she really mean them? He wanted to believe her. But Satara had made similar avowals.

She'd even told him that she loved him.

How could she have toyed with him like that? But Simone didn't seem to be the type of woman who would lie about her feelings. She laughed guilelessly. Lived her life in the open.

Touching her was like touching the sun. Warm, bright. Soothing.

He rose up above her so that he could look down and stare into her eyes. He could see forever in them. Sliding against her body, he cupped her face in his hands and kissed the tip of her nose before he slid himself inside her.

A groan escaped his lips at how good she felt. Biting his lip, he drove himself deep inside her while staring into those eyes that were filled with kindness for him.

And in that moment, he discovered a blistering truth. He'd sold his soul for the wrong thing.

He should have sold it for Simone's love. To be part of her world for all time . . .

It was so unfair that he'd met her now when he had no choice except to leave. Shivering at the thought, he pressed his cheek against hers and listened to her short, sharp breaths as he quickened his strokes.

Simone cradled Xypher to her as she let the strength of his body carry her to the ultimate height of pleasure. Who would have ever dreamed that a demon could be so tender? But he was. He held her as if she were unspeakably precious. As if he were afraid she'd break.

The only part of her that was in jeopardy of that was her heart. She'd lost everyone in her life who meant something to her.

Only Jesse had been a constant. And now she'd have to lose Xypher. It wasn't right.

She moaned as he drove himself so deeply into her body that it touched her very soul. She lifted her hips, drawing him in even deeper, until she felt herself slipping.

Screaming out, she came in a bright burst of release.

He laughed in triumph before he moved even

quicker against her. And when he came, he growled like a wild animal who'd been temporarily tamed.

Simone held him against her in the darkness and listened to the sound of his ragged breathing in her ear. "I won't let go of you without a fight, Xypher. Hades can't have you back. I won't let him."

Xypher winced at those words that cut into his heart. The fact that she said them meant the world to him. But he knew better than to put stock in words whispered in a lover's arms. Such words were empty more times than not.

Besides, words were easy. It was the doing that was hard. People started down the road with good intentions, but the moment the road became rough or difficult, they'd abandon it. There was no reason to believe Simone would be any different from anyone else.

He wasn't worth fighting for. All he could offer her was a broken future.

But it was nice to pretend that he could put faith in her conviction. That she would fight for him and not throw him to his enemies . . .

"Xypher?"

He slid to her side and pulled her into his arms. "Yes?"

"Did you love Satara?"

"I thought I did, but I realized too late that I have no understanding of love. It's a human emotion."

"My father felt it."

"He was an exception, as was your mother."

She looked up at him. "You don't believe in love, do you?"

"I think it exists. I just don't think it will ever exist for me."

She sighed before she snuggled back down on top of him. "What happened to make you hate Satara the way you do?"

He paused, his hand in her hair, as unfettered pain tore through him. He'd never told a single soul what had happened, but as he lay here with Simone, the truth came pouring out before he could stop it. "I made a bargain with Jaden to accept her punishment."

"What?"

He let out a tired sigh. "I showed Satara how to walk into people's dreams. I allowed her to use my powers and manipulate them."

"Why did you do that?"

"For the same reason you dance with Jesse. Dreams were the only place where I could have emotions. Whenever Satara joined me there, I felt like a man. And I thought I felt love for her. At the time, I was willing to do anything to make her happy."

"But you didn't love her?"

He sank his hand in her hair and spread it out over his chest. He savored the cool, tickling sensation of it. "No. And she didn't love me, either, even though she said she did. She was using me and my powers so that she could attack people and torture them while they were helplessly asleep."

Simone's heart sank at what he described. "What?"

"That's the curse of the Skoti. If we visit one person too much, we can burn them out and either kill them or make them go insane. Satara was using my powers as a way to assassinate those she didn't like."

Xypher drew in a sharp breath as he remembered that fateful day. Satara had been dressed in red, her blond hair flowing around her like an angel as she ran to him and threw herself into his arms.

"Xypher, help me, please . . ." Her eyes had sparkled with her tears.

He'd never seen her cry before.

"What's wrong?"

"Zeus and Hades are going to kill me. You can't let them."

"Kill you for what?"

"For the dreams you taught me. They . . . they said I was doing something wrong, but the people I killed deserved it. You believe that, don't you?"

"Of course."

She'd smiled at him then and he'd been lost. "Please don't let me die, Xypher. I love you. I'll always love you."

Gods, what a fool he'd been to believe her.

Simone swallowed as the knot in her stomach tightened. She knew what he'd done. "You summoned Jaden."

He nodded. "I gave him my soul if he would make the other gods believe I was the one who'd tortured the humans. Satara had promised me that once I was dead, she'd come to Tartarus and feed me seeds from the Destroyer's garden."

Simone frowned as she tried to understand. "Why eat seeds?"

"They would have killed me completely. Every facet of my being would have been wiped out of existence."

Simone gasped at the horror of what he described. "Why would you want that?"

He took her hand and rubbed it down the scars that marred his chest. "I didn't want to bleed for all eternity for something I didn't do. I was willing to die for her and I wanted her to make sure that I didn't continue to suffer."

Simone winced at the pain she felt for him. "She didn't carry out her part of the bargain."

"No. Instead she came and laughed at me for being so stupid." His eyes flared red. "There for a time, she'd even helped them to torture me. I would stare at her, wanting a part of her flesh so badly that I could taste it."

Simone covered her mouth with her hand as bile rose in her throat. "How could she do that?"

"She's a soulless bitch, and now you know why I can't go back to hell without taking her with me. I'm not the only man she's fucked over, but by the gods on Olympus I want to be the last."

Yeah, now she understood, but the understanding didn't change the fact that she didn't want him hurt. Or worse, dead.

"I would *never* betray you like that."

His gaze softened, but deep inside his eyes, she saw the doubt that tore at her.

How could she ever prove herself to a man who'd been so deeply betrayed?

Simone laid her head against the worst of the scars on his chest and took his hand into hers. Somehow she was going to prove it to him. He wasn't going to be alone in this fight anymore.

"Satara deserves to pay for what she did." How could anyone, after having been given so much, turn on the very person who gave it? It was cruel beyond cruel.

"Believe me, she will. If I have to descend into hell and drag her out by her throat."

Simone shook her head at him. "There's the little ray of sunshine I know so well. Ever out to cheer people up."

"Well, it could be worse."

"How so?"

"I honestly don't know. But it's something humans say so I thought it would be appropriate."

Simone laughed until she saw the writing on his arm. "What is this?"

He covered the hand she held there. "It's a reminder I wrote of why I have to have Satara's blood. Why I can't give up my quest no matter the temptation."

Simone tightened her hand over the words. How sad that he had marked them there. And she wondered if there would ever be any way to erase them and replace them with something far kinder.

Stryker paused as he caught sight of his sister at his desk, writing. "What are you doing?"

She jumped, then pulled a book down over her paper. "Writing a letter."

"To whom?"

"It's personal." She got up and sauntered over to him. "I have good news for you. The gallu have found the Dimme."

Stryker lifted a single brow in interest. "Really?"

She nodded. "One Dimme could take out the Destroyer, yes?"

That was the theory. "We need her."

"No . . ." Satara said with an evil smile, "*you* need her. But there's one small problem."

"And that is?"

"Do you remember when Dionysus almost opened the portal to Kalosis and Apollymi sent her Charonte out to stop him?"

Of course he did. Apollymi had been livid that day. "They were sent to keep Acheron from dying, but yes, I remember. What of it?"

"The Charonte didn't all die. Apparently a large number of them survived and they're guarding our Dimme."

Stryker choked. "Charonte are guarding a Dimme? Is the world coming to an end and I missed the memo? How the hell did that happen?"

"I'm not sure. But if someone . . ."—she gave him a meaningful look—"will loan me some of his Spathi Daimons, I might be able to get my hands on the Dimme. Then we can use her to kill my Xypher problem and your Destroyer problem. What do you think?"

It sounded like a good idea, but also a risky one. While his Spathi were highly trained and excelled at killing, so were the Charonte. The last thing he wanted was to deplete his army. However, if he could kill Apollymi and claim her powers as his own, it would be worth losing a few dozen soldiers.

"Very well, sister. You'll have your pick of my soldiers. Just remember that if you fail in this, it's all on your head. I know nothing about your plan."

"Don't worry, Stryker. I'm not about to fail, and by tomorrow both of our problems will be solved."

FIFTEEN

Xypher came awake to the oddest sensation of his existence. A woman snuggled against him. He lay there on his side in silence, just feeling her against his spine. Her right arm was draped over his waist, while her thigh was nestled between his. Her cheek lay against his shoulder and her breath tickled his skin.

He closed his eyes, savoring every nuance of her against him. Was this what being human felt like? Did human males take this for granted?

How could they? To have someone trust you enough to lie unconscious against you while you did the same, and for both of you to awaken un-harmed . . .

It was heaven.

No, Simone was heaven.

Why couldn't he have been born human? Born to this time and place so that he could stay with her. The fact that he couldn't was even more cruel than the torture he'd endured in Tartarus. He wanted to crawl inside her and stay there forever.

But it wasn't meant to be and all the dreaming in the world wouldn't change the fact that once this reprieve ended, he'd be right back in hell where memories of her would torture him forever.

How would he be able to stand it?

His heart heavy, he carefully rolled over so as not to hurt her. She whimpered in her sleep before she moved and smacked him in the nose with her elbow.

Ow! He rubbed the tip of his nose and blinked back involuntary tears.

"You're going to pay for that," he whispered against her skin.

Pulling the covers back, he stared at her naked body. Her curves were lush and full, her nipples slightly puckered. Her hips were flared and rounded, while her legs were parted just enough for him to see that she was still moist. It was the most inviting sight he'd ever beheld.

The frown returned to her face before she

grabbed at the sheet to cover herself and rolled away to cocoon in it.

Xypher laughed. She was a cantankerous thing in the morning. So much for all her talk about beginning her day with a purpose. More like she began her day with pouting. Amused by that, he leaned down to nibble the underside of her breast.

Simone came awake to small licks that caused her stomach to contract and her body to melt. Opening her eyes, she saw Xypher staring up at her with a look so intense that it stole her breath.

"What are you doing?" she teased.

"I'm licking you," he said, before he drew one nipple deeper into his mouth. "I couldn't be this close to you and not touch you. Besides, you owe me for my latest shiner."

She rubbed at her eyes. "Latest shiner?"

"My nose. You slapped me while you were sleeping."

"No I didn't."

"You're right. You actually slammed your elbow into my nose."

She brushed the hair back from his eyes and touched his nose where she'd accidentally hit him. "Oh, my goodness. I guess I'll have to kiss it and make it all better."

His look was wicked and warm as he crawled up her body. "I've got another boo-boo for you to kiss."

She looked between their bodies to see his erection. "Hmmm, and what a big boo-boo it is, too."

Xypher kissed her, his heart pounding at the way she teased him without malice. He honestly loved the newness of it.

People were afraid of him. They were angry at him.

No one had ever laughed with him or played with him.

And it was then he came to the most shocking conclusion of all.

He loved her.

Deep inside in a place where he never looked, he felt that love blazing. It burned and it ached, and it would do anything in the universe and beyond to keep her safe. The knowledge lifted him up.

And terrified him to the depth of his soul.

No! The scream of denial ran all the way through him. He didn't want to love anyone. Love was for weak-minded fools.

Glancing at his arm, he read the words he'd branded there . . .

It's a tool used to manipulate and ruin anyone who is stupid enough to hold it.

Don't be stupid.

Love destroys.

He'd given his love to Satara and she'd thrown it back in his face and then lashed him for his foolishness. But Satara had never treated him like this. There had been no laughter. No tender touches. No early-morning blushes and kisses that warmed him all the way to his core.

And in the horror of his realization over Simone was the knowledge that he'd never really loved Satara. He'd wanted to know love so badly that he'd contorted the concept of it to fit a relationship that it had no part in.

This time love had come up behind him and clubbed him on the head when he hadn't been expecting it. These emotions took him by surprise, they weren't conjured by some inner need he had.

When he'd met Simone and thrown her into her car, she'd been nothing more than a pawn.

Now she was his world.

And there was nothing he wouldn't do for her. How the hell had that happened? Yet there was no denying it. The worthless demonspawn who'd been wanted by none had given his heart over to a human *misafy* . . .

Simone moaned as she felt a shift in Xypher's touch. It was tender and sweet. Almost reluctant.

And at the same time it was masterful. His hands roamed her body, giving her pleasure and making her sigh.

Lifting his hand, she kissed his scarred knuckles. Then she took the pad of his forefinger into her mouth to gently suckle it.

Xypher rolled with her, pulling her on top of him. Smiling, Simone straddled his waist and stared down at him with an expression of kindness.

He'd never seen anything more beautiful or welcome. "Love me, Simone."

"What?"

"Make love to me."

Simone nodded. There was something needful in his eyes. Something that said this meant more to him than just a physical act. Wanting to make him understand that she would never hurt him, she kissed his lips softly as she slid herself onto him.

Xypher threw his head back as she slowly moved against his hips. It was an exquisite torture. Slow and steady. One so fierce that all he could do was tremble.

He was helpless against his woman and her guileless charms.

The light cut across her body, making it glow. She leaned over him, letting the ends of her hair brush against his chest and stomach while she rode him ever so gently.

Biting his lip, he lifted his hips, driving himself into her even deeper. Needing to feel as much of her as possible.

Simone smiled at the beauty of Xypher. She ran her hand down his muscular chest, cupping and stroking the tawny flesh. She couldn't imagine going back to her life without seeing his face every day. It would kill her.

In no time at all, she'd grown accustomed to his being a permanent fixture in her life.

She never wanted him to leave.

Normally when someone was around her all the time, she got irritable with them. Even Tate. But Xypher was like Jesse. Even when he was annoying, it was charming and she didn't mind it in the least.

His eyes searing her, he took her hand into his and led it to his mouth so that he could nip the side of her flesh. God, those lips were beautiful. Leaning forward, she ran her tongue over the stubble on his chin. It was so rough and masculine. She loved the sensation of it prickling her skin.

Xypher wrapped his arms around her and lifted his hips, meeting her strokes.

The warmth of his body and the feel of his skin on hers—it was more than she could stand. Staring into his eyes, she came in a blinding white moment of searing peace.

Xypher laughed deep in his throat as he felt her climax and watched the pleasure play out across her features. He loved the way she felt in his arms, the way her brows drew together an instant before she came. And the sound of her contented purrs as her body spasmed against his.

Burying his head against her shoulder, he gasped as he felt his own release finally come. Grinding himself against her, he held her close as he released himself inside her.

She collapsed against him. He held her there,

tracing lines over her back while her breath fell against his nipple.

"That was a nice start to the day."

He kissed the top of her head. "Yes, it was."

Simone sighed contentedly, stretching like a newborn kitten against him. "Now I don't want to get up. I just want to stay here in your arms for the rest of the day . . . You think Jesse could teach my classes?"

He chuckled at the thought. "I think watching him try could be highly entertaining."

"Well, I'd ask you to go do it, but that would defeat the purpose of my staying here . . . I wonder if I could retire early and live on the streets? What do you think?"

"Living on the street wouldn't work. Not enough privacy for what I want to do with you."

She smiled. "Very good point."

Her alarm clock started blaring.

Xypher growled at the piercing sound. "Rip that out of the wall." He flung his hand out at it, but she quickly diverted his blast.

"Don't you dare. I love that alarm clock."

He snorted. "You get attached to the damnedest things."

After rolling away from him, Simone switched the clock off and smiled at the truth behind that statement. She really did get attached to the oddest things and Xypher had to be the strangest of all her attachments.

He yawned as she returned to bed. "You sure you want to go back to teaching today? We didn't make much progress yesterday on training you to conceal your powers."

"Well, I'll have to mix with normal people eventually. Do you think it'll be worse today than yesterday?"

He brushed her hair back from her shoulders. "Have you learned your body's signals for changing?"

"It's a weird burning behind my eyes before they go weird."

"Then you should be fine. When you feel that, then you know to get out of public view as quickly as possible. If it happens in class, tell them you have a stomach bug and you have to run to the bathroom."

She wrinkled her nose at the thought. "That's gross."

"Well, then wear sunglasses and tell them you have an eye infection."

She nibbled the stubble along his jawline. "You know, that's not a bad idea."

"Of course the glasses won't be much use when the horns pop out of your head or the wings out of your back, but—"

She shrieked at the thought. "No they won't!"

He smiled evilly. "No. But that look on your face was worth it."

Laughing, she pushed him back on the bed.

"That's it, I'm going to beat you down and make you sorry."

Xypher froze as he braced himself for her attack.

But instead of her giving him pain, she tickled him. It took him several seconds before he realized her intent. By then she was pouting.

"You're not ticklish. Well, that stinks." She sat back and crossed her arms over her chest, hiding the breasts he loved to tease.

"I'm sorry," he said, trying to cheer her. "If it'll make you happy, I'll pretend to be."

"No, it's okay. Can't have everything, I suppose." She paused at the edge of the bed. "But you come darn close."

"Close to what?"

"Being perfect. Only you're more than that, Xypher. You're wonderful."

Xypher couldn't move as she left him to go to the bathroom. He couldn't breathe as those words sank into his consciousness. *She thinks I'm wonderful* . . .

No one had ever thought such a thing about him before. Pain in the ass. Rude. Violent.

But wonderful . . .

That knowledge hit him like a punch in the gut.

As he started to get up, Jesse appeared in the doorway with a stern look on his face. "What are your intentions?"

"I was getting out of bed to shower and dress."

Jesse's eyes narrowed. "Not that. Toward my girl. You two have been locked in here like two horny bunnies all night long, and before you break Simone's heart, I want to know if you intend to do right by her. Or do I need to go recruit some demons to kick your ass?"

He'd like to see Jesse try—in fact he'd pay for that entertainment. But while he was offended the ghost would think that of him, he would expect no less from Jesse who was only trying to protect Simone.

"I would never hurt her, Jesse. Or you. But I can't stay here and you know it, so don't make me feel any worse about leaving than I already do."

Jesse frowned at him. "You really are decent up under all that bluster, aren't you?"

"No. I'm still the same angry bastard who'd sell his own mother's heart to make Satara pay. Nothing has changed."

"Except you love her."

He had to bury the surprise deep inside before he betrayed himself. He wasn't about to give that knowledge up to Jesse or anyone else. "I don't know what you're talking about."

Jesse snorted. "Yes you do. I can sense it and you know I can."

And he hated that. But there was nothing to be done for it. So he narrowed his gaze on Jesse. "Don't you dare tell Simone."

"Don't worry. It's not my place. But if I were you, I'd let her know before it's too late."

That was so much easier said than done. "What do you know about it?"

"I'm a ghost, Xypher. I thought I had all the time in the world to tell the people around me how I felt about them and to build my future. But in one heartbeat, a cement truck driver looked down to change his radio station, weaved into my car, and in the blink of an eye, I lost everything."

He glanced away, but even so Xypher saw the pain in his eyes. "The last memory I have is my girlfriend holding me while the rain poured down on us, mixing with my blood as it ran over her. She was telling me that she loved me and begging me not to die. I didn't want to go."

His voice broke from the emotions he was trying not to show, but Xypher felt and saw them anyway. "There was so much I wanted to say to her, but the wreck had crushed my windpipe and I couldn't make a single word come out. I tried so hard to stay with her, but it wasn't meant to be . . . I couldn't even lift my arm to touch her one last time."

He locked gazes with Xypher. "So, yeah, I have a better understanding of your situation than you do. Been there, done it, and it still aches deep inside me that I never once told Julie how much I loved her. Three seconds was all it would have taken. Three seconds I wish to God I had back. Think about it." He vanished from the room.

Xypher sat in silence as he realized that for a kid, Jesse had a lot more sense than he'd given him credit for. But the problem was, it wasn't that simple. What good would it do to tell Simone he loved her when he couldn't stay? It would only hurt her more and that was the last thing he wanted to do.

No. It was best to keep his love to himself. Locked inside him, it would hurt only one person—him. He preferred it that way.

Pushing himself up from the bed, he went to join her in the shower.

"You didn't dream again last night, did you?"

Xypher paused in his shaving to look at Simone in the mirror. "How did you know?"

"I was thinking of it while I was in the shower. I'm not sure why, but I had a thought. Did you dream while you were in Tartarus?"

"No. Hades took that from me so that I couldn't use it as a way to escape my torture."

"Do you think that's why you haven't dreamt here?"

He rinsed his razor in the sink. "Jaden returned all my powers to me. I should be able to dream without a problem."

She paused by his side. "Did you try to dream?"

How could he explain to her that he was living the best dream of all just by being here with her? "Not really."

"Maybe that's it then. Maybe you just need to try."

How he wished it were that simple. There was something more to the fact he wasn't dreaming, but he didn't want to think about it right now.

All he wanted to focus on was her. Kissing her hand, he returned to shaving.

Even though they were no longer joined by the cuffs, Xypher spent the rest of the day with Simone. He told himself that he'd go after Satara tomorrow. He just wanted one more day with the woman who made him laugh.

A woman who thought he was wonderful . . .

Even Jesse and Gloria came out after the classes to hang with them while they walked around the French Quarter and had dinner at the Alpine Restaurant.

"Have you lived here your entire life?" he asked as they walked along the shops on Royal Street, back toward her condo.

She smiled. "I have. Except for the time I spent in the children's home after my father died."

"You don't speak much about your foster parents."

She hooked her arm in his as they walked. "Carole and Dave. They were wonderful people. They'd wanted their own kids, but Carole had been unable to have any. Originally, they wanted to adopt a baby, but finally they gave up and decided to take in older children. I was the youngest of four they adopted."

"So you have siblings?"

"Not really. My adopted siblings were out of the house by the time I came along. We exchange Christmas cards, but honestly we're barely more than strangers. The only thing we had in common was the O'Learys. And I do miss them a lot. Any time I was ever sad, Carole used to take me down to Fifi Mahoney's to try on wigs and to play with their makeup. She had a smile that could light up an entire room."

"Like yours."

She paused to look up at him. "You think so?"

"Absolutely."

Simone was warmed all the way through by his compliment. They walked on, arm in arm, joking and teasing until they reached her condo.

"So what happened to your foster parents?"

She took a deep breath at the sadness that question conjured. "They died in a car wreck my first year of college."

"I'm really sorry."

"It's okay. It was a long time ago, but it left me scarred for years. I kept thinking that I was cursed to lose everyone I ever cared about." She shook her head. "There for a time, I'd even get up in the middle of the night just to make sure Jesse was still with me."

Xypher drew a sharp intake of breath. And now he was going to have to leave her, too . . .

No, he could never tell her he loved her. It would be cruel.

Simone opened the gate to her condo, then paused as she saw someone slumped over at the end of the small walkway. Rushing toward the person, she was stunned to find Kyle Peltier there. He had a vicious wound in his stomach. Blood was steadily pouring out of him.

Trembling, he reached up and grabbed Xypher's shirt. "The gallu are attacking Kerryna in her condo. Help her. Please!"

Xypher shot to his feet. "Get him to Sanctuary."

Simone swallowed. "What about you?"

"I have a fight to join. Jesse, go with Simone and make sure nothing happens to her. If she needs me, get me immediately."

SIXTEEN

Xypher went running toward Kerryna's condo. From the outside, it was identical to Simone's, except it had a small mirror that dangled from the knocker—a mirror that was designed to keep the gallu out.

If only it'd worked.

He ran to the door and tried the knob.

It turned.

Opening the door, ready for battle, he was surprised to find the place completely empty. He entered the house slowly, expecting an ambush.

With nothing but silence humming in his ears, he went room to room looking for the Dimme.

Or her body.

There were no heartbeats in the place. But everywhere he looked were the remnants of battle. Furniture was busted, shelves were on the floor. It was obvious Kerryna and Kyle had put up a tremendous fight.

But the question was, why had she been here without Xedrix?

"Damn it," he breathed. They must have taken her with them when they left.

Xypher went rushing back to find Simone struggling to get an unconscious Kyle into her car. He took the whelp from her and swung him up in his arms before he flashed them to Sanctuary.

Carson came to his feet with a stern scowl as he saw Kyle's bleeding body. "What happened?"

"He was attacked." Xypher took Kyle into the room where Carson had tended him when he'd been wounded.

"Thanks for getting him here."

"Anytime. Now if you'll excuse me, I have some bad news to deliver."

Xypher turned to Simone.

"What bad news?" she asked.

"I think they took Kerryna."

Her face pale, Simone staggered back from the shock. "The gallu? Why?"

"To use her, I'm sure."

"Does Xedrix know?"

Xypher glanced back to Kyle's bleeding body. "I'm going to take a wild guess that he doesn't. I think Kyle must have been on watch duty. We need to get to their bar again and tell Xedrix what's happened."

She couldn't agree more. "All right. Flashy thing coming up . . . no nausea this time. We hope."

"Hang on." He looked at Jesse. "You, too. Gloria, hold on to him so we don't get separated."

The next thing Simone knew, they were at the club, which was hopping with college students and locals. They were all standing behind the stage where Xedrix had brought them in originally.

A band was playing loud, dark wave music.

Xypher took her hand and led her toward the dance floor. In the crowd, it was impossible to distinguish the Charonte from the humans. The only way she could tell the difference was her demon sense that picked up on them whenever they drew near one.

"Where's Xedrix?" Xypher asked a tall, dark-haired demon who was serving drinks.

"He's at the bar."

Xypher made his way over to the area that was marked with neon tubing and a hand-painted sign on the mirror with the club's logo of vampire teeth with three drops of blood falling from the lips.

Xedrix sat on one of the stools, watching the crowd and drinking absinthe. He tensed the moment he saw them approaching.

"What's up?"

Simone decided she'd take the heat for being the harbinger; as Xypher had noted earlier, since she was female Xedrix was less likely to hurt her. "It's Kerryna. We found Kyle Peltier wounded. He said the gallu had taken her."

The glass in Xedrix's hand shattered as his eyes glowed a terrifying red. "What do you mean she was taken?" He grabbed one of the demons who was walking past and threw him onto the bar.

The humans around them quickly took their drinks and moved away.

"Where is Kerryna?" Xedrix demanded.

The Charonte paled. "Last I saw she said she wasn't feeling well. She was headed upstairs to the office to lie down. She said not to tell you. She didn't want you to worry. Said she'd be back before you missed her."

Actual smoke came out of Xedrix's nostrils in a frightening display of anger. "Why did you leave her alone?"

"She was sick so she went with the bear upstairs. I only did what your Katika told me to do."

Xypher frowned. "How can she get sick?"

Xedrix turned on him with a ferocious growl. "She's not sick. She's pregnant with my simi."

Simone gaped. *This was bad.*

Xedrix shot off the stool, but before he could do anything, Xypher grabbed his arm.

"Take me with you to Kalosis."

Xedrix scowled at him. "Are you insane? Have you any idea what Stryker would do to you if you showed up there?"

"I don't care."

Xedrix cocked his head in a questioning manner. "Your vengeance means that much to you?"

Xypher locked gazes with Simone before he answered. "My vengeance means nothing to me anymore. Send me in there and I'll get Kerryna out for you."

Xedrix stepped back. "What are you saying?"

Xypher paused as he thought carefully about how much he wanted to tell them. This wasn't only about getting Kerryna back—this was about protecting Simone. She meant more to him than anything.

Even his vengeance.

"I understand why you won't stay with Kerryna in Kalosis. You protect Simone and I'll get Kerryna out of there for you. I swear it."

The demon curled his lip. "Stryker will never allow it. He'll kill you the minute you show. The gallu want to use her, they won't give her up without a war."

"Stryker is half human and half god. His powers won't stand against mine."

Xedrix's mocking laughter rang out. "You're

half *Greek* god . . . Have you any idea what Apollymi would do to you the minute that scent crosses her nostrils? You won't make it a foot before she skewers you. I'm the only one who stands a chance there. By the gods, I'm going to take it."

Jesse cursed.

Simone turned to glance at him and he pointed over Xedrix's shoulder. There in the shadows, leaning against the wall, was Kerryna and she looked terrible.

They rushed to her side.

Xedrix picked her up in his arms and cradled her close. "Are you all right, *me arita*?"

Kerryna gasped as if she were fighting a wave of severe nausea. She clung to Xedrix while tears brimmed in her eyes. "They've given me Aperia."

Xedrix's face paled.

"What's that?" Simone asked.

Xypher cursed. "It's a slow-acting poison that's deadly to demons."

"I have twelve hours," Kerryna said, her voice breaking. "If I kill Xypher and the Destroyer, Satara will give me the antidote."

Xedrix looked up at Xypher. "You're one dead son of a bitch."

"No!" Kerryna snapped, cupping his face and making him look at her. "We can't do this."

An angry muscle twitched in Xedrix's neck. "I'm not going to let you die. I don't care who I have to kill to save you. I will."

Simone cleared her throat to get their attention. "Can't we get the antidote?"

Kerryna shook her head. "Satara has it all and she's guarded by a thousand Spathi Daimons and gallu demons. It's hopeless. She wants Xypher dead. His life is the only thing she'll trade the antidote for."

Simone refused to believe that. "There has to be another way."

Xypher turned to her as he remembered someone who not only was connected to Apollymi and Satara, but one who also owed him a favor. "I have an idea. Give me your phone."

Simone did.

He opened it and dialed Acheron who answered on the first ring. "I need a favor."

Acheron laughed. "Really?"

"But not from you. I need to talk to Katra."

"Why?" There was no missing the ice in Acheron's tone. Not that Xypher blamed him. Katra was Acheron's daughter and he was sure the Atlantean would do anything to protect her.

But right now, they had a much more pressing problem. "I need someone who can walk into Kalosis, kick Satara's ass, and save the life of an innocent . . . Dimme."

Acheron cursed. "You're not asking much, are you?"

Xypher ground his teeth before he uttered the word that galled him. "Please, Acheron. This isn't about me. It's about saving a mother and her unborn baby." He seriously hoped that would work on Acheron's conscience.

"Where are you?"

"Club Vampyre in the Warehouse District. Do you know the place?"

"No, but I'll be there shortly."

He hung up and looked at Xedrix. "I have the cavalry coming. Trust me."

Shifting Kerryna to one side, Xedrix reached over onto the wall and pulled down the lever for a fire alarm. It rang out in a deafening tone that drowned out everything, even the music.

Every human in the club ran for the doors while the demons gathered around Xedrix.

"We're closed for the night," Xedrix announced to his staff. "Tyris, call the fire department and tell them a drunk customer pulled the switch by mistake. Let's get this place cleared out."

While they waited for Acheron, Xedrix took Kerryna to the bar and set her on a stool.

"What are you planning?" Simone asked Xypher. "And don't say 'nothing.' I've learned to know you better than that."

He glanced to Kerryna before he answered. "I'm tired of seeing innocent people get hurt. I'm going to stop this once and for all."

"And if you can't?"

"I will."

Simone felt a fissure in the air an instant before Acheron appeared with an extremely tall, unbelievably beautiful blond woman who was obviously pregnant. She must be the mysterious Katra.

The Charonte hissed as soon as they saw them, then fell to their knees.

Acheron looked around with one brow arched high. "This was wholly unexpected." He scowled at Xypher. "Where did the Charonte come from?"

Xedrix rose slowly to stand before Acheron, but he made sure to keep his eyes downcast. "Forgive us, akri, for our lack of vigilance. I ask for no mercy for myself, but for my men, spare their lives. They only followed me and did as I told them. I'm the one you should kill, not them."

Katra gaped at the sight of the demons. "So this is what happened to all of you. I'd wondered. Nice to see you guys again. I'm glad you survived. Have no idea why you're in a club, but still glad you're all here." She looked at Acheron and indicated Xedrix with a tilt of her chin. "Xedrix is of particular interest to you."

"How so?"

"Well, one, he's your mother's favorite of all her demons, and two, he's the older brother of your Simi."

Acheron frowned at her disclosure. "Really?"

Katra nodded.

Xedrix looked every bit as puzzled as Acheron. "Simi?"

"Xiamara," Katra said quietly.

Xedrix's jaw went slack. "My sister lives?"

Katra smiled affectionately at the demon and nodded. "And is spoiled absolutely rotten."

Xedrix's eyes softened. "Bless you, akri, for your kindness and mercy. I have grieved for centuries over the fate of my simi sister."

"Brace yourself," Acheron said in a deadpan tone. "Xirena lives with us, too."

Kerryna put her hand in Xedrix's.

The demon seemed pleased by the news. "Then I can die happily, akri, knowing they are alive. Thank you."

Acheron rolled his eyes. "I'm not going to kill you, Xedrix. Simi would torture me for eternity if I even considered it. By the way, how did you guys end up in a bar in New Orleans of all places?"

Kerryna laughed, then grimaced as if a wave of pain hit her. "The bear, Kyle Peltier, found them after they'd escaped from Kalosis. They were trying to eat a tourist, but Kyle stopped them before they'd killed him and explained that if they wanted to live here and not die, they'd have to follow rules and make a home. He took his own money and invested it in the bar and showed Xedrix how to run it all. The two of them are still partners."

Katra narrowed her gaze on Kerryna. "I remember you from Vegas. You're the gallu Dimme who escaped."

"And I you, goddess. I well remember you trying to kill me."

"She's not evil, Kat," Xypher said quickly, stepping between them. "She's been hiding out, trying to fit into the world, too."

Simone moved forward. "And she's the one Satara poisoned. The only antidote for it is in Kalosis with Satara. As an expectant mother yourself, you can see why we can't let her die."

Xypher nodded. "I was hoping you could help us."

Acheron met Katra's gaze. "You know I can't go in there without ending the world. You're on your own."

Katra smiled. "I know. I'll be right back." She patted Xedrix affectionately on the shoulder. "Don't worry, Xed. Kalosis is the one place Satara and Stryker can't touch me. You know what my grandma would do to them if they tried."

Xedrix nodded.

As she started to fade, Xypher stopped her.

"Wait, Kat. I want to go with you."

Katra frowned at him. "You sure?"

Xypher nodded, then looked at Simone. "I have to do this."

"I know," Simone said quietly. "I just wanted to tell you something before you left."

"What?"

"I love you."

Xypher couldn't breathe as those words hit him

like a physical blow. He cupped her cheek in his hand. "It's not possible."

"Trust me, it is, and you better come back here or I'm going to be really upset at you."

He pressed his cheek to hers and inhaled her precious scent. "Have no fear," he whispered in her ear. "I will be back to pester you."

"You better."

Xypher did the hardest thing he'd ever done in his life. He moved away from Simone and joined Kat. "Let's go."

Katra reached out and touched his arm before she opened the portal to Kalosis.

Xypher watched Simone's beautiful face until it dissolved into blackness.

Heartbroken, he blinked as they materialized in what appeared to be a giant hall of some sort. There were Daimons gathered all around as if waiting for something.

Or someone.

Kat turned to her left and it was there he saw a large throne. And in it sat Stryker with Satara standing off to the side.

"You're not dead," Satara said as she saw Xypher. "Pity."

Katra laughed at Satara's comment. "He's not going to die, cousin. Give me the antidote."

"Oh, I can't do that," Satara said in a simpering tone.

"Yes," Kat said, mocking her, "you can."

"Nope, 'fraid not." Satara pouted prettily. "I had an accident. It's all gone."

Kat lifted one finely arched brow. "Have you lost your mind? Do you know what Xedrix will do to you once I tell him it's gone?"

"Xedrix? The demon? He's dead."

"No he's not." Kat crossed her arms over her chest. This game aggravated her since she could tell Satara was lying. She'd known good and well that Xedrix was alive. "He's the father to Kerryna's baby. You couldn't have picked a worse enemy. Unlike Xypher, he can get in here alone anytime he wants to and he will have the backing of the Destroyer when he tears your heart out. Guess I better go tell him to sharpen his claws."

Kat began to fade.

"Oh, wait, you mean this antidote?" Satara pulled a small vial out from between her breasts. "I just remembered I had it."

"Oh, I'm sure."

Satara handed the vial off to a Daimon who brought it forward and gave it to Kat. The vial was of clear glass with a bright red liquid inside.

Kat assured Xypher it was the serum with a nod of her head.

Grateful Kerryna was taken care of, Xypher moved to stand in front of Stryker's throne. "While I'm here, I want a truce."

Satara blinked at Xypher's words as if she'd misheard them. "What?"

"You heard me. I've come to terms with our past. And I want you out of my life completely. No more demons, no more poisons. No more bullshit. You leave me alone and I'll leave you alone."

Satara appeared aghast. "Really?"

Stryker leaned over to speak to her. "I'd take this deal, Satara. I doubt you'll find a better one elsewhere."

Satara's eyes narrowed suspiciously. "Why is this so important to you?"

He knew better than to answer that question with the truth. That would only hurt Simone. "It isn't and neither are you. I only have two more weeks on earth. I'd like to enjoy them."

"So that's it?" she asked.

"That's it."

Satara laughed bitterly. "And you really expect me to believe that you'll just let me go about my life while you go back to hell? In peace. No harm, no foul?"

"Yeah."

She came off the dais to approach him with a sneer. "Do you think I was born yesterday? I know you better than that. You have no intention of seeing this met."

Xypher shook his head. "You don't know me at all. You never did. I want peace and I want Simone left alone."

She tapped her fingers against her upper arms

before she spoke in a low, lethal tone. "Then kill yourself."

It was Xypher's turn to blink in disbelief of what he'd heard. "What?"

"You heard me, Xypher. If you want peace and are willing to bury the hatchet, then do it. Kill yourself."

"Satara!" Kat snapped angrily.

"Don't Satara me, Kat. I know how to play this game. Better yet, I know how to win it." She turned her attention back to Xypher. "So what's it to be?"

Xypher stood there in silence as he considered her offer. "How do I know you're not lying?"

"I swear on the river Styx that if you kill yourself, I'll never go near Simone again. She'll be completely safe from me or any of the demons and Daimons here in Kalosis. I'll even send her a birthday card every year for good measure."

Xypher looked at Kat, whose face was ashen.

"*Don't*," his inner voice ordered. But as he considered it more fully, it made complete sense. He was going to die anyway. What difference would two weeks really make? Other than giving him more memories of Simone to torture himself with.

More time to love her.

More time for her to love him.

No, it would be easiest on both of them to end it all now. Rip the Band-Aid off and let the wound start to heal.

His heart breaking, he nodded. "It's done, then."

Kat gaped. "You can't do this, Xypher."

"Yes I can. It's the only way I can guarantee Simone's safety."

Satara paused at the side of a Daimon to draw a short sword from his waist. Her walk was seductive as she neared him. She angled the sword at his heart. "We have a bargain?"

He nodded.

Satara stabbed him straight through the heart. "Sorry. I didn't want you to change your mind about dying."

Xypher staggered back, gasping as the pain swept through him.

He sank to the ground.

Kat knelt by his side. "Xypher?"

"Don't tell Simone what I did. Let her go in peace . . . please. Tell her it was quick."

Kat held him close, but hers wasn't the face he wanted. He wanted to see Simone one last time. But in doing this, he was protecting her and that was all that mattered.

He glanced down to his arm where his vow of vengeance was written. The words dissolved while he struggled to breathe.

It was over now . . .

Kat watched as the light went out of Xypher's eyes and he expelled his last breath.

Satara smiled.

Kat curled her lip at the smugness on Satara's face. "You selfish bitch."

"Oh, shut up, Kat. You have what you came for, now go."

Kat stood to her full height, dwarfing Satara. "One day, someone's going to give you exactly what you deserve. I can't wait to see it."

And with that, she returned to the club.

Refusing to look at Simone, Kat handed the antidote to Kerryna who smiled her thanks before she drank it.

"Where's Xypher?"

That question from Simone tore through her. *I don't want to do this . . .*

But she had no choice. Turning around, she felt ill. Simone's face looked so hopeful—it was obvious she was expecting Xypher to appear at any second.

Swallowing the lump in her throat, she reached out and took Simone's hand into hers. "He didn't make it, sweetie. He went down in the battle."

SEVENTEEN

Simone staggered back. No. It couldn't be. "That's not funny, Katra. I don't like to play those games."

"I wish I were playing, but I'm not."

Simone saw the look of horror and pity mixed on the faces of those around her and it snapped her back to when she was a child.

"The poor thing saw it all. Her mother and her brother died right before her eyes. It'll haunt her forever."

It was the same expression they all had now—staring at her like she was a freak. And deep inside they were all grateful it was her and not them. They wouldn't say it, they were too polite for that, but she knew the truth.

Jesse held his hand out. "Simone, are you okay?"

How could she be okay? Xypher was dead.

She felt that burning in her eyes that signaled they were changing to red. She wanted the blood of whoever had killed him. "Tell me what happened," she demanded, her voice a demonic growl.

"I promised him that I wouldn't. He wants you to live in peace and to go on with your life."

Go on with her life . . . She was tired of picking up the pieces and going on.

"Did he get his vengeance against Satara?"

Katra looked away sheepishly and suddenly Simone had total clarity.

"So that's it, then. He chose vengeance and death over coming back to me. At least he died happy. He got what he wanted."

Kat had to bite her tongue to keep from telling her the truth. But now she understood why Xypher had asked her not to. If Simone knew he'd given up his life to save hers, it'd kill her.

Just like it would kill Katra to lose her husband. To have him sacrifice himself for her would only hurt more and she would never have peace from that guilt and anger.

Simone looked to where Xedrix stood beside Kerryna, holding her hand.

She would never touch Xypher again. Drawing a ragged breath, she turned toward Gloria and Jesse. "I want to go home."

Acheron stepped forward. "I'll take you."

"Thank you."

He held his hand out and she took it. The instant she did, they were all back in her house. No, not all of them. Xypher was missing.

"Is there anything I can do?" asked Ash.

She shook her head. "I should probably check on Kyle and see how he's doing."

"We already did. He's fine. He'll be recovering shortly and shouldn't have any lasting damage other than a couple of scars."

"That's good. I suppose that describes all of us, huh? Thank you for bringing me home, Acheron."

"You're welcome. My number is in your phone. If you need me for anything, call."

"I appreciate it."

Then he was gone.

Jesse and Gloria stood off to one side, watching her with a worried expression.

"I'm all right, guys. Why don't you go and play records or something?"

Jesse swallowed. "You're scaring me, Simone."

She was scaring herself. She hurt so bad inside that she couldn't even cry. It was as if she'd been gutted and there was nothing left except an empty hole where her heart and soul had been.

Wanting to be alone, she pulled her coat off and dropped it on the floor on her way to her room.

The bed was still rumpled from their earlier play.

She shoved that thought aside. If she didn't mean any more to him than that, he certainly didn't mean it to her. Her anger simmering, she snatched at a pillow to make the bed.

And it was then the scent of Xypher hit her hard. She hugged the pillow to her chest and inhaled the warm masculine scent.

That was what shattered her numbness. Grief and anguish came boiling up until she wanted to scream out in pain.

Instead, she sank to her knees as racking tears assaulted her.

Xypher was gone.

"Damn you, you bastard. Damn you!"

But the problem was, she didn't want him damned. The thought of him in Tartarus being tortured . . .

It was more than she could stand.

Xypher stood in the center of a cell he knew even better than the back of his hand. Over the centuries, he'd counted every grain of sand. Had saturated them all with his blood.

Now he was back.

The chains came out of the ceiling and laced themselves around his wrists. For once he didn't fight as they lifted him from the ground. His arms burned from the weight of his body.

But that pain was nothing compared to the one aching in his chest.

Simone.

I'm protecting her. He repeated those words over and over again and they alone gave him comfort. He would rather suffer eternal torment than have her hurt.

It was worth it.

The door of his cell opened.

Xypher braced himself as he saw the god of the Underworld. Tall and dark, Hades was dressed in black. He cocked his head to study him. "I didn't think you'd last a month out there. Looks like I was right."

"I'm in no mood to talk, Hades. Just start the torture."

"Interesting. My prisoners so seldom beg me to hurt them. And to think, right now, you could be in Simone's arms and not hanging here like so much meat."

"Leave her out of this."

"That, unfortunately, I can't do."

Fear gripped Xypher's heart. "What do you mean?"

"You know, Xypher, I really hate you. Truly. I

have to say torturing you has been one of my greatest pleasures. And now, just like always, you're pissing me off."

"I'm strung up here, waiting to be beaten. Tell me, how in the hell could that possibly piss *you* off?"

"Because I have to let you go, you bastard."

Disbelief coursed through him. "What?"

"The bargain I made with Kat . . . remember? I allow you to be human for a month and if within that month's time you find your humanity, you're free. You selflessly sacrificed yourself for another. And it didn't even take you a month. Damn you."

Xypher still couldn't believe what he was hearing.

The chains uncoiled so fast, he fell to the floor.

"Get out of here, Skotos. I can't hold you any more."

Simone was still rocking in the center of her floor when her phone rang. She looked at the number and saw it was Tate.

Drawing a ragged breath, she cleared her throat and answered.

"There's another demon kill."

"Are you sure?"

"Absolutely. You know the drill . . . we're at the corner of Rampart and Esplanade."

"I'll be right there." She hung up and dried her eyes before she went to Jesse's room. She found him and Gloria necking on his bed.

They broke apart as soon as they saw her.

"Um, we were just—"

"It's okay, Jesse. I'm meeting Tate and didn't want you to get worried. I'll be back shortly."

"Are you sure about this? Don't you need some time?"

"Life goes on, right?" It was the one lesson she'd learned. "It's not like I have a funeral to plan or anything. Besides, I can do with the distraction." She shut the door and headed for her car.

You could use your demon powers.

Yeah, she could, but right now she didn't want to think about that part of herself. She wanted her life back the way it'd been before Xypher had changed it. Most of all, she wanted to be free of the pain lacerating her heart.

It didn't take her long to reach the crime scene. The police lights were glaring in the darkness.

She got out and headed for Tate, who was standing alone, staring at the covered body. "Don't you ever take a day off?"

"Not when the kill is this freaky." He looked past her shoulder. "Where's—"

"He's gone. Let's leave it at that, okay?"

By his expression she could tell he was taken aback by the news, but he didn't press it. "Jane Doe. Same exact wounds as Gloria and our guy in

the Market who had gas that spontaneously com-
busted him into flames. Want a closer look?"

"Like a screwdriver through my eye socket.
Sure, let's have a look-see."

"Ooo, welcome back, Ms. Snark. I've missed
you."

Simone didn't comment as he uncovered the
body and she took a look at the poor woman.
Tate was right, and as she bent down, an unmis-
takable trace odor hit her.

Kaiaphas.

The woman's body reeked of the demon.

She closed her eyes as they began to turn and
forced herself to calm down. So Xypher's brother
had been the killer they were looking for all this
time.

Surely Xypher had smelled him, too. Why
hadn't he told her?

She rose slowly to her feet. "You're going to
need the body to spontaneously combust again,
Tate."

"Yeah . . . I need something better than that."

Simone looked up above them. There was a
house with an eave that was loose.

That should do the trick.

She moved Tate back with her arm an instant before she used her powers to dislodge it
further.

It came crashing down on the body, decapitat-
ing it.

"Problem solved."

Tate gaped at her. He held his hand up. "I don't want to know what you just did. My report is complicated enough."

Simone started to respond, but the sensation of being watched returned to her. It crawled over her skin with a malicious intent.

This time, because of her powers, she could pinpoint it. "You'll be fine, Tate."

She stepped back as the photographer came running to take more pictures. While Tate dealt with him and the police officers, she slipped away into the darkness toward the source of her discomfort.

"Kaiaphas," she called. "I know you're there."

He appeared directly behind her, sniffing her hair. "You smell like cattle and demon. Have you any idea how provocative that is?"

"Great. I have demon pheromone. Just what I've always wanted."

Kaiaphas laughed. "Xypher didn't tell you anything about your family, did he?"

"No."

"Your father, Palackas, was one of the most brutal killers we've ever known. Before he was enslaved, he was known to ravage entire villages, killing women and children and anyone who got in his way."

"You're lying!"

"No I'm not. Why do you think his master was

so determined to have him back? He was too dangerous to ever be unleashed."

He was lying and she knew it. "My father wasn't like that. He was a good man."

Kaiaphas grabbed her by the head and whispered something she couldn't understand.

In her mind, she saw her father as a young man. No, not a man. He was a demon. His eyes were red as fire, his teeth jagged and sharp, as he stormed through an ancient village killing everyone he saw.

How could this be?

"I knew Palackas had spawned. I just wasn't sure it was you. You smelled like your mother . . . but there was no scent of Palackas on you."

"How do you know what my mother smelled like?"

"I was there, Simone. Don't you remember?"

She gasped as she went back to that night. She was again in the backseat, looking out the window.

There were two men . . .

No, there was a third. He'd leaned down and snatched her mother's necklace from around her neck. Then he'd turned as if sensing her. Frozen, she couldn't move. All she could do was pray that the headrest on the seat blocked her from his view.

Then the police sirens had pierced the air.

The men in the store had scattered.

No, they had vanished where they stood . . .

Unadulterated rage tore through her. "You bastard!"

He laughed. "Make it look like a human death, my master had said. If Palackas wants to live like one, he can die like one. And so he did. I killed his family knowing he wouldn't live without them. A mighty demon taken down by a single gunshot through his head . . . but you know that, don't you? You found his body."

Shrieking in outrage, Simone turned on him and blasted him with one of the energy bursts Xypher had shown her.

Kaiaphas dodged it and laughed. "You didn't really think such a puny trick would work on me?" He slapped her hard. "You know why your mother never came to see you after her death? I ate her soul, just as I ate your brother's. And now, I'm going to taste yours."

"Taste this." She head-butted him in the lips, splitting them open.

He staggered back. Letting the power she'd inherited from her father course through her, she scissor-kicked him, then punched him hard enough in the gut to lift him off his feet.

Kaiaphas's skin started boiling as those serrated fangs came out. He dodged her next punch and kicked her in the side.

Lifting her by the neck, he threw her down on

the ground. Out of nothing, he manifested a sword.

Simone looked about for a weapon, a limb . . . something.

There was nothing around.

"Try this."

She jerked to hear the deep voice in her ear, and found a man there who had one vividly green eye and one brown one. He was gorgeous and he held a small sword out to her.

Not questioning anything, she seized the sword. The moment her hand touched the hilt, a shimmer of power went through her entire body.

She heard whispering voices in numerous languages.

"Simone." It was her father's voice.

"Daddy?"

"Close your eyes, little one, and we will guide you."

Trusting her father implicitly, she did as he said, and the moment she was blind, she saw everything clearly.

Even the wind was visible to the demon inside her.

Kaiaphas advanced and she parried. The harder he rained blows onto her sword, the easier she could parry them and fight him. The more she deflected, the angrier Kaiaphas became.

"You're going to beg me for mercy, just like your whore mother."

She ground her teeth until she heard her father again in her ear. "Anger is your enemy. Move forward not in anger, but with purpose."

And the moment she did, her blade sang true. It deflected Kaiaphas's thrusts and planted itself deep within his demon's heart.

"That is for my mother," she said, her eyes tearing. "And for my baby brother whose future you took. Burn in hell, you son of a bitch." She snatched her sword out of his chest, twisting it as she did so.

An instant later, he burst into flames. His cries echoed out in the darkness.

Suddenly, there was applause behind her.

Simone jerked around to see the man there who'd given her the sword. "Who are you?"

"Don't ask questions you already know the answer to."

"You're Jaden."

He inclined his head to her in a mocking gesture.

She looked down at the sword that was unlike any she'd ever seen before. The black hilt was tinged with red. Black roses and vines were etched down the blade that curved ever so slightly. "Why did you bring me this?"

"I promised your father peace. I told him that no demon would ever hurt his last remaining child. As Xypher told you, I can't kill myself to fulfill a bargain. I can only provide a means."

She held the sword out to him, but he refused to take it.

"That belongs to your bloodline, demonikyn. Guard it well. A demon's sword is the best protection from others of its kind. With it, you can kill any demon who comes for you or one of yours."

"Thank you."

He laughed. "Don't thank me. I do nothing that I haven't bargained for."

He started to fade.

"Jaden, wait!"

He solidified in front of her.

Simone tried to speak, but words wouldn't come. She wanted to ask about Xypher and yet she couldn't.

"He gave himself up for you," Jaden said in a stoic tone.

"What?"

"It's what you wanted to know, is it not? Xypher allowed Satara to kill him in exchange for her word that she would leave you alone. He gave up his vengeance to keep you safe."

"No, he took his vengeance."

Jaden placed a hand on her shoulder, and there in her mind, she saw Xypher in Kalosis. She heard the words spoken clearly and she watched as he died in Katra's arms.

"No!" she cried, unable to bear it. "You have to help him."

"There's nothing I can do."

"You make deals. Xypher said you have the power to do anything. *Anything*."

"What are you suggesting?"

"If you free Xypher from Tartarus, you can have my soul."

"Do you understand the bargain you're making? Once I take your soul from you, you are the property of whoever I give that soul to. You will be a bound demon, subject to the whims of your master. No will of your own. No future. Nothing."

"I don't care. Xypher died for me. I can't have him punished for that."

"He died to keep you safe."

"I'll be safe while I'm bound. He'll have what he wanted. Please, Jaden. I can't live knowing he's being tortured."

"Very well." He handed her a dagger. "Open a vein, sister."

Xypher flashed himself into Simone's bedroom, expecting to find her there.

It was empty.

Closing his eyes, he sensed for presences in the condo. There was no Simone, but Jesse and Gloria were in Jesse's room.

Without thinking, he flashed in there to find the two ghosts completely naked on the bed. "Oh, gods, I'm blind." He spun around to give them his back.

"Don't you knock?" Jesse said, until it must have dawned on him that Xypher was back. "Oh, my God, you're dead."

"Not as dead as you are, ghost-boy. Where's Simone?"

"She went out on a call."

"Where?"

"Didn't say. Call Tate and ask. His number's on the fridge."

Xypher left them to go to the kitchen where he quickly located Tate's business card. Picking up her cordless phone, he dialed the number.

He answered on the second ring.

"Tate? It's Xypher. Where's Simone?"

"She said you were gone."

"I was, but I'm back and I'm trying to find her."

"Well, she was here a second ago. I see her car across the street so she must—"

Using his powers to trace Tate's location, Xypher manifested in front of him before he could speak another word.

Tate looked around. "Damn, you're lucky no one saw you. Incognito, boy, in-cog-ni-to."

"I don't have time for that. I need to find Simone."

"Hey, Doc? Can you come here for a second."

"I'll help you look in a sec," he said to Xypher before he went over to the officer.

Xypher growled before he felt that rift in the air.

Jaden.

A bad feeling went through him as he honed in on it and went to search for him.

He rounded a corner and froze. No! That single word was branded into his mind as he saw Simone on the ground.

Terrified, he ran to her and gathered her up in his arms. But the moment he touched her, he knew.

She was dead.

He glared up at Jaden. "What have you done?"

"I didn't do anything. She did."

"Don't you dare play that bullshit game with me. What bargain was struck between you?"

"She wanted you out of Tartarus."

"You fucking bastard. I was already out of Tartarus."

"I know."

"You knew and still you made the deal?"

He shrugged. "I wanted to know how far she'd go."

Impotent fury roiled through him. Unable to think, he lowered Simone to the ground and charged at Jaden.

Jaden caught him and swung him back, pinning him to the side of a house. "You better think twice, demon, before you come at me." The fury of hell burned deep in those dual-colored eyes.

Jaden's fangs flashed as he spoke in sharp, clipped words. "Had Simone stayed alive, you would have watched her die of old age, while you continued to live eternally in your current form. Is that what you wanted?"

Xypher blinked in disbelief. "What?"

Jaden shoved him back, then released him. He pulled a small vial of a white substance from the inside pocket of his jacket. "She's free of her human life span now. She won't age and she won't die."

"But she's bound."

Jaden inclined his head. "So she is." He stared at her soul for a full minute before he held it out to Xypher.

"What's the price?"

"You two owe me a favor. One day, I'll be back to collect." He closed Xypher's hand over the vial, then vanished.

Xypher couldn't breathe as he stared at her soul in his hand. He couldn't believe what Jaden had done for them.

Why?

It was so against everything he knew about the demon broker.

Don't look a gift horse in the mouth. He knew what Jaden had known, there was nothing in this world or any other that he wouldn't have done to free Simone.

His heart pounding in joy, he took the vial to her body and released her soul.

She opened her eyes and looked at him. "Xypher?"

"Your worst nightmare has returned."

Jaden took a moment to glance back at Xypher and Simone, who held on to each other with everything they had.

He remembered a time when he'd done the same. "Whatever you do, don't betray each other."

The band on his neck heated and pierced him. Wincing, he left them and returned to his master. The blistering winds cut through his body as he stood, waiting.

"What did you do?"

"My job."

A disembodied slash opened his left cheek to the bone. Jaden cursed at the pain of the wound.

"Worthless dog. You let the daughter of Palackas go?"

"I fulfilled a bargain that was struck in good faith."

Another slash cut across his torso so deep it forced him to his knees.

"Your compassion disgusts me."

"Yeah, well, you don't exactly thrill me, either." Jaden realized he should have kept his opinion to himself as he was thrown against the wall.

"One day, dog, you'll learn obedience."

Jaden swallowed as his clothes were stripped from him. He knew what punishment was to come and it was going to hurt like hell.

Yeah, Xypher and Simone owed him more than they could ever dream.

Xypher sighed as he collapsed against Simone who was still purring in satisfaction.

"I like demon sex," she said, rolling over to pin him to the bed.

"I told you, you would."

She laughed, then kissed him senseless. "Thank you, Xypher."

"For what?"

"For trying to protect me."

"I'm not the one who bartered my soul for your freedom from hell."

"No, but you gave up your life to keep me safe. I think that makes us even."

He cupped her face in his hands. "I love you, Simone. And I swear with every part of me that you'll never doubt that."

She took his right hand into hers and kissed his knuckles. "Don't worry, I won't."

Simone smiled before she lay down over him and held him close. Closing her eyes, she realized that Xypher had given her much more than just his love. He'd given her a family and taught her things about herself she'd never known.

For the first time in her life, she had a real future to look forward to.

And a family that would be with her no matter what.

Turn the page for
a sneak peek of the most anticipated
Dark-Hunter novel yet

ACHERON

Available April 2009
from St. Martin's Paperbacks

June 23, 9527 BC

Acheron sat on the railing of his balcony completely drunk as he watched the elaborately dressed guests arriving for the birthday party in the palace below. His back was pressed against the building while his legs were stretched out before him in a precarious balance. He wasn't sure how much he'd imbibed at this point.

Unfortunately, it wasn't enough to kill him. But if he were lucky, he might yet tumble from his perch to the rocks a hundred feet below and die horribly there.

That would definitely fuck up his twin brother's birthday celebration. For the first time in weeks, he laughed at the thought of Styxx dropping dead in front of the gathered nobles and dignitaries.

It would serve them right.

"It's my birthday, too," he shouted, knowing no one could hear him. Even if they could, they wouldn't care.

Not even Artemis could be bothered to celebrate with him. Why? Because she was afraid someone would see them together . . .

Gods forbid.

Acheron turned his head and winced as pain tore through him. He hated the fact that she alone could give him so much anguish. So careful he'd been to shield himself from the callousness of those around him. But Artemis, she cut him on a level no one else could touch.

And like everyone else, she didn't care how much she hurt him.

Then again, he should be grateful. At least this year he wasn't celebrating the anniversary of his birth in prison . . .

Or a stew.

Ever alone. Even when he was in a crowd, surrounded by people, he was alone.

Truthfully, he was tired of it. No one wanted him. The only reason his so-called family cared whether he lived or died was because if he died, their beloved Styxx died too.

"I've had enough."

Even though he was only one and twenty, he was as tired as an old man. He'd lived beyond his years and wanted no more pain. No more loneliness.

It was time to end it.

The voices he heard in his head were louder now. They were calling him home . . .

Acheron stood up on the railing. The winds from below rushed up, over him, fanning his hair out as he stared down at the black sea. He dropped his goblet and watched as it tumbled down below, vanishing from his sight.

One step.

No pain.

Everything would end.

"It's time," he breathed. There was no one here to stop him this time. No Ryssa to pull him back. No father to tie him down and prevent it. No Estes to call for a physician.

Freedom.

Closing his eyes, he let go and stepped off.

Fear and relief whipped through him. In a moment, he'd have his long sought after peace.

Suddenly, something hard struck his stomach. Acheron gasped at the pain. He opened his eyes out of reflex.

Instead of falling, he was now rising, away from the sea. The sound of the waves crashing against rocks was replaced by the heavy fluttering of giant wings. He turned to see a demon holding him.

"Let me go!" he shouted, trying to free himself.

She didn't. Not until she'd returned him to the balcony where he'd been.

Acheron staggered back as she perched on the railing and watched him closely. She had long straight black hair that fell over skin that was marbled with white and red. Her eyes glowed in the darkness, white irises, surrounded by vivid red. Like her hair, her wings and horns were black.

"What are you doing?" he asked, his voice filled with venom.

"Akri should be more careful," she whispered kindly. "Had Xiamara been a moment later, you would have died."

"I wanted to die."

She cocked her head in a gesture that reminded him of a bird. "But why, akri?" She looked over her shoulder to where the people were still arriving. "So many come to celebrate your human birth."

"They don't come for me."

Xiamara frowned at him. "But you are the prince. Heir."

He laughed bitterly. "I'm heir to shit and prince of nothing."

"Nay. You are Apostolos, son of Apollymi. Revered by all."

"I am Acheron, son of no one. Revered only within the confines of a bedroom."

She stepped slowly down before him. Her wings tucked themselves around her body. "You don't remember your birth. I understand. I was sent here by your mother with her gift for you."

He was trying to follow her words, but his mind was too numbed by drink. The demon was insane. She must have him confused with someone else. "My mother is dead."

"The human queen yes. But your real mother, the goddess Apollymi, is alive and wishes you all of her love. I am her most faithful servant, Xiamara, and I am here to protect you as I've protected her."

Acheron shook his head. He was drunk. Hallucinating. Maybe he'd already died.

"Get away from me."

The demon didn't. Before he could escape, she placed a small orb on his heart.

Acheron screamed out as pain tore through him. Never in his life had he felt anything like this and given the tortures they'd put him through, that said much. It was like there was poisonous fire in his veins, ripping through him.

From the center of his chest where the orb rested, his skin changed from tawny to blue . . .

And as the pain and color unfurled through him, images and voices screamed out, piercing his eardrums. Scents assaulted his nostrils. Even his clothes burned against his skin. He fell to the ground and curled up into a ball as every sense he had was assailed.

"You are the god Apostolos. Harbinger and son of Apollymi the Destroyer. Your will is the will of the universe. You are the final fate of all . . ."

Acheron kept shaking his head in denial. No. It couldn't be. "I am nothing. I am nothing."

The demon lifted his head. "Why are you not happy? You are a god now."

Fury rode him hard as he grabbed her. He didn't understand his powers or anything else that was happening to him, but all the years of his life, all the degradations and horrors tore through him. Those he let travel from his mind into hers.

The demon cried out as she slung her head back. "Ni! This was not supposed to happen to you, akri. Not this . . ."

He grabbed her and forced her gaze to meet his. "It was bad enough when they thought me the human son of a god. Can you imagine what they'll do to me now? Take these powers away from me."

"I cannot. They are yours by birthright."

Acheron fell back, banging his head against the stone floor. "No!" he shouted. "No! I don't want this. I only want to be left alone."

Xiamara tried to embrace him.

Acheron pushed her away. "I want nothing from you. You've done enough damage to me."

"Akri—"

"Out of my sight!"

Her eyes glowed with reluctance. "Your will is my own." The orb she'd held against him appeared as a necklace about his neck. "If you need me, akri, call and I will come."

Acheron pressed his hand against his skull that ached and throbbed with new voices and sensations. He felt as if he were going mad, and perhaps he was.

Don't miss

THE DARK-HUNTER COMPANION

from *New York Times* bestselling author
SHERRILYN KENYON
(with Alethea Kontis)

*The absolute must-have guidebook for die-hard
fans and the newly converted.*

An informative, entertaining, original companion
to the Dark-Hunter novels—features include:
plot breakdowns for each book, an index of
characters, a directory of known Dream-Hunters
and Were-Hunters, a rulebook to the world of
the Dark-Hunters, instructions on how to deal
with a Daimon, Atlantean pronunciation guide,
original art from the Dark-Hunter manga novels,
an interview with Sherrilyn Kenyon, and more!

Now available from
ST. MARTIN'S GRIFFIN
ISBN: 0-312-36343-5

...and visit
www.kenyonfearthedarkness.com
to receive an exclusive free story—and other special
features—from the world of the Dark-Hunters

Look for these novels in Kenyon's *New York Times* bestselling Dream-Hunter series

DREAM CHASER
ISBN: 0-312-93882-9

UPON THE MIDNIGHT CLEAR
ISBN: 0-312-94705-4

THE DREAM HUNTER
ISBN: 0-312-93881-0

Available from St. Martin's Paperbacks

www.sherrilynkenyon.com
www.HunterLegends.com
www.kenyonfearthedarkness.com

Don't miss the next sensational novel
from *New York Times* bestselling author
Sherrilyn Kenyon

DEVIL MAY CRY

ISBN: 0-312-94686-4

"Irresistible." —*Publishers Weekly*

Coming in April 2008 from
ST. MARTIN'S PAPERBACKS

www.sherrilynkenyon.com
www.HunterLegends.com
www.kenyonfearthedarkness.com